Harriet B. Cooke

Memories of My Life Work.

The Autobiography of Mrs. Harriet B. Cooke

Harriet B. Cooke

Memories of My Life Work.
The Autobiography of Mrs. Harriet B. Cooke

ISBN/EAN: 9783744787086

Printed in Europe, USA, Canada, Australia, Japan

Cover: Foto ©Raphael Reischuk / pixelio.de

More available books at **www.hansebooks.com**

THE

AUTOBIOGRAPHY

OF

MRS. HARRIET B. COOKE.

"With invocations to the living God,
I twisted every slender reed together,
And with a prayer, did every osier weave."

NEW YORK:

ROBERT CARTER & BROTHERS,

No. 530 BROADWAY.

1861.

To

Those Beloved Teachers and Pupils,

Who by Their Prayers,

Their Christian Efforts, and Their Sympathy,

Sought to Lighten the Labors

And Cheer the Heart of Friend and Teacher,

This Work

Is Affectionately Inscribed.

PREFACE.

I offer no apology for the subject-matter of this work. The *truth* is exhibited in a plain, unvarnished statement of facts. For the manner in which these delineations have been made, I am in a measure responsible; but, standing as I do upon the threshold of the eternal world, the fear of criticism should not make me shrink from any attempt to glorify my heavenly Father. Had the reputation of authorship been my only incentive for bringing these pages before the public, they would long since have been consigned to oblivion. Often, as I have reviewed the dealings of God with me, I have desired to leave my testimony to His mercy and faithfulness; but the thought of sending it forth in the form of a *printed book* never entered into my mind till it was suggested by a few pupils and afterwards urged by several Christian friends, who felt that a record of such an experience might tend to strengthen many weary, sinking pilgrims, and encourage them in their efforts to educate our youth for God's service; and that by this testimony I might leave

> " Footprints that perhaps another,
> Sailing o'er life's solemn main,
> A forlorn and shipwrecked brother,
> Seeing, shall take heart again.

I have, with this view I trust, prepared this record of God's dealings with His most unworthy servant; and if I have been permitted to be the instrument of good to any, to Him be all the glory. And while I bless Him for the grace that enabled me to "go forward," trusting to His promise, and clinging to the crucified One, I praise Him for the fulfillment of those promises, and look back upon the precious seasons of light upon my pathway as oases in the dreary desert of the lonely pilgrim's life.

And thus I commend this simple effort to God's blessing, with the prayer that in it I may not have "labored in vain, or spent my strength for naught."

I trust that these sketches will not be unwelcome to many who have listened but are now far away, but will prove

> " As pleasant books that silently among
> Our household treasures take familiar places,
> And are to us as if a living tongue
> Spake from the printed leaves, as pictured faces.
> Therefore, I hope, as no unwelcome guest
> At your warm fireside when the lamps are lighted,
> To have my place reserved among the rest,
> Nor stand as one unsought and uninvited."

CONTENTS.

AUTOBIOGRAPHY.

CHAPTER I.

EARLY LIFE.

Our early days—How often back
We turn on life's bewildering track,
To where o'er hill and valley, plays
The sunlight of our early days.

I NEVER was a *child*. Trained by an ambitious father, and an industrious and intellectual mother, my earliest recollections find me at the age of four, seated in my little chair, beside my mother, learning "to make papa's shirts," and committing to memory from her lips, interesting passages from "Thomson's Seasons," and other favorite authors. She was fond of poetry, and from her I soon learned to love the early writers of her ancestral home. Indeed so far as reading was concerned, it was these or nothing. Moore, Byron, and Bulwer had not cast their blighting influence over the youthful mind, nor had the teeming press disgorged its "millions of yellow trash," to pollute and destroy the intellect and the heart.

1*

True, there were romances in rich abundance, but so extravagant were they in their exhibition of character, and in their developement of life scenes, that a reflecting mind could hardly fail to become satiated and disgusted in their perusal. Such was my experience as I turned from them to the study of History and the English classics.

My early religious education was confined to a strict observance of rites and ceremonies; but although I read the bible occasionally, of its precious truth and doctrines, I was entirely ignorant. Proud, vain, and self-conceited, it was my boast that "my *heart* was good;" my motto, "the *generous*, love and hate with all their heart," and well did I honor this motto.

At the early age of twelve, I was deprived of the care and protection of a father, whom I almost idolized. I well remember with what pride I looked upon his manly form and noble bearing. In my view he was no common man. With the enthusiastic ardor of youth and the generous confidence of a sailor's daughter, I regarded my father as a being, far above his kind—my beau ideal of perfection. I never dared to disobey him, and yet there was no terror mingled with my affection. Even now I can almost hear his voice in song, or the soft tones of his flute, as they melted the soul to tenderness and love.

Never shall I forget the morning of that day which brought the sad intelligence, that my mother was a widow,—that I was fatherless. He died far from home, from friends and sympathy, and his body was committed to ocean's waves to rest amid its waters, 'till the morning of the resurrection :

> "With white upturned brow,
>   He lies where pearls lie deep;
>   And the wild winds rave, and ocean waves
>   Sing requiems o'er his sleep.

No tidings respecting his illness—no last words, or messages of affection, ever reached our ears;—they were all buried with him in the deep. The circumstances attending and succeeding his death were such as for a long time to occasion peculiar emotions, amounting sometimes almost to the hope that we might yet possibly see his face again. A passing barque that had spoken his ship, was greeted with the intelligence of the death of its captain, but the ship itself was never heard of more. Undoubtedly it foundered at sea, and none survived to tell the story of his death or of their own calamity, yet often afterwards, in the stillness of the night would the thought find indulgence that the passing greeting of the two vessels might have been misunderstood, and that he might yet be restored to us.

O what trials then came over my young heart; what blighting of bright prospects, what crushed affections, what disappointed hopes and dark days followed. Wonderful was the mercy of God, in those seasons of trial and poverty. My poor mother was strengthened for her trying duties. The widow's God was near to help her, and through His blessing on her unwearied efforts, her children were educated for respectability and usefulness. Thanks be to God for such a mother: her children do, indeed, call her blessed, and they praise the Lord that she was spared to them and to the Church of Christ. "The righteous shall be in everlasting remembrance." "The memory of the just is blessed." They rest in heaven.

Just fifty years after the death of my father, I unexpectedly came across a letter which he had written to me, when I was but ten years of age. With what mingled emotions did I look upon the sacred relic, and in its expressions of earnest affection recall the oft repeated admonition, "My dear H. love and obey your mother; imitate her example; I ask no greater boon for my child."

Much responsibility rested on me, as the eldest of four children, and the dependence of my mother on me for comfort, companionship, and assistance in training her young charge, gave, perhaps, a maturity to my character, that did me good service in after life. Possessing a bold, ardent and independent mind, I was generally the leader in every daring enterprise. Once I remember being in imminent danger of drowning, through one of my youthful impulses. A few of us—school girls—had wandered along the banks of the Connecticut, in search of recreation. Seeing a boat most invitingly empty, we agreed to take possession of it, and have a sail. I volunteered to loosen the rope, and push it from the shore. I succeeded admirably in this attempt, but losing my balance, I was compelled to spring into the water. The assistance of a kind sailor saved me from being swept away by the current, and probably from being drowned.

CHAPTER II.

TEACHING.

AT the age of sixteen I commenced my pedagogical career. Allured by the glowing representations of interested seekers for teachers, then not so easily obtained as now, and by a desire to "see the world," I was induced, in the year 1802, to exile myself from my early home and take up my residence in the Green Mountain State. There I became acquainted with character in all its varieties, native and cultivated. Very different was the new world into which I was now introduced, from the sober, staid habits of old Connecticut. My mind and character were affected by the change. The descendants of the Allen's of revolutionary history were among my tried friends, and with a new zest, and with a fresh accession of patriotic zeal, did I listen to the recital of the thrilling scenes connected with the early story of that enterprising portion of independent America.

Here my whole mind was given to worldly influences and pursuits. While kindness and affection shed their sunlight around me, I gave myself up to the enjoyment of the passing hour. No one cared for my soul! no friendly voice whispered "prepare to meet thy God." Separated from all the restraints of home, and the tender watchfulness of maternal solicitude, "why," I have often asked, "was I preserved from ruin, when so many, in similar circumstances, make shipwreck of character and future happiness?" It was the God of the widow who followed me with His blessing; it was the Father of the orphan who watched over my youthful steps. Fearless of the future, and reckless of consequences, while suffering, on one occasion, from a distressing headache, which unfitted me for the duties of school, I was induced, by the advice of an indiscreet companion, to try the effect of opium. Ignorant of the quantity that might be taken with impunity, I ate, in the course of the morning, a piece equalling a hazel nut in size. Strange feelings warned me of my danger, and I sought sleep at the house of a friend. Scarcely had my eyes closed upon what threatened to prove my *last* sleep, when the alarm was communicated by the thoughtless friend whose suggestion had induced the dangerous remedy, and the efforts of the physician and neighbors were put in requisition to preserve a life that I had so carelessly jeopardized.

For twelve hours these efforts seemed unavailing. I was not permitted to recline on a couch or bed. I slept as they dragged me from place to place. It was the depth of winter—snow was plentifully applied, and yet I slept. Emetics were administered, but without effect, and not until the midnight hour was any relief obtained. Then I awoke from my long, restless sleep, in such a bewildered state that weeks elapsed ere the faculties of my mind resumed their natural powers.

A few days previous to this occurrence, a man lost his life in consequence of taking, by mistake, a much smaller quantity of the drug than I had eaten.

Thus, again, the orphan's Father watched over the thoughtless one. But even this warning excited no apprehensions respecting the life beyond the grave. Truly of me it might be said, " She obeyed not the voice; she received not correction; she trusted not in the Lord; she drew not near to her God."

CHAPTER III.

> "Sower Divine!
> Sow the good seed in me,
> Seed for eternity.
> 'Tis a rough, barren soil,
> Yet, by thy care and toil
> Make it a fruitful field,
> An huudred-fold to yield.
>   Sower Divine?
> Plough up this heart of mine."

MY removal to Middlebury, in 1805, to join my mother, who had previously removed from Connecticut, and thus once more to complete the family circle, was an important era in my life. Here I found a general interest awakened in the minds of the people on the great subject of the soul's salvation, an interest so new and strange to me that I resolved to keep aloof from every effort to affect my feelings. Up to this time I had never attended an evening meeting, unless on some *great saint's* day, when, though there was much to please the eye and the ear, there was little, under the *presiding administration*, to touch the heart. I say this with no sectarian feeling, for if I know my own heart, I believe I can truly say, " I love the church of God in all its branches."

A few friends had been for a long time in the practice of collecting at my mother's, to spend the Sabbath evening, as we said, in *rational conversation*. As the religious interest in town increased, the question arose among the female portion of our party, "is it right for us to spend our Sabbath evenings in visiting, when there are those collected for prayer who would rejoice to see us with them?" Influenced by the urgent invitation of a friend who had herself been benefited by these meetings, we resolved henceforth to spend the Sabbath evening in a manner more befitting holy time, and promised to accompany her to the house of prayer. Our friend Catharine met us at the appointed hour, and we went like *strangers* going to a *strange* place. Half way there, we espied the little company of our male friends, who had formed a part of our Sabbath evening circle, as we thought, approaching us, and not having sufficient independence to invite them to accompany us, or perhaps fearing that they would persuade us to a walk, we turned from the public road, and passed unnoticed to the place of meeting.

We were scarcely seated before those same friends whom we had sought to avoid, entered the room. Had Van Amburgh let loose half his menagerie upon us, it could scarcely have created a greater sensation. Looks of gratified surprise, passed from eye to eye, and the beaming countenance of Dr. A., who was then acting as our pastor, spoke his delight. With the affectionate solicitude of a father did his earnest gaze rest on the youthful band, while all his energies seemed aroused and concentrated on this one point—to attract our attention and to effect our hearts. The words chosen as the basis of his remarks accorded well with my feelings. Had he placed before me the threatenings of the law against sinners—had he dwelt on the misery of the lost, I should have listened calm and unmoved. I had been *baptized* and *confirmed*, and in accordance with my early instructions I was prepared for the Kingdom of heaven; but when the man of God arose and repeated, with deep feeling and solemnity, "God is love,"—when he spread out before us the exhibition of that love in the forbearance and patience manifested towards us—His watchful providence guiding our wayward and inexperienced steps—guarding us from dangers—supplying our wants, and, above all, giving his only Son to suffer and to die for us, and freely offering salvation to all who would accept of this Saviour—when he contrasted this exhibition of his love with our forgetfulness of Him—our ingratitude, rebellion, and rejection of his Son, my heart was touched; I felt that I was *the one* to whom the words of this ministry had been sent. From that moment a fire was kindled in my soul that was not quenched till the blood of Jesus extinguished it forever.

On questioning the young men of our party how they were induced to attend the meeting that evening, they frankly acknowledged that, influenced by similar views of duty to our own, they had formed a similar resolution; that when they first saw us they were on their way to the place of prayer, and fearing that we were out for a walk, and would expect them to attend us, they turned into another street, and were equally surprised with us, when, on entering the room, they saw us quietly seated there.

Before that revival of religion passed away, *all* the members of our little party were, as they hoped, adopted into the family of the Redeemer. But there were some circumstances attending my own conversion too striking to be hastily passed by. My early education had made me an Arminian. I had no belief in the doctrine of native depravity. I felt no need of regeneration; that work had been accomplished at the baptismal font! The reasonings of sceptical relatives had made me almost a deist, and of course the doctrines of justification by faith, and of eternal punishment had no place in my creed.

But now the arrow entered into my soul, and I knew not what it was that had barbed its point. I left my home for a six months' sojourn, in a neighboring town. Engaged in teaching, I felt that there was something wanting to my instructions that I could not impart. Often, as I returned to my room at night, have I wept over the second chapter of Romans—particularly the verses that reprove the unfaithful teacher - resolving to commence a new life on the morrow, but the following night found me again weeping over the disappointment of my hopes, and thus, week after week passed, and still I remained in ignorance of the *cause* of my distress. I knew not—at least I *felt* not—that I was an enemy to the God who had made me, and who claimed the homage of my best affections; that I was a despiser of the salvation of Him who had died to redeem me; but I experienced a continual dissatisfaction with every thing that I attempted to do; nothing seemed to be done aright if done by me. No christian friend whispered that there was help for me only through the merits of the Redeemer; none pointed me to the offers of salvation so freely bestowed, while pride kept me from appealing to any one for direction, in this time of need.

My return to Middlebury in the autumn, brought my feelings to a crisis. I found my sister much in the same state of mind with myself. Our friend Catherine, had yielded her heart to the Saviour, and she was the only one who urged upon us the duty of submission to God. At a communion season in September, my distress became insupportable. Then it was that the horrors of *eternal* death, seized upon my soul, and filled me with unutterable and fearful forebodings. My heart was filled with a deep sense of its alienation from God; I felt that I was indeed a sinner in His sight, miserable, blind, and wretched; and as I looked into the dark " chambers of imagery" within my heart, I became fully convinced that nothing but the blood of Jesus could cleanse the pollution there. I returned home to throw myself upon the mercy of a crucified and divine Redeemer, and then in the solitude of my chamber, I found peace in believing.

During all this season of deep conviction, while debarred the privilege of christian counsel and encouragement, *I read no book but my Bible*, and when my mind opened to the blessed assurance that the blood of Jesus cleanseth from all sin, *all the doctrines peculiar to our Holy Religion*, which are essential to salvation, were perfectly clear to my mind. I could but feel, that *I had been taught by the Holy Spirit*, through the word of God. Truly, I might say with the Apostle, "I neither received it of man, neither was I taught it, but by the revelation of Jesus Christ." Gal. i. 12.

On the 7th of October, 1806, Catherine B., my sister, and myself, with twelve others, united with the church of Christ in Middlebury, and publicly "avouched the Lord Jehovah to be our God forever." "Not unto us—not unto us, O Lord, but unto Thy name be the glory, for Thy mercy and for Thy truth's sake." The feelings of my heart were, "Let every thing that hath breath, praise the Lord."

CHAPTER IV.

MY MARRIAGE.—TRAINING OF CHILDREN.—
THE COVENANT.

Two years after the public consecration of myself to the service of my Saviour, I made in my Journal the following record. "A new era has commenced in my life. I have exchanged a single for a married state; have left that home, in the bosom of which I have enjoyed many happy hours, for a situation most responsible. For the goodness of God in granting me a companion, who, I have reason to hope, has sought and obtained the pearl of great price,—an interest in the Saviour, with whom I can journey through life, in one mind, one faith, and one Lord, I hope I am not wholly insensible." He was one of the little company of friends who so singularly met, early in the revival of 1805, in that "place where prayer was wont to be made," and who dated from that evening their first serious impressions.

How necessary is it that a woman placed in the responsible situation of a head of a family, should possess firm and correct principles; a heart warm with love to God and to her fellow creatures. Actuated by that benevolence which seeketh not her own, but the good of those around her, she will strive to imitate her Divine Master. Continuing, fervent in spirit, and faithful in the discharge of duty, she will fully prove that "the price of a virtuous woman is far above rubies." "The heart of her husbaud will safely trust in her, she will do him good and not evil, all the days of her life. Her children shall rise up and call her blessed; her husband also, and he praiseth her."

Agreeably to the above representation of the inspired penman, is the description given by Wilberforce of a happy family. "Can a more pleasing image be presented to a considerate mind," says he, "than that of a couple happy in each other, uniting in grateful adoration to the author of all their mercies, commending each other and the objects of their common care, to the Divine protection, and repressing the solicitude of conjugal and parental tenderness by a confiding hope, that through all the changes of this uncertain life, the Disposer of all events will assuredly cause *all things* to work together for good to them that love Him, and put their trust in Him; and that after this uncertain state shall have passed away, they shall be admitted to a joint participation of never ending happiness." If it is indeed true, that such a degree of happiness is attainable in this imperfect state, how interesting to us to consider the means by which it is acquired.

The pathway of married life, is often beset with difficulties, and many times there are "fightings without and fears within," aye, and the rebellious feelings of a proud unyielding spirit, will sometimes cast their shadows athwart the hearth-stone of domestic affections, and darken the brightest sunlight of a happy home. There is one lesson often learned too late to be of much benefit—too often, alas, it is never learned—that to constitute real, substantial happiness in married life, not only must perfect confidence between husband and wife be established, but they must learn to assimilate themselves to each other's temperaments and feelings. Too often, each expects the other to conform to his, or her views of right and wrong. They have come together to journey on through life, forgetful that education has imparted different views; that religion, even, does not entirely assimilate tastes, and at once correct natural propensities, and unless they can agree to yield in minor points, disagreements persisted in, may finally produce estrangement and dissensions, while a willingness in the wife, to yield to the influence of a superior mind, will strengthen the government of both, and produce a confidence and affection, that will always cast light upon the family circle.

One after another a little group gathered round

our fireside, filling their parents' hearts with bright anticipations of future comfort, and demanding much parental care and maternal solicitude. Those only can sympathize in such solicitude who themselves have watched over these opening "buds of promise," who have felt the throbbings of the mother's heart, as she brings her little ones and lays them on the altar of sacrifice, and consecrates the young immortals to the service of her heavenly Father—whose eyes have pierced through the thick veil of coming years, and shuddered at the thought of temptations to be resisted, of struggles against the enemy of souls, of the power of sin within and of the fearful influences clustering around the pathway of the feeble pilgrim of earth. The fairest and the frailest of the infant band soon passed away from earth—transported, as a tender bud, to blossom in the paradise of God.

The work of training children for usefulness here and happiness in the world to come, involves an amount of responsibility which few mothers are suitably qualified to meet. It calls for *self government*, for how can a mother govern her child who has yet to learn to control her own feelings and temper? It requires *knowledge of mind*, in order to discriminate correctly, and understand thoroughly, the different dispositions which will be exhibited in the family circle. There is the impetuous one to be restrained, the self-willed and the obstinate to be subdued, and the timid, the mild and retiring, to be brought forward and encouraged. To effect all this, various plans must be devised, much perseverance and patience exercised, and, above all, there must be a *firm, unwavering faith* in His promises who has said, " I will be a God to thee, and to thy seed after thee," constantly animating to renewed efforts in the labor of love.

Too often parents have no settled plan of action. The father, immersed in business—his mind filled with carking care, grows remiss in the performance of his home duties. He passes by, as trivial offences, faults in conduct and dispositions that are rapidly making their impress for evil, on the future character of his children, and perhaps leaves to an injudicious, weak, and indulgent mother the training of the youthful despot, or the victim of passion. A case in point. Visiting, some years since, in the family of a neighbor, I became deeply interested in the conversation of Mr. ——, an intelligent lawyer, whose remarks were always instructive. His wife, unqualified to enjoy or join in the conversation, sat evidently annoyed that she was a cypher in the circle. Determined to disturb us, she called her little son to her, and commenced a spirited discussion with " Young America." The boy became very noisy. " James," said his father, " sit down in this chair by me." " I don't want to—mother wants to talk with me." " Sit still, sir," reiterated papa. The mother's eyes flashed unspeakable thought and feelings. " Ma! I want some sugar plums; you promised me some." "Why, Jemmy dear, so I did;" responded the mother, "here, dearie, come to me and get some, and ma owes Jemmy ten cents to buy some more with. Mr. ——, give me ten cents for Jemmy—dear boy." The pleasant interview was broken up, the poor father evidently *felt* this interference with his authority, and I returned to my home to meditate on the influence of such a training on the youthful mind. Yet this woman claimed the promises of God for her children, and was loud in her denunciations of unfaithful parents.

Another instance may be mentioned. Seated at my window in the house of a lady with whom I was boarding, her son, a wild, ungoverned boy of twelve years, was worrying the cook, who could neither by threats nor kindness, control him. "I will tell your mother, and she will punish you," said the incensed woman. "Punish me! will she," replied the "youthful patriarch," "do you think I'm afraid of it? Why, she has promised to whip me a hundred times, and she never does it—*she daresn't do it!*" Such mothers as these have often expressed to me their strong hopes that their children would become Christians in early life. On what could they reasonably base such expectations? Certainly not on the assurance, "Train up a child in the way he should go, and when he is old he will not depart from it." Children are quick to detect inconsistencies in those on whom they are dependent for example and instruction. " You must not *comperdict* and tease mamma," said a little lisper to her brothers, "don't you know mamma never tells lies?" What a testimony from the lips of infancy to the firmness and truthfulness of a parent! It matters not how much *is said* to children on the importance of loving the Saviour, on the wickedness of neglecting their duty to God, on the ingratitude of forgetting him who is the Bestower of all their mercies, if they see the love of the world predominate in the hearts of their mothers—if greater anxiety is manifested by them for their personal appearance than for the cultivation of their hearts, pride and vanity will be engendered in the youthful mind, and a distaste for religion and a love for the world will " grow with their growth," until it strengthens and ripens into positive aversion to every serious thought and feeling. The daughter of such a mother once boldly asserted that *her* mother did not pray, she *knew* she did not. On being asked *how* she knew it, she replied, " because I never see her go away alone by herself."

The mother's influence—who can fathom its depths? Who can estimate its effects upon the mind of the poor prodigal, who has wandered far from his home and from his God? Poets have spoken out the heart's emotions at the recollection of the home scenes of early childhood. With what feelings of awakened sensibility have many in after life, who have broken through all restraints, and made shipwreck of character and bright hopes, recurred to the times when a pious, perhaps a sainted mother, stood out on the heart's memories the very embodiment of all that was lovely and of good report.

> "My mother's voice! how often creeps
>   Its cadence on my lonely hours,
> Like healing, sent on wings of sleep,
>   Or dew to the unconscious flowers;
> I can forget her melting prayer,
>   While leaping pulses madly fly,
> But in the still, unbroken air
>   Her gentle note comes stealing by,
> And years, and sin, and manhood flee
>   And leave me at my mother's knee."

Never was parent more abundantly repaid for all her early trials and difficulties through years of widowhood and self-denial than was I when the remark of a beloved son was repeated to me, made in reply to a friend who was speaking of the temptations to which young men were peculiarly exposed in our cities.

"You and I, C——," said the friend, "know well what these temptations are, and how fearful their influence on the youthful mind."

"No, *I do not*," was the prompt reply, "I was never led astray into such scenes."

"Is it possible? And what influence, let me ask, preserved you from these temptations?"

"My mother's," was the ready response, "I cannot now recollect an instance when I was in danger of committing outward sin but the thought of the effect it would produce on my mother's happiness restrained me."

My feelings, views, and resolutions in relation to my own children will be best exhibited by a recurrence to the records of their early days. I read in my journal, under date of "May, 1816," while all of them were yet almost in their infancy, the oldest being not eight years of age: "My feelings have been greatly tried by the misconduct of our dear L., dear with all his faults. The Lord direct his parents to the best means of correcting and instructing our children. Suffer not our prayers in behalf of these loved ones to ascend in vain; suffer not our warnings and instructions, however unfaithfully given, to be lost upon them. I have no greater joy than to see my children walking in the truth. Oh, that they all may be accepted in the Beloved, and if their lives are spared, prove a blessing to the church and to the world." Often in their early years I was so much affected with my great failures in duty to my children, that I felt that I was unfit to perform these duties as a Christian mother, and I was ready to sink into despondence and almost despair. When I read that the Almighty had said of His faithful servant Abraham, "I *know him*, that he will command his children and his household after him, and they shall keep the way of the Lord," and again, when the Divine direction sounded in my ears, "ye shall lay up my words in your heart, and in your soul, and bind them for a sign upon your hand, that they may be as frontlets between your eyes. And ye shall teach them to your children, speaking of them when thou sittest in thine house, and when thou walkest by the way, when thou liest down and when thou risest up. And thou shalt write them upon the door-posts of thine house, and upon thy gates, that your days may be multiplied, and the days of your children." I felt that there was great deficiency in the training of my loved ones.

Impelled by this feeling, I then began to think more earnestly upon the condition and privileges of the Abrahamic covenant. The more intently I studied, the deeper was the impression, that parental obligation and responsibility were not sufficiently insisted upon by the ministry of Christ,—that believers were not enlightened as they should be, on the great subject of training the children of the church for the Redeemer's service,—that while they thought and talked much of the necessity of prayer for their conversion, they forgot that another duty was enforced by the word of God : "Fathers, provoke not your children to wrath, but *bring them up in the nurture and admonition of the Lord.*"

Often have I heard parents, with sad disappointment, exclaim, "I feel sure that in his infancy, I consecrated my child to God—that I sought, by faith, to secure the blessings of the covenant for his soul," while I well knew that the *early* education of that son, had been one of worldliness and folly.

Says one, in a sermon on the influence of education, " Though men are never made Christians in heart, merely by a course of early instruction, and discipline, independently of the special influences of the Holy Spirit; are they not frequently made so, by a course, in connection with such influences? And would they not *uniformly* be, if the instruction and discipline in question, were not more or less neglected? Is there not fulness and firmness enough in the promises of God, to furnish ground for such an opinion? Can any thing be plainer than the language, " train up a child in the way he should go, and when he is old, he will not depart from it?" Has not God promised to bless the means of grace, when they are faithfully used? Has he not, by a particular covenant, given such a promise to faithful parents, in relation to their children? May they not plead that covenant, and when they are unsuccessful in their plea, is it not because they have broken their part of this covenant, by not performing their whole duty?"

By baptism, the children of the believer are adopted as the children of the Church; now, if the Church instructed these her children, as she should, and in this were seconded by parental faithfulness, then, I believe we might expect with great confidence, the *very early* conversion of such children.

One, whose memory is still precious to the hearts of many, who daily listened with delight to his instructions, the late Dr. White, Professor in the Union Theological Seminary of New York, in a discourse on the Abrahamic covenant, remarks, "that the promise to be the God of Abraham, and his seed after him, implies that the promise is spiritual and its blessings eternal," and adds, "it is the duty of christian parents to train up their children strictly in the ways of virtue; to restrain them from all courses of immorality, and sinful and dangerous pleasures, and to cause them to conform their lives to all the requirements of the gospel. Do any say, "this is too hard a requirement, they *can not* do it? We can only answer them by replying, "*it is their duty*,—God will strictly require it of them, and will admit of no apology to justify or extenuate their failures."

In the days of primitive christianity, and even of our pilgrim fathers, the children of the Church were carefully instructed in their religious duties, and restrained from intercourse with the children of the world, and the general result, was, a blessing on their efforts, and their youth were distinguished for early piety. Now, it is impossible to discriminate between him who has been dedicated to the service of God, and him who acknowledges no such allegiance, and thus, the minds of our children are filled with worldliness and pride, and they become an easy prey to the destroyer.

As my mind dwelt with increasing interest upon these topics, and my soul became more deeply imbued with a sense of responsibility, I sought to find those among the people of God, who would freely enter into my feelings and aid me with their counsel and sympathy. Conversing with a christian friend one day, on this subject, I learned that her husband and herself had set apart a particular hour, for special prayer for their children—it was the very hour chosen by my husband and myself to commend our loved ones to the fatherly care of our covenant God,—and we then agreed that this hour should henceforth be remembered by us, as a time in which to plead for each other's children, till *a'l* should be embraced in the family of the Redeemer. This covenant was carefully observed and its object was eventually fully attained. Frequent allusions to these seasons in my journal, show with what interest they were observed, and what encouragement they afforded to the anxious mother.

Very interesting to me, were my stated seasons for religious instruction and retirement. Every morning I required each child to repeat a text, of his or her selection, and to explain it as well as they were able. This seemed much to interest their feelings and to elicit thought. After giving my own views of the verses selected, in as simple language as possible, I would kneel with them before the mercy-seat, and supplicate the blessing of God upon their souls. If any one had been refractory, the particular case was mentioned, and intercession made for the individual, *by name*. This seldom failed of producing a good effect. Often have I been solicited by the weeping offender to go with him or her, to pray to God to forgive their sins, and make them to love Jesus. Every Saturday evening, I devoted an hour to instructing them in the catechism, and I strove to make the explanations so simple, that even children could understand them. In after life, I saw the benefits resulting from this course, in the ability exhibited by them, in their efforts to defend the doctrines of salvation, and in their freedom from doubts, respecting their truth.

CHAPTER V.

PECUNIARY EMBARRASSMENT.

> "Adversity, sage, useful guest,
> Severe instructor, but the best;
> It is from thee alone we know,
> Justly to value things below."

IN the winter of 1813, my husband was persuaded to enter into mercantile business, and formed a partnership in trade, with my brother. Many reasons were urged, in favor of such a change. The place first chosen as a residence, was peculiarly unpleasant, from the fact that the church was in such a state of dissension and declension, that we could not enjoy the stated preaching of the gospel. We therefore removed to Middlebury, and were for a time most happy in the society of early friends. Business prospered at first, but an unfortunate contract, made by my brother, previous to his connection with my husband, to furnish supplies for the fleet, on Lake Champlain, during the last war with England, for which, owing to governmental difficulties, he was never compensated, brought disaster and failure. As my husband had endorsed my brother's notes, he was involved in the common ruin, and our family was thus at once reduced to comparative poverty.

Of the trials of that season, none can conceive, who have not been placed in similar circumstances; it proved a fitting discipline for the severer chastisements that were soon to succeed. My brother sought a home in a southern city, hoping there to retrieve his shattered fortunes, but my husband remained for the purpose of effecting, if possible, a compromise with their creditors. After occupying several months, in a vain attempt to accomplish this object—at the close of a week spent in most agitating conflicts of feeling— there seemed no alternative, but that the doors of a prison were to close upon him. The trial came at last. An unfeeling creditor would make no compromise, and late one evening, having spent a day of agonizing forebodings, my husband returned home, to tell me that *that* night he must sleep in the debtor's room. Oh, the distress of that hour! it seemed as though my heart would surely burst; "the *wormwood* and the *gall*, my soul hath them still in remembrance."

Oh, season stained with ingratitude, with repinings and rebellion. Never, since I hoped in the mercy of the Redeemer, had I been sensible of such irreconciliation to the government of God. I could see nothing but judgment—an angry God, chastening me in wrath. I tried to pray, but my heart rebelled, and I dared not repair to the mercy-seat for help. All night, I struggled in this terrible conflict, "without were fightings, within were fears." I finally became alarmed at the state of my heart, so opposed to the dealings of that Being, who had so long borne with my waywardness, and who had bestowed so many blessings upon me. I knelt before the mercy-seat— I besought the Lord to turn from me his fierce anger— to hush the storm within; to say to the overwhelming billows, "peace! be still!"

I could not approach him with that filial confidence which would enable me to look up and see the hand of a Father directing the rod that smote me. All was darkness within and without. I could only cry, in the agony of my Spirit, "all Thy waves and Thy billows have gone over me. Thou hast covered Thyself with a cloud, that my prayer should not pass through. I have transgressed and have rebelled— Thou hast not pardoned."

Gradually light dawned upon my mind, and peace again visited my soul. A sweet resignation to the will of my Father succeeded this storm of passion, and I was enabled to say and *to feel*, "Even so, Father, if it so seemeth good in thy sight." Then I ventured to seek an interview with my husband, and found him calm, cheerful and trusting in God. Could the sympathy of friends have compensated for the severity of this trial, it would indeed have fallen lightly upon us. They could not remove, but they did much to alleviate the suffering. A remark, made to me by a young friend who was at this time a member of my family, who afterwards labored as a missionary among the Choctaws, and whose dust reposes upon their prairie grounds, long dwelt upon my mind and influenced my feelings in after life.

"I know not, Mrs. C., what the Lord designs by his dealings with you, but one thing I have observed in Christian experience, that such distressing trials of circumstances and feelings are generally a preparation for some peculiar work to which God has appointed His people."

Friends crowded around the "prison house," to offer aid and sympathy, and by their efforts in a few days the husband and father was restored to the bosom of his family. Again the journal of the past speaks the language of the heart:

"And now what shall I render to the Lord for all His benefits? He has restored the loved one to the family circle, and again we bow together around the family altar to offer our *united* praises to the Father of all our mercies. But what an experience has been mine! The 'chambers of imagery' have been opened to my inspection; the Searcher of hearts made me sensible of deep and hidden iniquities. He showed me my weakness, my inability, if left to myself, to exercise one holy affection. He taught me from whom cometh my help, and He made me willing that He should direct all my concerns, and enabled me to cast all my burdens and cares on Him."

Soon after this our family circle was again broken. My husband journeyed to one of the Southern states in quest of business; and I, with my children, took board in my mother's family till we should be summoned to join the absent one in the land of strangers. Wearisome days and months were those, and yet much mercy was mingled with the trials of our temporary separation. My time was spent in instructing my children, visiting the sick, and comforting the afflicted.

In the summer I taught school and thus was able, by my own efforts, to remove from my husband during his absence the burden of supporting his family from his slender means.

CHAPTER VI.

MY BROTHER'S DEATH.

AT the close of August, 1819, the dear brother who had sought a southern home was called away from earth to enter upon the rest prepared for the people of God. The yellow fever, which had that year clothed so many families in mourning, passed not him by, and he, "the only son of his mother, and she a widow," departed in the midst of his usefulness, and left many mourning friends to weep over disappointed hopes, and high expectations of future good, effected for the Christian church.

Generous, manly and ardent in his affections, he early decided to relieve his widowed mother from the charge of his support, and thus was he necessarily deprived of much of the instruction and discipline of school which he might otherwise have enjoyed. His great desire was to acquire wealth, and for this purpose he entered a mercantile establishment where his indefatigable labors were well appreciated.

But years must elapse before his great object could be attained. Thoughtless upon the great subject of the soul's salvation, *all* his desires centered upon this one engrossing object, and his sisters saw, with much anxiety, the influence that it exerted upon all his actions. Expressing to them, one day, his determination to become a rich man, and his vexation that the future did not open with brighter prospects, one of them said to him, " Brother, we should tremble to see your wishes gratified. It is *our* desire that you should become a Christian, and for this our petitions ascend daily to our heavenly Father. We do not believe that God will suffer you to prosper while your heart is so bent on worldly prosperity."

" Well, then, sis," was his angry reply, " I wish you would stop praying for me."

But a few months had passed ere a deep and thrilling interest in the subject of religion pervaded the minds of the community, and his own was soon affected by the question, " what shall I do to be saved?" His distress was at times almost insupportable, and one night, so intense were his feelings, that, almost bereft of reason, he bade farewell to his mother and sisters, declaring that they would never see him more. Friends followed and arrested his steps, as with wild insanity he was hastening to the river to make the fatal plunge. The voice of prayer prevailed; the Holy Spirit subdued the proud heart, and he sat meekly and humbly at the foot of the cross.

A short time passed and I beheld him present himself, in company with a younger sister, and eighty companions, most of whom were in the morning of life, in the house of God, to profess his faith in the Redeemer. Previous to their admission to the church this interesting group united in singing the hymn, " Grace, 'tis a charming sound," etc.

For several years he pursued a consistent Christian course. All the time that he could command when not engaged in business he devoted to the improvement of his mind, and so sedulously did he study, that he became a cultivated and intelligent Christian. Thrown much, however, into the society of men of the world, he gradually relaxed his hold on the Saviour and became worldly; feelings and pursuits were indulged that he had hitherto considered wrong for the follower of Christ, and his friends often feared that he was a stranger to the constraining love of Jesus. But the eye of the compassionate Saviour still rested on the wayward youth; he was arrested in his career of worldly prosperity and at once plunged into pecuniary embarrassments from which no earthly hand could extricate him.

By the failure of the Government to remunerate him for advances made to supply McDonough's fleet on Lake Champlain during the last war, he became a ruined man. Determined to make a vigorous effort to retrieve his great losses, he left his northern home, to seek, in a southern city, the means honorably to discharge the heavy debt that burdened him.

Furnished with introductions from some of the first merchants of New York and Philadelphia, he landed in Charleston, South Carolina, in the year 18—, and took lodgings in a hotel adjoining a fashionable theatre. As he stood, one evening, debating in his mind whether to indulge in the tempting pleasure, where no earthly eye could recognize him, or to take his stand at once decidedly for God and religion, the thought was suggested to his mind, "I am now to commence a new life—God has smitten me for the worldliness of my spirit—shall I provoke Him to inflict severe chastisements, or by prayer and penitence return unto Him whom I have justly offended, and in the strength of the Redeemer consecrate myself anew to his service?" A moment sufficed for the decision; raising his foot, he brought it with energy to the ground, and with his accustomed decision said, " Henceforth I will live for God."

Retiring to his room to seek aid from on high, he marked out his future pathway, and while life was spared he never departed from it. The letters, which were designed merely to introduce him to fashionable society, he destroyed, and presented only those which would assist him in his business. For two years he labored unremittingly in the cause of his blessed Master. In a letter addressed by his partner to our mother, after his decease, the writer states that " he devoted from four to five hours every Sabbath to the instruction of children, and during the week many hours were spent in teaching adult blacks to read ; in short, during the last year, his whole time, when freed from the business of the firm—in which he was truly faithful—was spent in doing good to others."

He was superintendent of two Sabbath schools, and was unremitting in his efforts to devise means by which the greatest amount of good might be effected. Every Saturday evening was devoted by him and his teachers as a season of prayer for a blessing upon the instructions of the coming Sabbath.

Said a friend who was present at the last meeting he was permitted to attend, " He remarked the necessity of being prepared for death, and of being able to give a faithful account of our charge, and observed that some of us might be in eternity before the next Saturday night. True; he who mingled his voice with ours that evening in the praise of God, was mingling it in far more exalted strains with the spirits of just men made perfect before another Saturday night rolled around.

On the Sabbath he was unwell, but attended as usual to his Sabbath school duties. A physician was called in the evening and he was immediately placed under medical treatment for fever. Said his pastor, Dr. Palmer, of Charleston, who visited him on Monday, " I found him with a high fever, and in much bodily pain, but comfortable in his mind. At his request I prayed with him, and my heart was enlarged in his behalf. On arising, I observed him in the attitude of fervent devotion. He afterwards told me that on that occasion he felt a sudden and very remarkable relief afforded to his bodily sufferings; that they all left him, as it were, in the twinkling of an eye, and that his spirit was remarkably composed and tranquilized. I saw him again on Wednesday, and found that his disease had considerably progressed, and that his physician had pronounced it one of the most malignant and alarming cases of yellow fever that had come under his knowledge. He received my visit with peculiar gratification, and with an animated smiling countenance grasped my hand while I took a seat near his bedside.

" He then requested me to assure his dear mother and sisters, that he was as affectionately attended, as though he were under their roof; that his Christian friends generally, and particularly, the affectionate couple who had taken him into their family, were to him mother and sisters. Repeatedly, during his sickness, he remarked on the goodness of God, in raising up for him such friends, and he desired me further to say, that in point of real Christian enjoyment, he was as highly favored, and as happy, as though he was surrounded by his numerous and valued christian friends, in Middlebury.

" He laid a solemn injunction on me, and even extorted a promise from me, which I gave very reluctantly, that I would not, in any public discourse, or in print, utter *any thing*, in praise of what he was, or what he had done, stating, as his reason, that such notice was due only to grey-headed veterans in their Master's service. I endeavored to convince him, that good might be done to others, by stating some things in relation to him, the praise of which we would still ascribe to Divine grace. But his purpose was immovable, and he would allow me to say nothing more, in any publication, than to state his name, his age, and the fact that he was a teacher in the Sabbath school.

"He requested me to address the teachers and pupils of the schools of which he was the superintendent, on the Sabbath morning after his decease, and make such improvement of the event, as I thought would do them good. On Thursday, I called to see him three times. He expressed some doubts whether he would not yet recover; said that there were some reasons why he thought the Almighty might see fit to restore him, and why he would desire it himself. He was perfectly willing to depart, and hoped his life would not be spared, and that his friends would not pray for its continuance, with any other view, than that of his unreserved surrender of himself to his heavenly Master's service.

"When I had prayed by his bed-side, around which were collected a group of young Christians, chiefly fellow-laborers in the Sabbath school, it was made a subject of special petition, that his useful life might be spared, that he might have more opportunity for doing good, &c. He gently reproved what I had done, by observing that Christians ought to pray for a brother present, in different terms, from what they might use in his absence. I have never seen such abhorrence expressed at every thing that looked like self-approbation or self-exaltation.

"Disinterestedness appeared a peculiar trait in his character. Throughout his illness, he preserved uniformly, a tranquil, happy, joyful frame of mind, speaking of his own death, and all the circumstances attending it, with the utmost calmness, and frequently with a smiling countenance.

"Yesterday another physician was called in for consultation, one of rather infidel sentiments. To him Mr. L. said, 'Doctor, I have had two physicians attending me ever since I was taken ill, one an infallible One, whose prescriptions never fail;' then taking up a small pocket testament that lay on his bed, and holding it in his physician's view, 'this' said he, 'is His book of receipts.' During the whole of yesterday, he seemed to be impressed with an increasing conviction, not only that his death was certain, but that his time was short; several times in the course of the day he affirmed that all would be over by ten o'clock this morning. At nine o'clock this morning, I called to see him; found him composed and in full possession of his senses. When I asked him if he knew me, he replied, ' it is my dear Dr. Palmer.' He addressed every one around him, with the utmost tenderness and affection : he insisted that his shroud should be made in his presence, and would not be satisfied, till it was brought to him, that he might see it with his own eyes.

" At a quarter past nine, he asked, what o'clock it was. On being told, he replied, ' the conflict will soon be over.' We sang the hymn, ' There is a land of pure delight, &c.; he said that Jesus was on the other side of Jordan, beckoning him to come, and frequently prayed to God to take him, and then would ask forgiveness, if he was too impatient to be gone. We knelt in prayer, and besought the Lord to afford him a comfortable, speedy, and easy passage. After a few gasps, his spirit fled, at the very moment at which he had all along said his dismission from the body would take place, precisely at 10 o'clock, August 27, 1819.

" He was by strangers honored—he is by strangers mourned; we knew his worth—we are drowned in tears. To the Sabbath schools, it would seem, that his loss is irreparable. It is a heavy stroke to our religious community, of which he was a very active, useful, and most exemplary member. Rich are the comforts which his mother and sisters may enjoy, in reflecting how he lived, and how he died—and how he now reigns."

Such was the testimony of his pastor, concerning

his life and his death, to which might be added similar testimonials, from other friends, to the triumphs of grace in giving him the victory.

"His entire exemption from delirium, was a remarkable circumstance in his case, as yellow fever is almost uniformly attended by derangement of mind. His skeptical physician, declared, 'that it was the greatest triumph of *Philosophy* he had ever witnessed,' and both of his medical attendants, asserted that his was the only case that they had ever known where the patient retained the full exercise of reason, after the black vomit had commenced."

The friend who had taken him to his own home, at the commencement of his illness, and who, with his companion, were truly brother and sister to the dear departed, gave us the above statement, with many additional circumstances that cannot here be recorded. One little incident deeply interested us. On the day previous to his death, my brother took a piece of paper, and wrote with his pencil, in large letters, "God is love," and requested that it might be placed opposite to his bed, where it would be constantly in view. Oh! what consolation was afforded to his bereaved mother and sisters, by these precious testimonies. "He is not lost, but gone before," was the language of our hearts.

"There may we meet, when a few more suns or seasons shall have cast their departing shadows upon his silent grave. Death separates, but it can never disunite those who are bound together in Christ Jesus. It is no more death but a sweet departure—a journey from earth to heaven. We are yet one family,—one in memory—one in hope—one in spirit."

> "When no shadow shall bewilder,
> When life's vain parade is o'er,
> When the sleep of sin is broken,
> And the dreamer, dreams no more
> When the bond is never severed—
> Partings, claspings, sobs and moans,
> Midnight waking, twilight weeping,
> Heavy noontide—all are done;
> When the child has found its mother,
> When the mother finds the child;
> When dear families are gathered,
> That were scattered on the wild;
> Brother, we shall meet and rest,
> 'Mid the Holy and the blest."

CHAPTER VII.

REUNION WITH MY HUSBAND.—HIS DEATH.

AND now came the trial of parting with a widowed mother, with bereaved sisters, with the friends of other days, to join my husband, in his far-off southern home. Many were the conflicts, the emotions of sorrow and of joy, that agitated my heart, at this time. I went forth as does the missionary to foreign climes, with the expectation that I should return no more to my own land. Traveling was then effected by the slow progress of the weary stage-coach, or by the tardy movement of the *steamless* vessel.

Previous to our departure, many Christian friends assembled to commend us to the protection of our heavenly Father. The parting hour arrived, and sad hearts and weeping eyes, testified that this was no common trial. Our poor mother who had just consigned her only son to the silent tomb, as she bade farewell to so many objects of fond affection, seemed overwhelmed with the thought that the ties to earth were fast being sundered.

For four weary days was our slow vehicle dragged through mud and rain, e'er we reached a temporary resting place, in the city of Troy. Late, on the following day, we embarked on board a sloop for New York,—the only steamboat that then plied upon the waters of the Hudson, having been already carefully packed away for the winter,—and *eight* dreary days were spent in *drifting* along, at the mercy of the wind and tide, before we reached that city. Disgusted with most of my associates; confined to a small cabin, with few intellectual resources; how irksome were the passing hours. Still, I found our tiny saloon, a fine place for the study of character—for observing the different dispositions and propensities of men—and above all for learning lessons of patience and submission.

Our steward,—a Portuguese, in size, a "son of Anak"—disturbed me much by the repetition of profane expressions, to which my children were compelled to listen. In vain I expostulated with him, he treated me with respect, but insisted that the habit was too powerful to be overcome. Determined to make another trial, I pleasantly offered, one day, to wash his cups and saucers for him, morning and evening, if he would desist from the practice, and added that it might prove a great relief to him, as we were probably embarked for a *long voyage.* The appeal to his selfishness prevailed.

"Ah, madam," said he, in his broken English, " you be so very good, I can deny you notting."

A week after my arrival in New York, when I went on board the vessel that was to convey me to Savannah, this same Portuguese was the first to greet me.

"Why, Pedro, how came you here ?"

" Ah, madam, you so *very good*, I follow *you*," and no more oaths were heard from his lips.

We embarked on board the Levant, and after a stormy passage of eight days, reached Savannah in safety. Here I left the friend who had thus far taken charge of me and mine, and proceeding to Augusta, the place of our final destination, arrived there on the morning of December 25, 1819, in season to partake of a Christmas dinner with my beloved husband. How did my heart bound to meet him from whom I had been so long separated. I hope I was thankful— I am certain I was rejoiced.

That winter passed happily away, in the society of of my best earthly friend, and in efforts to train our children for God. Many are the mournful records in my Journal, of my forgetfulness of recorded vows ; of my worldliness and unfaithfulness in my Master's service. I prayed to be delivered from this worldliness, that my soul might no more cleave to the dust. My heavenly Father heard my prayer, and answered it by blighting all my earthly prospects. The "desire of my eyes," was removed by a stroke,—my "house was left unto me desolate,"—"widow and orphans," was written against me and my bereaved children. What a change did a few short days effect in my situation. At one moment, I was blessed with the affection of a worthy and beloved husband, whose smiles brightened the dear domestic fireside—the next, solitary and sad, I was a stranger, in a strange land—destitute—desolate—afflicted.

During the summer, the fevers to which northern constitutions are generally susceptible, laid many a strong man low; and besides the care of our little family, and the performance of my husband's duties as an instructor of youth, we found our time fully occupied in ministering to the sick, who, like ourselves, strangers from home, had none to care for them in the hour of trial. Some we took into our dwelling, and little did I imagine, while watching beside their beds, how soon I must perform the same painful task, for a far dearer friend.

But the trying hour drew near, and this friend, who had never known what it was to be laid aside from active duties, since my acquaintance with him, was also visited by the fatal pestilence. Of *his* exposure to sickness, I never dreamed; but I often thought of the probability that to myself or to my children, the change of climate might prove fatal. This fear in my husband, turned all his solicitude from himself, and he watched over us with the tenderest anxiety.

How often did this beloved one speak of his present happiness, and dwell upon the prospects opening for future domestic comfort. A few evenings previous to his illness, he said to me :

"We want nothing to add to our enjoyment but the society of our northern friends."

He then made a calculation of the time it would require to liquidate the heavy debt, with which he was now wholly burdened, by the death of my brother, but which he was fast diminishing, by frequent payments from a generous salary.

"In four years," he said, "I think it can be accomplished, and then we shall be free from this pecuniary trouble, and we may be reunited to those whom we love."

"O do not deceive yourself," I replied, "with hopes that may never be realized. I feel, that with us, every thing future is most uncertain."

"But you know, there can be no great danger in *planning*, if we never execute. It is pleasant even *to talk* of meeting friends again."

Never shall I forget the deep emotions excited in my breast, on the evening of the succeeding Sabbath, as seated with him in our chamber, surrounded by our little family group, enjoying a delightful moonlight scene, we sang at his request the hymn—

> "Come we that love the Lord
> And let our joys be known."

We conversed on the blessedness of those, who behold the glories of Immanuel, and never, never sin." Our souls were raised above the world, and I believe that we enjoyed an elevation of feeling, a solemnity of spirit, that was peculiarly calculated to prepare us for the approaching trial.

On the next day, Mr. C. complained of feeling very unwell, and consulted a physician. Doctor S. seemed anxious, and bade him attend carefully to his prescriptions. As I urged him to eat some food that I had specially prepared for him, for which he had no appetite, I laughingly said: " O you *must* eat ; I shall not suffer *you* to be sick," the physician, with a look. and manner that struck to my heart, and which has since convinced me that he was aware of the danger that threatened him, said to me, "my dear friend, you are not Omnipotent !"

For three days, my husband was able to walk about the room, but complained much of his head. Some circumstances, since recalled to mind, have led me to believe that *he* was aware of his danger, though he carefully concealed it from me. He was unwilling that I should leave his room, even for a short time, and when I urged the claims of the family, his reply was,

" Let them manage for themselves now, I can not spare you, I want your society."

I did devote myself to him, and during this last week of intercourse, it now seems strange, that not a single word escaped us, respecting the probability of a separation. I thought it scarcely *possible.* I considered his indisposition as the result of a cold, accompanied by a slight fever, which a few days of quiet and seclusion from care, would entirely remove.

On Saturday, the distress in his head increased, and he became delirious, but as the Doctor had said that the fever would form a crisis on that day, or on the following Monday, I was not alarmed. His situation distressed me, and the physician, deceived by my appearance, supposed that I was aware of his danger, and therefore did not speak of it to me. Some favorable symptoms, awakened hopes in the mind of Doctor S., that he might recover. A partial restoration to reason, on Sabbath morning, gave me still greater confidence, and I then resolved, that as soon as the room should be cleared of visitors, and he had rested from the fatigues of the morning's interruptions, I would enjoy a conversation that I had desired to have with him. I wished much, that we might both be profited by this visitation, and both renew our consecration to God, and commence a new life. We did each commence a *new life* indeed. He, I trust, entered into glory—and I was left a widow.

When our friends had gone, Mr. C. complained of great exhaustion, gave his pet, as Maria called herself, a kiss, and fell asleep. I took my seat beside him, resolving to improve the first hours of his awaking. He did awake, but he knew me not—he knew me no more, unless he recognized me in delirium, and never again were the lips of my husband opened to address me, in the language of affection. Though the delirium continued, I entertained no apprehensions of the result of that crisis on the morrow to which I was looking with so much anxiety, and so much assurance that it would prove favorable.

Though many kind friends offered their services, I preferred to be his only watcher through the hours of that solitary night. As with the point of a diamond, are the sensations of that watch graven on my soul. No creature was near me, save a young servant, and my children, who were all in a sound slumber, unconscious of my distress. Every noise reverberated through the large building in which we dwelt, and as my husband's delirium increased, the loud howling of the watch dog, and the low moaning of the wind, seemed to excite in him a distressing terror. It was a night never to be forgotten ; yet it seems strange to me *now*, that through all those dismal hours, I never revolved in my mind the probability of the greater trial that awaited me; nor even when I collected my family in the morning, around the bed of the dear unconscious sufferer, to beg for a blessing on the means employed for his recovery, did I entreat for peculiar support under peculiar trials.

I have since thought, that God in mercy prevented

my suspicion of his danger, knowing that exhausted nature would sink under the fatigues of incessant watchings and distress of mind. He continued insensible to the anxiety of friends, and unconscious of the presence of the beloved ones, who gathered around his bed until twelve o'clock. At that time, a friend who had just entered, first conveyed to my mind the idea of danger, and just at the moment that the spirit was forsaking its earthly tenement, did I first learn that I was about to be bereaved. Stunned by the blow, I made no resistance to those who led me from the room to my chamber, and there, on my knees, I awaited, what even then, I hoped would be a favorable issue to this terrible crisis. But when the words of Doctor S. sunk into my heart,—

"All human help has failed," I *then* felt in all its bitterness that I was indeed *a widow*.

I was, literally, *alone*, with no female friend to comfort me in this time of trial, though surrounded by many who knew and respected the departed, and who would fain have sympathized with me, in the desolation which spread over my soul. Truly at such a time "the heart knoweth its own bitterness, and a stranger intermeddleth not with it." I was stricken to the dust, but not forsaken; cast down, but not in despair. Though the shock I received, from the suddenness of the blow, nearly dethroned reason, I was not left comfortless. Heaven was now brought near to earth; only a narrow passage—and it seemed *very narrow*—separated me from the friend and companion of my youth and riper years, whom I expected soon to meet in our Father's home. Eternity seemed very near, and so impressed was I with the belief that I should very shortly follow the departed one to glory, that the trial seemed more like the *temporary* separation of those who look forward to a speedy reunion. O could I then have viewed the long and weary way which lay before me; the privations and trials I was to meet in educating my children, and in providing for their support, surely heart and flesh would have failed, and I should have sunk beneath the stroke.

On the morning after my husband's death, as I sat weeping by the side of all that remained of *him* on earth, my little M. entered the room, and in her usually affectionate manner took my hand and said,

"Mamma, why do you cry?"

I pointed to her father, and spoke of the loss that we had all sustained.

"Mamma," she said, "do you believe that Pa has gone to Heaven?"

"Most assuredly, I do," was my reply.

"And are you crying because Pa has gone to Heaven?"

The reproof of the child was not unregarded, and often, in after times, when I have felt the bitterness of my trial in all its freshness, has this question recalled to mind, made me ashamed of the selfishness of my grief. Dear E. too, though but six years of age, was made a comforter to me. Sitting with me a few days afterwards, she asked permission to read the Bible to me. I bade her choose a chapter for herself, and she, opening the sacred volume, read the fifty-fourth chapter of Isaiah: "Thy maker is thy husband; the Lord of Hosts is his name; and thy Redeemer the Holy One of Israel."

"For a small moment have I forsaken thee; but with great mercies will I gather thee.

"In a little wrath I hid my face from thee for a moment, but with everlasting kindness will I have mercy on thee, saith the Lord thy Redeemer," &c.

It seemed to me truly as though God was speaking to me by the mouth of infancy. Again and again did I peruse that chapter, and from it derive strength that was to support me through new and trying scenes.

CHAPTER VIII.

MY ILLNESS.

IT was ascertained, that my husband's death was directly owing to the influence of a miasma, generated in a large marsh, which was about two miles distant from the building that we occupied, and as the situation was pronounced unhealthy, we were in a few days removed to the " Sand Hills," to spend the remainder of the summer months in the family of Colonel W. Doctor S. had pronounced my husband's illness a decided case of yellow fever, and I had scarcely become settled in my new home, in the midst of kind and attentive strangers, before the same disease attacked me; but it came not to me like a " thief in the night," for judging from my feelings that disease was approaching, I had taken such precautionary measures as greatly diminished the violence of the attack. " But for this," said my physician, " humanly speaking, you would have been laid beside your husband."

Never shall I forget my feelings at the commencement of this illness. I believed I was about to bid farewell to earth, and I desired "to set my house in order," while I had my reason. I examined anew the foundation of my hope—and though I found much, very much in my past life, that called for humiliation and repentance, I felt that the blood of Christ *could* and *would* cleanse me from all my sin. I felt *assured* that I had put my trust in Him, and that I should not be cast off. The promises of God seemed to be so suitable for every condition, and to contain such a pledge of covenant blessings to my dear children, that I was enabled to cast them all upon His fatherly care, and while they stood weeping around my bed, so great was the peace and joy of my soul that I could scarcely refrain from singing aloud,

> "Arise, my soul, with joyful powers,
> And triumph in my God."

For four weeks was I prostrated by extreme suffering. I was often deprived of my reason or was in a state of entire insensibility, but when conscious of my situation I fully expected to be summoned to join the loved ones who had preceded me to their heavenly home. Through the whole of this distressing sickness my blessed Father did not forsake me. His comforts and promises refreshed my soul, and before He brought me back to the activities of the world, He made me willing *to live, to suffer*, or *to die*, as He should direct.

CHAPTER IX.

WIDOWHOOD.

WITH returning health, the question presented itself, what shall I do?—in what business engage, in
order to support myself and my children? After
much prayer and consultation with friends, I determined to open a boarding-house, and in October, with
my pecuniary resources reduced to *nine dollars*, my
health still feeble from my severe and protracted illness, I commenced my new life of widowhood and responsibility.

The trustees of the Academy had kindly paid my
husband's salary to the close of the term, but this was
exhausted by the necessary funeral expenses, and by
my illness; and they also granted me the privilege of
educating my sons in the Institution, free of expense.

Now was the time to feel in its full force, the extent of my loss. Daily was I reminded by my ignorance of business, and my exposure to imposition of
every kind, of the affection of that dear husband, who
would never suffer me to be burdened by providing
for the family when he was near. The wants of a

large family of boarders to be supplied, and that liberally and satisfactorily—my children, too young to appreciate their loss, or their mother's care or anxiety on their account,—without resources, and in feeble health, my faith, and hope, and spirits, would at times all sink, and I could only cry out in my distress, "O that it were with me as in months that are past!" Often did I, in the agony of my spirit and the rebellion of my heart, desire that God would prepare my children and take us all to Himself.

One day—"a day of darkness and of gloom"—in which I had been more than usually perplexed and tried, I had frequently exclaimed in the spirit of impatience, "Oh! that I had wings like a dove, I would flee away and be at rest." The evening bell reminded me that the hour for our weekly lecture had arrived. I was too unhappy to desire to leave the house, but something whispered to my heart that the sanctuary was the place to find comfort, and I went. The hymns selected spake reproof to my rebellious heart, and I was awed in the presence of that God who knew *what was in my heart*; but when the minister of God arose and repeated for his text the very words that had so often risen to my lips through the day,—"Oh! that I had wings like a dove, I would flee away and be at rest,"—I felt assured that God had directed my steps to the sanctuary, and the message to my soul; and when he feelingly spoke of the cowardice and rebellion which often dictated that prayer; of our unwillingness to meet the discipline which our heavenly Father sees we need, and applies in parental love, my heart was humbled within me, and I trust I returned home penitent and submissive.

Many were the trials I experienced, on account of my children, and from anxiety, lest my sons should be corrupted by intercourse with irreligious and immoral companions; many the difficulties I passed through, in providing for my large family, but I think that after this reproof in the sanctuary I never suffered myself to sink so low in despondency. "Leave thy fatherless children and I will preserve them, and let thy widows trust in me," was a promise on which I rested in confidence.

Often, in a wonderful manner, did my Father, who beheld all my need, graciously supply my wants. Accustomed to carry every burden and lay it at the foot of the cross; to go and tell Jesus my every necessity and every trial, I was never sent from the mercy-seat without some token of His love, while supplies would sometimes be granted in a way so unexpected that it seemed as though the windows of heaven were opened for my relief.

The two succeeding years were marked by events of thrilling interest. They will ever live in remembrance, to awaken humility and gratitude; they were preeminently years of preparation for my subsequent career. I suffered much from pecuniary embarrassments, and often was so straitened for means that I could scarcely maintain abroad an appearance of respectability, and yet the fact was not suspected, as economy and close calculation, aided by my mourning garb, did me good service. My children had little idea of the sacrifices and privations to which their mother submitted that they might enjoy the advantages of good society, and the privileges of a good education.

The example of Mrs. Graham, of sainted memory, often inspired me with courage when heart and flesh seemed failing, who, when sitting down to her frugal meal of "*potatoes and salt*" could say, " I delight to do thy will, O my God."

" Peace with God," says her biographer, "and a contented mind, supplied the lack of worldly prosperity, and she adverted to this, her humble fare, in after life, to comfort the hearts of suffering sisters." Her experience and submission did serve greatly to encourage and strengthen mine.

Among the varied trials to which I was subject, was one of no ordinary character. Most of the boarders who resided with me during the winter, were accustomed to spend their summer months in traveling, or at their northern homes. Only two of the inmates of my dwelling professed to love the Saviour, and they kindly led in our family devotions, and asked the blessing of God upon our daily meals. On the evening previous to their departure, I was conversing with a Quaker gentleman, who was also a member of my family, and proposed that he should perform the latter service for us, as he did not hesitate to call himself a Christian.

"Well, Harriet," said he, "I will see what I can do for thee, the Spirit may not move me. I will see."

"May I then call on you to perform this kind office, and will you promise to oblige me?"

With one of his arch smiles, he nodded, as I thought, his assent, and left me.

When summoned to dinner, we were all seated before he made his appearance, and as he passed to his seat, which was always directly opposite to me, I cast upon him an appealing look, which was answered by an expressive bow, which quite assured me that he would not refuse my request.

"Mr. L.," I said, "will you ask a blessing for us?" With a most amusing smile, he fixed his eyes steadily upon me, and replied,

"Thee will do it thyself, Harriet."

No levity marked the group that surrounded my table, and no discomposure of spirit prevented me from performing the duty thus suddenly imposed upon me. God strengthened me for it, and I had no foolish fears in attempting it.

In the evening I was again summoned to take up the cross. As I was about to commend my family to the care of our heavenly Father for the night, I was interrupted by the entrance of several of my boarders;

of course I did not suppose that duty required such a sacrifice of feeling as would be involved in leading our family devotions before such a household. The Bible lay on the table beside me. "Well, Mrs. C.," said a young German, "who is to pray for us to-night?" I was startled by the question: "I think, Mr. D.," was the agitated reply, "that we must do our own praying."

"And why should not *you* do it for us?" said another, who was from my own New England. "I never could see why the head of a family, if she is a widow, should not take the lead in family worship; I boarded," he continued, "for some time with a widow lady who never omitted the duty, and her boarders all respected her for her consistent Christian conduct."

The approval of this course was unanimous, "and now, Mrs. C.," persisted the German youth, "I do not see but you must do our praying for us."

"I certainly can read the Bible," I said, with the feeling that I could proceed no farther. I selected the most devotional of the Psalms, and as I closed the sacred volume, with a feeling that I could not—that I dare not—resist, I kneeled in prayer in the midst of these impenitent young men who had taught me my duty, and again was I strengthened and assisted in the accomplishment of that which at first seemed wholly impossible.

There are those who may be disposed to cavil and

object to a female assuming such a responsibility; to convince such of its propriety, I have only to wish that a necessity as *morally imperious* may be laid upon them. The path of duty would be plain to them then.

If our heavenly Father deprives our families of their head and their guide, does He design to deprive them of their religious privileges?—and what widowed mother, deeply imbued with the spirit of her high obligations, can refuse to present her family to God for His blessing? Rather let her say with one of old, "In the name of my God, will I set up my banner." Thus saith the Lord, "Fear thou not for I am with thee; I will strengthen thee, yea, I will help thee, yea, I will uphold thee with the right hand of my righteousness."

"Give to the winds thy fears;
　　Hope, and be undismayed;
God hears thy sighs and counts thy tears,
　　He shall lift up thy head."

After a trial of nearly three years, finding that if I continued to seek a support from keeping boarders I should only become more and more deeply involved in debt, I resolved to change my plans of life. The circumstances leading to this change were mortifying and distressing. Here again was exhibited the evidence of a Father's care. I found that my expenses exceeded my income. As my boarders were mostly northern men, they generally spent the summer months at home, thus materially reducing my receipts while the expense of house rent and servants' wages continued through the entire year. The cotton market was not stationary, and unfortunately, in the autumn of 1822, just as I was settled, as I supposed, in one of the best locations in the city, I found on the return of business men that I had entirely misjudged. The market was removed to a distant point, and thither went those who would otherwise have formed a part of my family. Twelve boarders were all that were left to me, and when at the expiration of the first quarter the rent was demanded, I had not wherewith to answer the demand. What was to be done? Boarders were all located elsewhere. In what other business could I engage? The prospect was appalling. In the deep agony of my spirit I called upon the Lord, "when my heart is overwhelmed within me, lead me to the rock that is higher than I. I cried unto the Lord and He heard my prayer."

Though unwilling to make my situation known, as I could not even seem to be soliciting relief, at the earnest entreaties of a friend who had seen that my spirit was burdened, I made known to her my circumstances. She consulted her husband without my knowledge, and immediately, as I afterwards learned, a few kind friends met together and contributed an offering for the widow and fatherless. After paying the rent of a good house for a year, and providing me with many comforts they reserved the remainder for a future supply.

My first intimation of their kindness was received on the morning after taking possession of another dwelling, which by the urgent advice of one of these friends I had engaged,—though with many fears that I would not be able to meet the rent—when a receipt in full for a year's rent, which had been paid in advance, was placed in my hands by my landlord. I burst into tears, and gave praise to God who still continued His mercy to His wayward child.

During the remainder of the winter I taught a small school, and was thus enabled to furnish a scanty support for myself and my children. On the marriage of my mother, in the spring, I was urged to return to my northern home, and the wish to educate my children in their fatherland led me seriously to consider the practicability of such a removal. My eldest son had been sent to Middlebury a year before, and was preparing to enter college. My wish to return was very great, but I had not the means of defraying my expenses. I had incurred heavy debts while endeavoring to support a boarding establishment, and there seemed no probability that I should ever again see my friends in the home of my youth.

I finally agreed to allow a test proposed by a few friends, to decide the question. My furniture was sold at auction, and a dividend was made of its proceeds among my creditors. By almost all of them, it was generously returned to me, so that abundant means were thus supplied to defray the expenses of my journey to the north, and I determined to depart.

In the month of May, 1823, I took passage for Charleston, S. C., with my children and a small party of friends, who were returning home. That parting hour lives in the memory of the past. Farewells were exchanged with friends whom I expected to see no more on earth, and I went forth full of demonstrations of their continued interest, deeply sensible of my obligations to my heavenly Father, and more and more impressed with the truth that "here we have no continuing city."

> " Pilgrim, is thy journey drear?
>   Are its lights extinct for ever?
> Still suppress the rising fear—
>   God forsakes the righteous—*never*
>
> Storms may gather o'er thy path,
>   All the ties of life may sever;
> Still amid the fearful scath,
>   God forsakes the righteous—*never*."

Our passage down the Savannah river was slow and tedious, but early on Sabbath morning we anchored in the harbor of Charleston. Here the friends of my departed brother soon surrounded and welcomed me. Three weeks were delightfully spent in this interesting city, and here I found a band of Christians, who, in their devotion to their Master's cause and the hallowed influence of Christian affection, fully answered my idea of the fellowship that existed in the church in the days of its primitive simplicity.

I visited the grave of my beloved brother, whose praise and whose memory were in the church, and in the Sabbath schools of which he was a superintendent, and I formed many friendships among his friends, that I trust will be perpetuated in eternity. With much regret I parted from these interesting friends and scenes, again to embark on my homeward voyage.

CHAPTER X.

"We need not go to open haunts of vice
    To look for sin; the best of our frail race,
    May find it shrined within the heart's recess,
    Mingling with all his thoughts, his words and deeds.
    Since man is sinful, sure we need
    The Sabbath day to call us back to God;
    By prayer and penitence to fit us,
    To stand before Immanuel's throne."

A CIRCUMSTANCE occurred in connection with this voyage, which, as it is the second of the kind that has come to my knowledge, I record for the encouragement of those who reverence the Sabbath. I had engaged and paid for my passage to New York, with the understanding that the vessel would sail on the following Monday. Early on the morning of the Sabbath, word came from the captain—himself professedly a pious man,—that a favorable wind had sprung up, and that all the passengers with the exception of our party were on board, and we were urged to hasten our departure. I decidedly refused compliance with the request; referred to the agreement respecting the *time* of sailing, and desired that if any change was made my passage money should be returned. The captain in great perplexity came to see me. He pleaded his cause earnestly the passengers were clamorous to depart; a favorable wind promised a speedy passage; a rival vessel, the "President," had hoisted her sails and would reach the great city before them, and finally he begged that I would be less scrupulous and depart with him. I appealed to his religious principles, and to the command to "keep the Sabbath," and asked,

"Why is it, Captain B., that more vessels go out of port on the Lord's day than on any other?"

"Why," said he, with a smile, "it is a *good day*, because there are more Christians praying for us on this day."

"Those prayers," I replied, "are not offered for the mariner's *continuance* in sin, but that he may repent and turn unto the Lord."

As I steadfastly refused compliance with his wishes, he left me declaring that "he knew that I was a *Yankee*, because I was so determined to have my own way."

While I was at the tea-table he again made his appearance.

"Now, Mrs. C., I have given you a *whole day* to attend church, the President is on her way, out of sight, and the passengers declare that they will be detained no longer."

"Captain, I sincerely regret to be an annoyance to you or your passengers, but with my present views of duty I *can not* comply with your request."

"But some on board are so enraged that they are actually swearing about you."

"That is an additional reason," I said, smiling, "why I should fear to trust myself with them while conscious of doing what I believe to be wrong. I might meet the fate of the prophet of Nineveh. Now, Captain, no persuasion that you can use will affect my decision. If you feel that you must sail to-day, you go without me and my friends, for they all approve of this decision. If you choose to wait, you shall see us with the early dawn on board your vessel."

"Well," said the Captain, with a long sigh, "I do not intend to lose this company, so I will take up my anchors and pretend that I am about to set sail, but I shall only get my vessel out into the stream, and wait till morning."

Many angry glances greeted us as we ascended the vessel's side on the bright morning of Monday, but the addition to our company of a clergyman and his family, in consequence of the delay, quite restored the Captain's good humor and *we* secured a pleasant party of pious friends.

For six days no cloud obscured our sky; no unpleasant circumstance occurred to disturb our passage; bright moonlight nights and a calm sea, gave us the opportunity every evening, of collecting for the worship of God, and when Saturday night arrived we retired to rest full of bright hopes of anchoring in the habor of New York on the following morning, in season to attend upon the worship of God in the sanctuary. We were about entering the Narrows, and the beautiful island of Manhattan was looming up in the distance, when a violent gale drove us back to sea, and our Sabbath proved a severely sick and turbulent day. Early on Monday as with renewed hopes and with joyful looks, we were again approaching the city, the Captain summoned me on deck, and pointing to a vessel in the distance that had just risen above the horizon, exclaimed,

"There, Mrs. C., comes the President, still plodding her weary way along, while *we* are about to cast anchor in the harbor."

"Now, Captain, what do you think of *trusting God*, and obeying his commandments?"

"Ah," said he, "I see that it is the best way. I'll remember this."

At this discovery, a shout went up from the passengers and crew for the triumph achieved over the tardy vessel. We afterwards ascertained that contrary winds, on the day of their departure from Charleston, had driven them far to the south, and thus they were disappointed in their expected victory over us.

CHAPTER XI.

VISIT TO MY EARLY HOME.

> I miss the dear parental dwelling,
>   Which memory, still undimmed, recalls,
> A thousand early stories telling,
>   I miss the venerable walls:
> I miss the well-remembered faces,
>   The voices, forms of fresher days:
> Time plows not up these deep drawn traces,
>   These lines, no ages can erase.

WE spent but one night in New York, and then pursued our course towards my native state, to visit my mother who had recently returned to her early home. Language can not express my emotions, as I approached the scenes of my childhood and youth— scenes from which I had been exiled for more than twenty years. The sad lament of Naomi was in my heart: "I went out full but the Lord hath brought me home empty. Call me Mara, for the Lord hath dealt bitterly with me."

Change was written on all around me. "I said of the friends of my youth, where are they?"

> "All scattered—all sundered, by mountain and wave,
>   And some, in the cold, silent womb of the grave."

I looked for the pleasant grove where I had loved to wander in school-day thoughtlessness, with companions as full of glee as myself, and for the trees beneath whose venerable branches we had so often united our carols with the sweet songsters, who nestled unmolested in their leafy homes, and I hoped, even though time might almost have effaced them, to find some precious names inscribed on those trees, rendered sacred by the associations of years passed away. The grove "was not," for the axe of the woodman had not spared a single tree.

> "Not a *token* or *trace* could I view,
> Of the names that I loved,—of the trees that I knew;
> Like a tale that is told they had vanished away.
> And I thought the lone river that murmured along,
> Was more dull in its music, more sad in its song,—
> Since the birds that had nestled and warbled above,
> Had all fled from its banks, at the fall of the grove."

A few days after my arrival at my mother's, I was taken violently ill with typhus fever, and for some days no hope was entertained of my recovery. For nearly three months I was confined to my room, much of the time too delirious to be sensible of these apprehensions; but God in his merciful providence spared me to my children, and to the work for which he had been preparing me.

In September I returned to Middlebury, to a solitary home. Oh! how dark and desolate did every thing appear to me as I entered the scene of former joys and sorrows; how gloomy the prospect that opened before me. Four years previous to this I had left the place full of pleasant prospects, rejoicing in the expectation of being soon reunited to my husband ; but now I had laid him to rest and returned destitute, with no earthly means of support but the labor of my hands, dependent wholly on the promises of God. To supply present necessities, I resorted once more to keeping boarders, but the experience of one year, satisfied me that this was not my vocation, and I determined to abandon it.

CHAPTER XII.

TEACHING IN VERGENNES.

MY mind had become more and more impressed with the belief, that it was my duty to teach, and as circumstances all seemed to point to this as my future employment, most willingly, though with much fear and trembling, I assumed new responsibilities, and in 1825, commenced a school in the city of Vergennes. Here I found many kind friends—and *trials* in abundance. For four years I toiled in the midst of cares, and labors and sorrows of no trifling kind. My eldest son, then a student in college, had been entered there with the express assurance, that the expenses of his education should be defrayed by a friend who had voluntarily agreed to assume the responsibility, but by the removal of that friend from the post that he occupied, R. was cast upon me for support. This unexpected increase of expense continually weighed me down, so that at times it seemed as though I must sink under my difficulties. Anxiety lest his extreme youth should expose him thoughtless as he was, to the temptations that I knew surrounded him, added to my distress, and without Divine support I could never have sustained the burden. My health yielded to the demands made upon my strength to such a degree, that I passed day after day in such bodily anguish, that death seemed the only relief. But my heavenly Father did not forsake me—light was scattered in my pathway.

Once when called upon for the payment of forty dollars, for the board of my son, I had not even one dollar to meet the demand, and the individual to whom the sum was due, was like myself a widow dependent on her own efforts for support. I had no earthly resource; I carried my burden to God and plead with agonizing earnestness for a supply to meet the necessities of the present case. I do not think that the idea of *submission* entered my mind. I felt that I was pleading for the *widow;* that her wants *must be* relieved, and that God was in a measure *pledged* to hear my cry.

As I rose uncomforted and sad, and sat pondering upon my trials, rather suspecting that wrong feelings had mingled with my prayer, I saw that I had been *dictating* to my heavenly Father, instead of seeking help as an unworthy suppliant. I was condemned at my own tribunal, and again I implored not *money,* but *mercy* at the throne of grace. I plead for submission to the Divine will, and sought anew to cast all my burdens on Him who had never forsaken me. Peace of mind followed this renunciation of self, and I returned to my children with a mind stayed on God.

"Mamma," cried our youthful pet, as she came bounding into the room in her usual joyous manner, "Mamma, here is a letter for you, a boy gave it to me and then ran away, 'tis a dirty looking thing and I would not touch it."

It certainly was a "dirty looking thing." A sheet of yellow foolscap paper, that might from its appearance have been exhumed from the ruins of antiquity, contained these lines :

"Mrs C.—Enclosed you will find forty dollars which is sent for the benefit of yourself and children. Seek not to ascertain who is the donor, for you will search in vain.   A FRIEND."

As I removed from its soiled envelope the sum that would give relief, and enable me to meet a just demand, my soul bowed in gratitude and humiliation for the aid imparted, and the lesson thus taught of the dealings of God with his children. Long did I search for the generous friend who had thus been employed by the widows' God to extend relief in this time of need ; but to this day I am ignorant to whom under Providence, I was indebted for the gift.

At the commencement of my new life, as the guide

and instructor of youth, I solemnly consecrated myself to the work, resolving that while I would devote
my energies to the cultivation and discipline of *mind*,
a prominent object should be the education of conscience and the moral affections, and the formation of
such habits as should prepare for future usefulness.
In accordance with these resolutions, religious instruction and supplication for God's blessing on the labors
of the day, formed the first morning duty. Pupils
seemed interested in the simple and brief exposition
of the Bible and often evinced their interest by questions suggested to their minds while reading the Word
of God.

I had not pursued this course long, before I received
a visit from one of the trustees of the school. With
some degree of embarrassment and awkwardness he
said,

"He called to converse with me on the subject of
imparting religious instruction to the school. Some
persons, he found, objected to having the time which
should be occupied with the lessons *thus* employed.
Some were afraid of sectarian bigotry and influence."

He then hesitated as though seeking some more
weighty objections.

"Proceed, sir," I said, "say all that you wish on
this subject. Frankly state all your difficulties without any hesitancy."

Evidently afraid that I would consider him an opposer of religion, he very cautiously queried, "whether

it would not be for the best interest of the school, to suspend for a while any *remarks* on the Bible and confine the morning exercise to the reading of a few verses, till the people had become better acquainted with me and I had time to secure their confidence."

"Mr. H., when you invited me to take charge of this school," I replied, "I presume that you under-stood what my character *has been* and what my standing *now is*, in the church of Christ."

With somewhat heightened color he stammered out that "he did not know, that he had not made any inquiry in regard to that matter."

"You certainly then neglected an important part of your duty, in selecting a teacher for your children. Allow me to ask you a few questions. I have no doubt that you acknowledge God as the author of all your mercies, "is it proper then to thank Him for His goodness?"

"Certainly, certainly," was the ready response.

"We are *daily* dependent on this Benefactor, for the mercies we need and the blessings we receive;—How often should we return to Him thanks?"

"Of course, each day," replied my censor.

"We are *unworthy* of these blessings and yet we daily and hourly need them; should we not then, sir, *confess* our unworthiness and supplicate for their continuance day by day?"

"Oh! yes, of course."

"As individuals and as families we ought to do this; why not as a school?"

"I can not see why we should not," was the reply, after a moment's thought.

"When would be a suitable *time* to do this?"

"The *morning* seems to be the best time, but you would yourself be the best judge as to the most convenient season."

"Just so. A few moments ago, Mr. H., you said that the scriptures should be read in school; would you think it proper to explain any thing difficult to be understood—to give information respecting eastern and ancient customs, &c., in order that a deeper interest in the Word of God may be excited?"

"That is certainly important."

"Should not this be done when the Bible is read?"

"Of course," was his reply.

"Now, Mr. H., you have conceded all I wish. Liberty to read and explain the Scriptures and permission to praise God for his mercies, and to entreat future blessings and guidance; and you have decided that the *first part* of each day is the most suitable portion of time for this duty. This is just what I have done, just what I shall continue to do. I have no sectarian bigotry—neither shall I impose *my* creed or that of any denomination upon the minds of my pupils; but I promise you to strive to be faithful to the trust reposed in me, and to train your children for usefulness and Heaven."

"Well, madam, I am satisfied to leave the decision of this subject with you. Good morning."

CHAPTER XIII.

ATTENTION TO RELIGION.—OPPOSITION.

MANY and severe were the trials that clustered around me during my residence in Vergennes. Every attempt to excite an interest in the minds of my pupils, on the great subject of the soul's salvation, was met with decided opposition by a pleasure-loving group, who were determined that nothing of a serious character should interrupt the hilarity of the season.

An incident in the experience of that winter will illustrate my situation. Among some of my pupils I noticed a deeper feeling and more fixed attention to religious instruction. The alarm was given and speedily the watchword passed through the ranks of the enemy, "thus far, but no farther." A ball was decided upon, as the most effectual means of driving away serious thought. A morning or two previous to the time fixed for the proposed amusement, while many were expecting to hear me "come out in a severe tirade against this terrible sin," I took my place as usual at my desk, read a portion of Scripture and made a few remarks upon the twelfth chapter of Romans. On the verse, " Be not conformed to this world," I said, " it is sometimes difficult to satisfy ourselves *when* we are in danger of too great conformity to the world. I will give you a *test* by which you may always decide whether you are in the path of duty. It is this,—never to engage in any employment or in any amusement, in pursuance of which *you dare not ask the blessing and the presence of God"* No allusion was made to the expected ball, or to the efforts of the opposing party; the effect was just what I wished. But two or three from the school attended the gay gathering and thus the design of its projectors was frustrated.

Provoked at a discomfiture so unexpected they determined to persist in their opposition to the religious influence that seemed to spread. " Mrs. C.," said they, " need not imagine she can control the young people of Vergennes. If she does not like a *single* ball, we will give her a *regular course* for the season." Then followed grave canvassings on the important subject, and " committee meetings," and divers efforts to accomplish their purposes but without success; the affair ended with open expressions of animosity against me as the cause of their failure, when my only cause of offence in the matter was the giving of that simple *test* to the school.

Several times I had been asked, if I disapproved

entirely of worldly amusements; if I thought it wrong to dance, but I answered all inquiries of this kind by an appeal to my text.

In my journal for 1826, I find this experience recorded. "How different have been my feelings since this year commenced from what they were for some weeks previous. Then the darkness of midnight brooded around me, wherever I turned my eyes I found nothing to encourage me. Threatened with the entire loss of health, I could only look forward to protracted illness,—a burden to my friends—my prospects of usefulness as a teacher destroyed and my children without protection and support. My very soul shrunk from the trial, and like Jonah I gathered myself into my own little world of selfishness and almost suffered myself to cry out, 'I do well to be angry.' But my heavenly Father dealt not with me according to my deserts; He pitied my sufferings; He listened to my cries for help; He sent His spirit to show me the depths of sin within, and He excited the tear of penitence and the supplication for forgiveness. He imparted peace to my soul—even that peace of which no earthly trial can deprive us, and though afflicted with unexpected and severe pecuniary troubles, and though this clayey tenement oft threatened to drop into dissolution, and with difficulty I struggled through the duties of each succeeding day, still He gave me such a confidence that *all* these things would work for my good—such a cheerful acquiescence in His holy will as almost made the trial sweet and turned the poison into medicine.

"Separated from my children, I find it sweet to present them one by one, by name, and plead for God's blessing upon them. He knows their various characters and their exposedness to dangers, and he can do infinitely better for them than I can even desire. He has said, 'leave thy fatherless children and I will preserve them and let thy widows trust in me,' and I will cleave to this promise. I will continue to plead it, until all my children are gathered into the family of the Redeemer. It is sweet thus to commit them to His care.

> "Sweet on His faithfulness to rest,
>   Whose love can never end;
>   Sweet, on His covenant of grace,
>   For all things to depend.
>   Sweet in the confidence of faith,
>   To trust His firm decrees:
>   Sweet, to lie passive in His hand,
>   And know no will but His."

Weeks passed and an increasing interest in the subject of religion was manifest in the school. The tearful eye, the quivering lip, the anxious look, spoke volumes to the teacher's heart. Inexperienced myself in the workings of the Holy Spirit on youthful hearts, thus congregated together, I was afraid of myself. Had this fear driven me to more entire dependence on my Saviour it had been well; but the "fightings without," alarmed me and so excited the "fears within," that all my efforts were neutralized.

Another portion of my journal, which bears date a few weeks later than the preceding extract, tells the tale of my unbelief.

"This poor, beating heart, will soon cease its struggles and this war of feeling cease. My heart has been sadly torn by conflicting emotions. I retraced the feelings and the experience of the winter;—I thought of the repeated instances in which I had earnestly asked direction of God and resolved to be willing,—His grace assisting me—to walk in the path which He should point out, and of those seasons when I thought my will *was* wholly resigned to the Lord's. Were all these feelings delusive? I trust not wholly; but I had calculated too much on the strength of religious feeling in my own heart, and the Lord showed me that my strength is very weakness. I compared my privations with those experienced by the early missionaries. True, I am an isolated being, far from the friends that I love best; but I have many comforts denied to them—some dear and valued Christian friends—religious privileges—and opportunities for doing good; while those who go to heathen lands, are called to surrender all the dear delights of social life and refined society, the comforts of home and the commingling of the heart's best affections, and go forth to expected danger and perhaps an early death. Then I remembered my perverseness and was ashamed. How mysterious have been the dealings of God with me during the last twelve years, crosses and changes have followed each other in quick succession; 'waters of a deep cup have been wrung out to me,' but my God has not forgotten to be gracious, and He has kindly led me thus far in safety. To Him be all the praise."

The interest awakened in the school deepened. Often the pupils were unable to recite their lessons. Many in the town were distressed on account of their sins; meetings for religious instruction were multiplied and Christians were looking with intense anxiety to see the results of these efforts. Alas! it was soon too evident that we were looking to the creature for results, rather than in simple confidence to the Redeemer. And thus the enemy prevailed against us; the deep solemnity passed away, and we were left to mourn over our own fearfulness of opposition, and our unbelief.

Relating to a clerical friend soon afterward the experience of this eventful period, his only reply was, " Well, friends, I have but one thing to say to you; *according to your faith* has it been unto you." What a lesson of deep and thrilling import did I learn from this first manifestation of the grace of God to my school and of my own sinful distrust.

CHAPTER XIV.

REMOVAL TO MIDDLEBURY.

SOON after this another trial came. Once and again I had been solicited to transfer my residence to Middlebury. This place had been for years the home of my choice,—was the birthplace of my soul—the spot where I had passed most of the years of my married life and where I should find, as I had no reason to doubt, kind and sympathizing friends whose attachment had been often proved.

The first application had produced so favorable a change in my pecuniary affairs at Vergennes, that though my heart longed for the society of early friends and shrunk with dread from a repetition of the trials that had almost unfitted me for my work, I felt willing to resign myself to the disposal of my heavenly Father. I certainly had no great cause for attachment to the people generally. Good and noble ones I could count as friends, but *the many* were too selfish, too groveling, to estimate the privileges of good literary or religious institutions. "He maketh haste to be rich," seemed to be inscribed on every act; "who will teach us the way?" was the great inquiry. On this subject they were wide awake, ready to combine the energies of mind and body for the accomplishment of their object.

All things having been duly considered I determined to remain another year, but at the expiration of that time the invitation which had previously been extended to me to remove to Middlebury, was renewed. The prospects which such a change offered were certainly tempting to the weary, harassed pilgrim. Pecuniary embarrassments would be lessened; a large circle of Christian friends stood ready to support me, and it seemed like returning to my own home. Yet I must leave many to whom I had become warmly attached, and dear pupils who still preserve their places in my heart's affections. But now the path of duty seemed plain and I accepted the proffered situation.

Much opposition was made to this decision; urgent intreaties and severe remarks followed, but I could say "none of these things move me." I go at the bidding of my Master, expecting to encounter responsibilities and trials, but I go with the promise of my Father graven on my heart, "I will never leave thee nor forsake thee." "Let thy widows trust in me."

Very painful was the parting hour. Overcome by

the fecling manifested by many loved ones, I could but exclaim, "what mean ye to weep and to break my heart?"

With many cherished tokens of affection, I left these beloved friends and pupils, and in December, 1829, commenced my school in Middlebury. I was accompanied only by my youngest child. My eldest son had passed through his collegiate course and was then engaged in teaching in a distant state. The youngest was then connected with the college in Middlebury. At the age of twelve he had been invited by a friend of my brother, to become a clerk in a bookstore in Charleston, and there through the faithful instructions of that friend he consecrated himself, at the age of fourteen, to his Redeemer. By the aid of the friends of Christ in that city, he had been enabled to prepare himself for college and had entered the Institution where had graduated his father and brother. My eldest daughter, whose health required a change, had been for more than three years with her grand-parents in my native state, and there, in a season of deep religious interest, she had been received into the fold of the great Shepherd. Towards the faithful pastor of the church which admitted her to its communion, she ever expressed the warmest gratitude and affection, and she often referred to him as a model of Christian and pastoral fidelity.

CHAPTER XV.

"Till David touched his sacred lyre,
In silence lay the unbreathing wire;
But when he swept its chords along,
E'en angels stooped to hear the song.
So sleeps the soul, till thou, O Lord,
Shall deign to touch its lifeless chord;
Till waked by Thee, its breath shall rise
In music worthy of the skies."

THE winter of that year passed away pleasantly; religious instruction was communicated to the pupils daily, but no special seriousness was awakened until towards the close of the term, when one individual manifested deep anxiety respecting the salvation of her soul. She resolved to remain in the family during the short vacation, that undisturbed by study or new scenes, she might seek an interest in the Saviour. With much anxiety I left her, to pass a week with friends in Vergennes, but my heart was lifted continually in earnest supplication for the descent of God's spirit on the members of the school that I had just dismissed, and of that over which I had formerly presided in Vergennes.

I returned to Middlebury to find that the distress of poor E. had greatly increased, and that she was entirely unable to resume her studies. In view of her great guilt in so long rejecting the Saviour, her soul was agonized with the fear that there could be no hope for her. I pointed her to the "Lamb of God, who taketh away the sin of the world;" I read to her His precious promises, "Him that cometh unto me I will in no wise cast out." "He that believeth on me hath everlasting life." "The blood of Jesus Christ cleanseth from all sin," &c. Two days after this she cast herself on the mercy of her Saviour and He spake peace to her soul.

The effect on the school, was electrical, and with trembling and in tears many inquired, "what do these things mean?" It was evident that this and other circumstances were awakening an intense anxiety in the minds of the pupils. There were at that time but four professors of religion in the school, including two teachers, but we commenced a prayer-meeting to be observed on Saturday evenings by all who were disposed to attend.

The course adopted for religious instruction seemed signally blessed. God spake to the hearts of the youth by His own word; often while repeating the sacred Scriptures, were they so overcome as to be unable to proceed. A series of questions or subjects were selected, and one was given out every day, for each succeeding morning and the young ladies committed and repeated their answers from the Bible, which were then explained and applied. The attributes of God were given: "If God is omnipotent and omniscient, He must know the heart of man; what is His testimony in regard to it?"

" What His sentence passed on such a character?"

" Is there no escape from this condemnation?"

" Is Christ able and willing to save all who trust in His merits?"

" Is it your duty to make an immediate surrender of yourself to His service?"

" What is *your* determination respecting it?"

By the time that the questions had advanced thus far, a deep solemnity prevailed throughout the Seminary. My youngest daughter had spent her vacation with worldly friends and had returned more trifling than I had ever known her. Evidently annoyed by the increasing seriousness exhibited in school, she avoided the society of Christians, searched her music book for the gayest airs and most trifling songs, and for a few days, it seemed, as if she and her music teacher were resolved to close their hearts against the Holy Spirit.

A remark which I dropped concerning her and which was repeated to her by a trifling companion, first awakened her anxieties. " If mother feels so troubled about me ought I not to search my own heart and see what is wrong there?" was the thought that succeeded. She laid aside her books and studied only her Bible, and for weeks no smile of peace beamed from a face usually radiant with joyousness.

The solemnity of that morning when the answers to the question, " what is your determination?" were to be given, will never be forgotten by those who then stood before God to make their decision for eternity. One, who in the spirit of levity had boasted that she had a verse to answer that question, when asked what it was, replied,

"*Go thy way for this time.*"

"You dare not repeat it," said her friend.

"Listen, and see if I dare not," was the boasting response. This determination had been whispered to me by a friend, and I was prepared to meet it. As she arose from her seat to repeat the text that she had selected, I fixed my eye upon her, deeply expressive of the solemnity that filled my soul, and awaited her decision. She hesitated, her lip quivered, the starting tear told the conflict that was passing within, she sat down unable to utter a word and then the pent up feelings of her soul burst forth in audible sobs.

The scene was perfectly overwhelming, and as with the anxiety of a mother as well as of a teacher, I followed one after another as they rose to express their *desires* or their decision to live for God, no pen can describe my feelings, and when my child with streaming eyes and with an agitation almost convulsive, spoke forth her resolution, "I will arise and go to my Father and will say unto him, Father, I have sinned against heaven and before thee," my emotions were irrepressible. Her whole appearance bespoke her sincerity, and her evident distress produced a great effect on her companions. I could not add one remark; I could only offer a broken petition to our Father for His blessing.

The attention of the pupils to this absorbing subject now became general, and nothing but strength from God imparted at that time saved me from sinking under the weight of responsibility and the burden of my labors. From the dawn of day till the midnight hour, did these dear young friends crowd to my room, to receive instruction and to entreat that prayer might be offered for them. The distress of my own child deepened: at times she seemed almost in despair. Eternity opened upon her mind with new light and force and viewing herself as a *condemned* sinner, she could not believe that mercy could be extended to one who had so long resisted the warnings of an enlightened conscience, and the love of God manifested through his son.

In the study of the Bible she sought for that peace which cometh not to those who trust *only* in the *means* of grace, for salvation. Driven from this stronghold, she turned to the *prayers* of Christian friends, and for a time there placed her confidence. Sleep departed from her and the expression of her countenance, was a faithful index to the anguish of her spirit. In vain did I point her to the "Lamb of God," whose "blood cleanseth from all sin;" in vain assure her, that it was the unbelief of her heart, that deprived her of the peace which she so earnestly sought. The proud heart, the unbelieving spirit, yielded not.

Finding that I could say nothing to induce her to venture on the promises of God, I hazarded an experiment, with much fear and with many prayers. At the close of a week in which my apprehensions concerning her had been greatly excited, after urging upon her the freeness and the fullness of Christ's salvation, I said, " Well, Maria, I see that no motive, nor persuasion from the Word of God, has had power to move you to a decision. The spirit and the bride say come, but you heed not the gracious invitation. My children must not live in vain ; God has done too much for us to suffer this. He demands the consecration of our souls and bodies to His service. If you will not give the affections of your *heart* to Him, you must give your life and improve your talents for His service. You must resume your studies on Monday, and endeavor to prepare yourself to aid me in doing good." She cast a wild imploring look upon me and without a word closed her Bible, laid her head upon it and wept aloud.

On the evening of the succeeding Sabbath, my spirits and strength were exhausted by intense anxiety for many, smitten to the soul on account of their alienation from God, and for this child of prayer who was still bowed down in distress. I commended them to the mercy of their Redeemer and sought rest upon my bed; but could I sleep quietly while the agitated footsteps over my head gave sure tokens of the distress of one who thus at the midnight hour held converse with her own soul, and while the imploring cry for mercy from my own dear child reached me from an adjoining room, as she sent up her petitions in the stillness of the night?

"Mother, do pray for me," was again and again repeated, during that season of anguish. At last in agony of spirit she came once more:

"Mother," she said, with awful solemnity, "if there is mercy in heaven or on earth, pray for me, that I be not lost forever." After uniting with her again in prayer and listening to her heart-broken cries for mercy, I persuaded her to retire and seek rest and strength for the coming day.

On the evening of Monday, she with several others was visited by our pastor, and she often recurred to that conversation as the time when she first fully resolved to accept the offers of salvation and to consecrate herself to the service of her Redeemer. The affectionate interest manifested by her pastor for her spiritual welfare and the remarks he made, encouraged her to hope that her heavenly Father might extend mercy to her, and as soon as she was alone she gave herself to God in an everlasting covenant, trusting only to the merits of her Saviour for acceptance. She now saw that a proud heart and an unsubdued will, had held her thus long in slavery; that while her almighty Friend had been inviting her by the still small voice of the spirit, speaking by his word, to *look unto Christ* and be saved, she had presumptuously marked out her own way of salvation and virtually taxed the Almighty with injustice, because in the way of disobedience she found no peace or comfort.

Our music teacher, a young lady much devoted to the world, had been for some time disturbed by the appearance of the school. She felt that it was evidently the work of the Holy Spirit, but her heart loved not the things of the spirit and she strove against the convictions which agitated her mind. She determined that if others would be so foolish as to be influenced by the solemn considerations pressed upon the conscience, she would not relinquish the pleasures of the world for the *gloom* of religion. It was very apparent that there was a great conflict in her mind. She knew her duty but she had no heart to perform it. Contrary to the advice of friends and the monitions of conscience, she attended a scene of amusement well calculated to divert her mind from every serious thought, but this device of the adversary only proved the means of deeper impressions. Every day, during the succeeding week, God spoke to her heart by the faithful efforts of Christian friends. A letter from a beloved sister, who had heard of the interest excited in the school and whose prayers had long ascended in her behalf, came home with powerful effect to her soul. Feeling that by her folly and levity, this determined opposer was seeking to undermine all my efforts for the spiritual welfare of my pupils, I also addressed a letter to her which alarmed her; and with no common interest and fervency did the prayers of Christian friends petition the throne of grace in behalf of the careless worldling. The Spirit of God visited her soul, and on the succeeding Sabbath, the preaching of the word so powerfully affected her, that the proud heart was humbled and she wept aloud. Two days passed in agony of spirit, and while bowed down in the dust at her Saviour's cross, He cast a look of compassion upon her and gave her peace in believing.

Her first anxiety when relieved from the distress that filled her soul, was for the conversion of those who had been influenced by her example. She spoke to them of the preciousness of her Saviour, and urged them to commence with her a life of devotion to God. It was interesting to see those who had so recently trifled together, now bending with one heart and one spirit in supplication to their Redeemer; to hear their voices unite in ascription of praise to God, who had put a *new song* into their mouths.

CHAPTER XVI.

> " Earnest, without delay, thy Maker's face
> Seek, and the riches of his promised grace
> Go ask in prayer: O never yet in vain,
> Was bent the knee, His favor to obtain."

THE exercises of one day—the day succeeding that in which my own beloved child and Miss A. had dedicated themselves to God,—comes up with ever living interest to my mind. As I entered the school-room in the morning, the solemnity of eternity rested upon our souls. Every heart was full and every eye testified that God was there. I called the classes to recitation, for I considered it important that there should be no suspension of regular studies. As one after another rose to answer the questions put by their teachers, the falling tear and the troubled countenance, too plainly showed their inability to give attention to their lessons. As these *nominal* recitations passed on, I was continually requested by the young ladies, to permit them to retire to the private apartments of the dwelling, for prayer with Christian friends,— for each convert had become a missionary in the school.

After closing the morning exercises as best I could,

I retired to my chamber to rest and pray; but scarcely had I entered it ere Miss B., a teacher who had aided me much in this great work, came to beg me to visit a room where, she said, for nearly two hours a little company had been praying with seven impenitent friends and they felt that they could not desist, until God had heard and answered their petitions. I entered the room and there they still kneeled, pleading for their companions. Language can not convey an adequate idea of the solemnity of the scene which presented itself to me. Again and again, the the voice of prayer ascended, succeeded by a pause like the stillness of the grave, while heart met heart in its silent aspiration for mercy on the sinner; and still none could rise from her deep prostration.

After again commending them to the grace of God and pointing them to Christ, who only can remove the burden of sin, each of the little anxious group was sent to commune in solitude, with her Bible and her God. None of them were boarders in the Seminary, but they had come to school that morning, with the determination not to leave the house till they had submitted to Jesus; and before the week closed, all those dear ones were rejoicing in God their Saviour, and returned to their homes to " tell their friends how great things the Lord had done" for their souls.

In the afternoon of the day to which I have just alluded, as I stepped from my room to enter the study hall, I could hear the voice of prayer from almost every apartment. I entered the school-room and of fifty or sixty pupils usually assembled there, only eight or ten occupied their seats. There they sat still and solemn, and yet ashamed to join their companions. As I took my seat I said,

"How solemn is this place; this is none other than the house of God."

Every head was bowed and the countenances of all showed that their hearts responded to the remark. I followed it with a few observations and the feeling which had hitherto been restrained by pride now burst forth. It was no time for study,—a higher, holier influence pervaded the minds of all. I felt that the present moment might decide their destiny for eternity.

"If," said I, "any here feel that they cannot attend to their studies and wish to seek their companions, where they are lifting up their hearts in supplication to the Father of mercies, they are permitted to leave the room."

In a moment all had retired and it might truly be said, that there was scarcely a room in the dwelling, where the voice of prayer could not be heard.

At four o'clock our pastor visited the school at my request, and the marked expression of solemnity and grief depicted on the faces of the pupils as they entered the room, arm in arm, told more forcibly than language the deep distress and conflict within. Doctor Merrill could not repress the emotions of his soul: the strong man wept and it was some moments before he could so control the agitated feelings of his heart, as to be able to address his youthful congregation.

In the evening, as had been the case for some time previous, the house was thronged with pupils and their friends, who came to converse on the subject most interesting to them and to unite in prayer in their behalf. Our little prayer-meeting, which originally consisted of four, increased to a great number of worshipers, so that often two or three rooms could not contain all who crowded to the place of meeting. It was the remark of one who spent a night in the Seminary at the time, when asked, if he had rested well, "I did not sleep at all for there was scarcely an hour of the night that I could not hear the voice of prayer in some room near me."

On Saturday morning the classes were again called together for recitation, and again was it evident that they felt too deeply the injunction of their Saviour, "seek first the Kingdom of God and His righteousness," to attend to their studies. A class had been previously directed to select the first reading lesson in Porter's Analysis, as an exercise in parsing. On opening the book, teacher and pupils were struck by the appropriateness of the words to their present condition and feelings.

> "What sinners value, I resign,
> Lord, 'tis enough that thou art mine."

"We will look at the *meaning* of these words," I said. All *felt* their import too deeply to attend to their grammatical construction. "What shall we do to be saved?" was the great inquiry, and this just then was too absorbing a subject to permit attention, even to intellectual improvement.

Though anxious for the salvation of the souls of my pupils, I felt it to be very important that the studies of the school should not be interrupted. This discipline was necessary to prevent the mind from exhausting itself by its own emotions. It would help to counteract the tendency to substitute the mere impulses and sympathies of nature, for the sober decisions of judgment and the exercise of holy affections and principles. They were accordingly resumed on Monday, after an interruption of four days, and were not again suspended. The revival continued throughout the term and was characterized by deep solemnity and stillness. Day after day I trust, there was joy in heaven, over souls renewed and pardoned.

O what a time to feel the impotency of all our efforts without help from God,—and the necessity of His grace to give efficacy to the means employed. Never did I so sensibly feel that it was not by "might or by power, but by the spirit of the living God," that this work was effected. It was a precious season of refreshing to my own soul; but such views as I had of the utter worthlessness of my own works, the awful neglect of duty, the sinfulness of my own heart pressed upon me with a weight, that but for the gracious displays of Divine love through a Mediator, I could not have endured it.   But unworthy as was the instrument, God mercifully blessed the means employed; and during that interesting season about thirty, it was hoped, became the followers of Jesus and publicly consecrated themselves to His service.

CHAPTER XVII.

INTERESTING CASES.—A SISTER'S INFLUENCE.

> "Take up your cross and say farewell;
> Go forth without the camp to Him
> Who left heaven's throne, with men to dwell;
> Who died, His murderers to redeem:
> O tell his name in every ear;—
> Doubt not,—the dead themselves will hear."

MANY of the cases that occurred during this revival were very striking. A young lady in P. was just preparing herself to attend school in Montreal, when her parents heard of the revival in the Seminary. They had devoted their children to God in baptism and felt a desire that this child of prayer, might be placed in a situation favorable for religious improvement. Like many thoughtless ones her heart was too much attached to the world to desire such a privilege and she came to us with evident reluctance. She told me, however, very frankly what were the motives of her parents in sending her to Middlebury. We have reason to believe that these parents, while they used the means offered the prayer of faith. Every word of instruction seemed to produce effect. The young lady became deeply impressed in view of her guilt and danger, and in one week from the time that she entered

the school, she indulged a trembling hope of acceptance through a Mediator.

One of the little company like the woman of Sa-
maria, full of the love of Jesus, called her brother to
her room and urged him to commence with her a life
of faith and holiness. Supremely devoted to the
world—thoughtless of the hereafter to which he was
hastening, and remembering that a few days previous
his sister seemed as careless as himself, he could not
understand the great change that had passed upon
her. He sought an interview with a pious friend
whom he loved and respected, and with much agitation asked him, what these things meant?—were they
growing mad at the Seminary? Had his sister become
a fanatic? With the simplicity of a child of God, did
this faithful friend unfold the great plan of redemption—of its perfect adaptation to the necessities of
man as a sinner dependent on the mercy of God,
and exposed to eternal punishment; and urged him to
obey the heavenly call and trust in the Redeemer
alone for salvation. The word was blessed and the
man of the world became afterward a preacher of the
gospel to perishing sinners. Who can estimate the
extent and value of a sister's influence?

Another child of prayer and of early consecration,
was sent from parents who earnestly coveted the "best
gifts" for her and the same results followed. One
who was among the earliest of the convert band, afterwards entered on a life of missionary labor in Persia.

where she fully justified the high hopes that her friends entertained of her entire consecration to the cause of her blessed Master. She went forth to her work as one who had fully counted the cost—who understood the sacrifices she was about to make, and who cheerfully laid friends, home and native land,—the enjoyments of refined society and religious privileges—*all* at the foot of the cross, as an offering to her Saviour who gave Himself a sacrifice for sin.

In view of this visit of mercy to the school we were all led to exclaim, " What hath God wrought?" " Not unto us, O Lord, not unto us, but to thy name be all the glory."

> " Glory to God on high
> Let earth and heaven reply,
> Praise ye His name.
> Angels His love adore,
> Who all our sorrows bore,
> And saints sing ever more,
> Worthy the Lamb !
>
> Ye who surround the throne,
> Cheerfully join in one,
> Praising His name.
> Ye who have felt His blood
> Sealing your peace with God,
> Sound his dear name abroad,
> Worthy the Lamb !

CHAPTER XVIII.

> "I was a wandering sheep,
>   I did not love the fold;
> I did not love my Shepherd's voice,
>   I would not be controlled.
> I was a wayward child;
>   I once preferred to roam;
> But now I love my Father's voice,—
>   I love, I love His home!

In the spring of 1831, in consequence of encouraging appearances in the town, a series of meetings were appointed, and again my school shared largely in the blessing and my heavenly Father again brought salvation to my own home.

My eldest born,—the son whom in early life I had dedicated to God, hoping that he would become a minister of the gospel—perhaps, a missionary of the cross—was still living "without hope and without God in the world." Often had my soul been agonized on his account, and day and night had I presented his case before the mercy-seat. Five years before, while he was in college and I in Vergennes, a revival of religion in the Institution of which he was a member, in some measure affected his mind. O what days of distressing anxiety did I then pass through. I went to Middlebury a few days previous to the annual fast in April, and then sought to interest Christian friends to plead for him before the throne of grace. Well do I remember the morning of that day of fasting and agonizing prayer. I had written to several Christian friends to unite with me in my secret supplications, at the ringing of the first bell for service; and to the pious members of the class with which he was connected in college, I wrote, "If you can exercise faith for one who has sinned against great light, join a widowed mother in her supplicaitons this morning, for this son of prayer and object of agonizing solicitude." The request was not unheeded. They plead for the thoughtless one, and as I was afterwards informed, they carried God's own promise to his throne, "Leave thy fatherless children and I will preserve them, and let thy widows trust in me."

So overpowering were my feelings as the hour for the *concert* approached, that I could scarcely walk or stand, and when the bell struck the first note for the hour of prayer, I sank on my knees in utter helplessness and wretchedness. From the depth of my distress, I cried unto God—unto him who had heard my supplications in other days. All day did my prayer ascend for this impenitent child, and the night still found me pleading for his soul. So intense was my anxiety, that a beloved sister now a saint in heaven, said to me, "sister, you are wrong in indulging this *exce sive* and continual agitation of feeling,—it is affecting your health. I would say to you as a friend did to Monica, the mother of Augustine, 'It is not possible that the child of so many tears and prayers should perish.'"

But the harvest passed by and he was not saved.

Often since has the inquiry arisen in my mind, why were not these prayers heard? They were earnest— they were continued— they were made in the full belief that God was able to fulfill His own promises. The subject was perfectly absorbing. This one idea — the salvation of that child's soul, filled all my thoughts and was the burden of every prayer. In after times, when God graciously answered my petitions, I was able to see *why* the answer was then withheld. *My prayers were selfish.* I could not bear to be disappointed in the expectation in which I had indulged, that in their earliest years *my* children should all be the followers of the Saviour. This was *my* son; I had said much respecting my belief in the covenant, and I felt in some measure pledged to show in the early conversion of my children, what that covenant had done for me. I could afterwards plainly see that my distress partook more of the nature of self-inflicted torture, than of an humble submissive spirit, desirous only of the glory of God. I felt with Israel of old, "I *can not* let Thee go, except thou bless me;" but I said it with a fretful, impatient spirit, that could not be denied.

Time passed on and the thoughtless child continued unmindful of his great obligations to his Redeemer, nor did a sudden and severe illness, that threatened speedily to summon him into the presence of his rejected Saviour, serve to lead his thoughts to his own danger or to God. When five years later, the protracted meeting to which I have alluded, commenced in Middlebury—knowing that a vacation in the Institution with which R. was connected, would give him an opportunity to journey—my prayer to my heavenly Father was earnestly raised, that his steps might be directed to the home of his youth, and that this might be the time of mercy to his soul. He was the subject of prayer in the family circle and in the social prayer-meeting.

My situation at this time was one of no common anxiety and trial. A deep solemnity pervaded the minds of my pupils. Some were in great distress and one, R. S., gave me no rest day or night. Orphaned in early life, with an extreme degree of sensitiveness and refinement of feeling, she had been cast upon the world, with but one near relative who could sympathize with her in her youthful trials, and that one younger than herself. Disappointed in her expectation of deriving happiness from the world, she shrank into herself and became the subject of morbid sensibility. Henceforth, she determined to give her whole attention to the cultivation of her mind, and to seek within herself her resources for happiness.

When she looked around, upon her first entrance into the Seminary, and observed the interest evinced by many in the great subject of their soul's salvation, folding her arms and erecting her tall figure, in the pride of her heart, she exclaimed,

"Mrs. C. need not expect to make a Christian of me, I came here for intellectual improvement alone ;" and then she sat erect in her seat, when religious instruction was imparted, speaking with her piercing eye, a meaning not to be misunderstood, "talk on— *you can not move me.*"

But One greater than her teacher did speak effectually to her soul, and the rebellious heart was humbled. She sought my room, my counsel and my prayers. Very deep were her convictions of sin ; very unwilling was she to submit to the simple requisitions of the gospel. Yet while her whole soul rose against the plan of salvation, she *thought* that she desired an interest in her Saviour, above all other things. Accustomed always to "write bitter things" against herself, it was sometime after her Christian friends had hope for her that she indulged hope for herself. She was "too vile to indulge such a hope." I pointed to the Saviour's own words, "I am not come to call the righteous, but *sinners* to repentance." But she did "not feel this vileness, sufficiently."

"Show me the passage," I replied, "where Christ has told the sinner the *degree of conviction* that he must have, before he may apply to Him. If you are convinced that you have forfeited all claim to His mercy by your disobedience and rejection of His salvation, that is all that he requires. You may fearlessly apply to Him, to cleanse your soul from all pollution."

Sometimes it would seem as though she were just stepping into the healing pool, and then retreating in fearful agony, she would fly to me for direction and prayer. But the God of the orphan did not forsake her. She did at last cast herself, in all her helplessness and woe, upon His mercy, and the hope of sins forgiven, sent rays of comfort through her soul.

I often recall a little incident of her after life, with much interest. Her mother, whose memory she cherished with deep and sacred affection, while on her dying bed, called her to her side, and taking a string of gold beads, which were then much in use and which she had worn for many years, fastened them on the neck of her child as her last gift. Treasured near her heart, though unseen by human eye, they kept their place for years. After her consecration to God's service, she told me, that if Jesus would accept of such an unworthy laborer, she wished to devote herself to missionary work, and to prepare herself for usefulness "somewhere in this wide world." She remained some time in the Seminary as a pupil and afterwards as a teacher. As we sat side by side one day, in a missionary convention, where the claims of a dying world were urged upon us, I saw her loosen something that seemed suspended from her neck, and gathering the string of beads that had so often spoken to her of a mother's love, carefully wrap them in a paper on which she wrote with a pencil these words, that I did not hesitate to read as she sat beside me:

" The last gift of affection, from a dying mother to her orphan child—now consecrated to God's service."

She was overcome by the effort and our tears flowed together.

A few years afterwards this beloved friend might be seen toiling beneath the scorching sun of India, with a holy band who had gone forth to their labor of love as pioneers in the great missionary work. Faithfully did R. perform her vow of consecration, until her work was accomplished, and her beloved Redeemer gave to her the welcome summons, " Come up hither." " Enter into thy rest." Her ashes repose far from her natal soil; but her spirit rejoices in God her Saviour.

CHAPTER XIX.

> "Say dost thou mark that beaming eye?
>   That countenance serene?
> The smile of hope and love and joy,
>   Where gloom so late has been?
> More beautiful, that sight appears,
> Than all the charms that nature wears."

AT the commencement of the revival, to which reference has been made, my eldest daughter and three pupils were all very ill with typhus and remittent fevers. Anxiety on their account,—the care that I was necessarily compelled to bestow on them, and my great solicitude that this day of grace, might prove to the pupils the day of salvation, joined to my anxiety respecting my son, would have proved too heavy a burden, had I trusted only to human strength.

On the Sabbath morning previous to the protracted meeting, I requested prayers for my impenitent son, that his steps might be directed to Middlebury at this juncture and that he might be brought to repentance. The Spirit of God aided us, and we all felt that we were near the mercy-seat. As I rose to leave the room at the close of the exercises, one much loved, who has since gone home to her Father in heaven, took my hand and said, "Be of good courage such prayers will be answered ; your son will be made whole."

The religious exercises commenced on Tuesday, and continued with increasing interest for three days.

Some there were who inveighed loudly against "such a waste of time ;"—"the Sabbath was given for religious instruction and that was sufficient for all such purposes." These remarks reached the ears of our pastor and he replied to them by reading the thirtieth chapter of the second book of Chronicles, from the twenty-second to the twenty-seventh verse.

Such was the state of feeling in the Seminary, and such the anxiety to attend, that I dismissed the school during the public exercises and many of my pupils at that interesting season, gave their hearts to God.

Dear Maria when not occupied in nursing her sister, was constantly employed in efforts to lead her young friends to her Saviour. Her drawers were filled with notes, written in reply to her earnest entreaties to forsake all for Christ, and she labored not in vain. One memorable evening when I had invited our pastor to attend a meeting in the Seminary, the dining room was filled, and so intensely solemn were the minds of all and so deep the feelings of distress exhibited by many, that Doctor M. proposed after the services had continued for a while, to separate the assembly. He requested those who had no hope in the Saviour, to retire to the parlor, where he and a Christian friend would meet them, while those who could pray should unite in one or two rooms for that purpose.

It was an affecting sight to witness the separation of that little company. Before they parted they sang the eighty-third of the Village Hymns, and the suppressed sob and streaming tears, testified to the effect produced. *They* passed silently and sorrowfully to the appointed place,—*we* retired to pray for a blessing on their souls. The prayer of agonizing faith was offered ;—we *expected* and we *received* a blessing.

During a momentary pause, the door opened and Mr. G. entered to say, that two of that little company had chosen Christ for their Saviour. "Do not cease to pray." O with what renewed animation did the supplications of that little band ascend. Another soul bowed in submission to Jesus and gave her heart to him. The voice of praise and thanksgiving went up from that dwelling that night. Every one felt that God was there, of a truth. When the minister had departed, I entered the room—to me a holy place—where souls had been born to God, and there sat one convulsed with distress, who a few days before could not be made to feel. She was one of the best and the dearest in the school—a fine scholar and so amiable and exemplary in all her deportment, that I feared she would be wrecked on the quicksands of morality. But here she was writhing under a sense of the plague of a wicked and proud heart. I urged her to retire to her room, and I would follow her there; "*never*," she replied, with her accustomed decision, "*I will never leave this room*, Mrs. C., till I have submitted to God."

I was startled by the determined tone and look that accompanied this resolution. "Why then, Helen," said I, "do you not *now* submit your heart and rebellious will to the Saviour?"

"I have tried, but it won't yield; *but it shall yield*, and this pride shall be subdued."

I told her that all *her* efforts would be powerless to effect this great work, without the influence of God's Holy Spirit. She must look to Him to accomplish it and to lead her to the Lamb, whose blood cleanseth from all sin; she must believe His promises and trust wholly in Him for salvation. I prayed with her and left her with her Bible to the mercy of God.

Again at the midnight hour I sought the solitary suppliant: "Helen," I said, "are you still rebellious against your God? Has not your proud heart yielded to His claims?"

"No, Mrs. C., but it shall yield, I will never leave this room till I love God."

Early and faithfully instructed by pious parents, she was well aware of the requisitions of the gospel, and of her obligations to Him who had sacrificed His life for her. Again we prayed together, and exhausted by labor, anxiety and excitement, I retired to bed, yet I could not sleep.

At two o'clock a gentle tap at my door, announced to me a welcome visitant. She entered and throwing her arms around my neck, she exclaimed,

"O, Mrs. C., I believe God has forgiven my sins; I do believe that I have given myself to the Saviour forever."

From that hour Helen B. became a decided Christian, and she has since been eminently useful as a teacher of youth.

On Tuesday of the week following the series of meetings, R. arrived. A short time previous to the closing of the term in the Institution with which he was connected, much religious interest had manifested itself among the pupils, and he had been so much affected by it, as to feel very uncomfortable under its influence and to desire to be beyond its reach. As soon, therefore, as the close of the term released him from his duties, he departed for New York with no other design than to drive away the serious thoughts that oppressed him. There he found no relief; a feeling of anxiety scarcely amounting to conviction for sin, rendered him restless and unhappy. No change of place or scene seemed to restore his peace of mind, and he therefore suddenly resolved, contrary to his previous intentions, to visit the scenes of his boyhood and youth.

As he drew near to Middlebury a casual conversation in the stage coach, first revealed to him the fact that a revival of religion was in progress in the Seminary. His first impression was to take the return stage, and hasten back to New York without even letting his mother know that he had been so near to her, but sober second thoughts led him immediately to abandon such a purpose, though he determined to manifest as much indifference as possible to the subject that even then engrossed his thoughts.

His arrival, though so unexpected, did not cause in our minds much surprise; the supplications that had been offered for the attainment of this very object had prepared us for it. Yet so affected was his sister Maria at meeting him, that she could only give him a kiss of welcome, and, bursting into tears, leave the room.

"What is the matter with Maria?" said her brother. I looked steadily at him and replied, "R. this visit is in answer to prayer, and so earnestly has your sister pleaded for your conversion that her heart is full, and can not repress its emotions. We hope that you have been directed here to become a Christian." Such a greeting as this effectually repressed every manifestation of indifference, and deepened the impressions that had already been made upon his mind.

We had one or two meetings every day of that week, all of which he attended, but as yet I perceived no deep anxiety on account of sin, though he was serious and attentive. Friday was observed as a church fast, and there were religious exercises throughout the day. I felt that the time was now come that would decide his future destiny. I wish I could describe my feelings in prayer at this season, but language is inadequate. It was all God's work to show me the difference between prayer that saves the soul, and selfish supplications. God's glory was the great object constantly and distinctly before my mind. I believed that his glory would be promoted by the conversion of one who had so long refused subjection to the yoke of Christ, and therefore I laid hold of the covenant. Here I had a *strong hold*. I had God's promise to be, not only *my* God, but the God of my children. I felt that I did trust His promise, and that his faithfulness would not fail. All that day I was looking for its fulfillment; I *knew* it would come, and I watched in silence.

At the close of the afternoon service R. and I walked home together; not a word was spoken—my heart was too full for utterance. I retired to pour out its yearnings at the throne of grace. When I descended to the parlor R. was not there; with anxiety that could not be repressed, I followed him to the Music room, whither he had repaired with Miss A. and his brother. Such were my feelings at the moment, as I leaned unobserved against the door, that I could scarcely withhold the bitter cry, "*depart hence*," but a blessed Comforter whispered to my soul, "trust him with Jesus."

I returned to my chamber, calmly resigning all my

interests into His hands " who careth for us."   When we collected for family worship, as was our wont directly after tea, I requested that the second part of the 119th Psalm might be sung.   How did my heart respond to every line of that beautiful song:

"My spirit faints to see thy grace,
  Thy promise bears me up;
And while salvation long delays,
  Thy Word supports my hope."

The younger members of the family attended a meeting that evening designed expressly for youth, and as R. lodged at his uncle's, I saw him no more that night.   In the morning he came not as usual, but about eleven o'clock I was called to my room, where I found him walking the room in considerable agitation.   He handed me a note from our pastor, whom he had just visited.   It contained these words:

" My dear sister, have you *faith* to hope that the last unconverted member of your family is now one of God's dear children?   I believe it is even so.   I have had a long conversation with R., and I trust he has made an entire surrender of himself to God's service."

I could read no further before I bowed with the returning prodigal before our heavenly Father, to thank him for His great mercy to one who had so long rejected Him.

That evening this new-born child of grace stood up before the thoughtless companions of other days, and declared his resolution to serve God during the remainder of his life.

> "Yes, I am thy servant, most bountiful Lord,
>   The son of thine handmaid so dear;
> Who taught me the precepts contained in thy Word,
>   And gave me to God in her prayer;—
> Yes, I am thy servant, eternally thine,
>   And thou art my heavenly King,
> Of covenant mercy, transcendent, Divine,
>   My soul will eternally sing."

How did my obligations to my Father in heaven press upon my soul as I looked upon *all* the loved ones of my family, gathered for the first time in many long, weary years, but now united by a double tie, as the sons and daughters of the Lord Almighty. Together we bowed before the widow's God, and the Father of the fatherless, and then we felt the sweet assurance that though separated on earth, though all the attachments to home and native land, and dear domestic comforts might be dissevered, and henceforth we might be pilgrims on earth, the time would come when we would meet, "an unbroken family, before the throne of God—*no wanderer lost.*"

In one year from that time my family was again united around the bed of one of the loved number, to witness her departure to another and a better world.

CHAPTER XX.

WILLIAM AND HIS ROOMMATE.

DURING this season of deep interest, which extended to the town and the college, more than one hundred, exclusive of those in the Seminary, expressed hope in the Redeemer. One evening two young friends from the college, sought my counsel and sympathy. Their minds were filled with doubts—their souls with fears. They were both professing Christians, but peace of mind had departed from them. To my question,

" Do you pray?" their only reply was, " God has covered himself with a cloud, that our prayers shall not pass through."

" What efforts are you making for the conversion of sinners around you?"

" *We* can do nothing;—we have no hope for ourselves,—how then can we direct the sinner to Jesus?"

" You *have* hoped in His mercy; you *have* labored

in His cause; what has brought this darkness upon your souls?"

"We can not tell?"

"It is evident to me that the adversary has gained some advantage over you. You have yielded to temptation, neglected duty, and God sees it necessary to correct the wrong feeling or act. This want of evidence of your acceptance with Him, is the legitimate result of a departure from God and calls for an humble and penitent spirit. Now, does a refusal to perform known duty imply a *penitent spirit?* and can you expect God to restore to you the joys of His salvation, while you live in the violation of covenant vows? Did you make it a *condition* of obedience to the command of your ascended Saviour, when you consecrated yourselves to His service, that you would be diligent in His work just so long as He would impart the comfort of a good hope to you?"

The questions startled them. "Never!" was the prompt reply.

"And yet this is the language of your conduct."

They acknowledged the correctness of the inference, but still felt that their efforts were paralyzed by the feeling that God would not accept their work. Almost despairing of saying any thing to benefit them, as they rose to depart I proposed that they should retire to their rooms, and *write down* a determination to this effect; that if the Lord would give them peace and comfort in believing, they would prove faithful disciples and laborers in His vineyard,—but if this blessing was withheld, they must be excused from the work. This proposal sent them with sad hearts to their home. God made it a word in season to them. The morning found them at their work as followers of Jesus, and I heard no more of dark distrust and despondency.

About fifty individuals, we have reason to hope, had during these two revivals in the school found a personal interest in the great salvation. Many of those who had been under my instruction in Vergennes partook of the blessing and referred to that memorable season, when the seed sown seemed to have been scattered in stony places, but which in after time took root and brought forth fruit to the glory of God.

Many were the letters that I received from beloved pupils of other days, informing me of their resolutions to serve the Lord. One ascribed her first serious impressions to the morning instruction. "It was never forgotten," she said, "and though I never told you of the effect upon my mind,—when I left school it followed me, like an accusing conscience; till I cast myself on the mercy of the Redeemer."

Another ascribed her convictions of sin to a parting word dropped as she left me, "Remember, God is love;" and still another, to a farewell charge given with the parting kiss,—"Meet me in heaven." Some referred to the recollections of disregarded instructions, and others to private conversations.

In the course of a few months my heart was rejoiced to hear of about one hundred and fifty dear pupils, who had determined to live for God.

I would not speak boastingly of these mercies, for the work was all of the Holy Spirit,—and to the Triune God be all the glory; but these are bright spots in my existence, upon which I delight to dwell. Many sad hours have been cheered by the hope of meeting these redeemed ones in the heavenly world, and with them of praising our Father for His great mercy forever and ever.

To a missionary friend, who was a teacher in my school during the last revival, and who has for years devoted her life to the cause of her blessed Master, in the land of the Moslem, I wrote, requesting her to send me any recollections of that season, so interesting in its details to both of us. Her reply somewhat embarrassed me, for while I looked for a recital of her own experience with the anxious, she gave me what she considered the causes under Providence of the interesting work that had filled so many hearts with rejoicing and with hope. I give it in her own words.

"You ask me to mention any thing that particularly interested me in the Seminary, while we were together in Middlebury. With great pleasure I will do so, but I only mention those things very briefly, for were I to write out the impressions that I received there, especially with respect to the religious instructions,—the manner and the character of them—which are still clear and vivid in my mind, it would require a much longer letter than you would care to read, or I have time to write, just now.

"That morning hour for religious instruction and prayer, was I am sure, to me *the* blessing, that went with me through the whole day and was ever felt in after life; there was in the method the plain, practical instruction, adapted to the wants of each day, such power and spirit, as I knew you could have received only from on high, in the recesses of your closet, before you came in to us.

"*That hour*, I believe, the Lord will show in eternity to have been the beginning of eternal life to many souls. Before and after my connection with your Seminary, I was accustomed to hear more or less daily religious instruction at the family altar, and at the opening hour of school, in different Institutions, but it was usually such as did not *prick the conscience*. The Lord, it seemed to me, enabled you to bring truth to the conscience, so that the guilty soul would feel, *God knows it—God sees me*. Hence, sometimes I would hear it whispered, ' Somebody has been telling Mrs. C. about *me*."

"I recollect well the course of lectures that you gave on the Ten Commandments. Although I had been a professor of religion for many years, it seemed to me that these little daily lectures, stripped me of every particle of goodness and showed me my heart full of deformity and sin. Yet with hope they sent me to Christ, for cleansing and clothing. I was well aware that by my friends I had been considered a model of filial piety, and thought myself very nearly perfect on that head, but one morning in your lecture on the fifth commandment, you told me how I had disobeyed my mother and grieved her affectionate heart, years and years ago. I knew that you could know nothing about it; even *I* had forgotten it till that memorable morning, when your words brought to my mind every particular of the *time*, the *place*, and the *manner* in which I did it. I never spoke of it to you, but I wrote to my mother, and asked her forgiveness. She, loving soul, did not remember the circumstance.

" The precious seasons of revival in your school,— the teachers' and pupils' prayer-meetings—the recess, five-minute gatherings for prayer—though not peculiar to your Seminary—are still remembered with no common interest, and the benevolent society and missionary associations,—which, I believe, you have brought to greater perfection in B.—I always felt were superior to any I had enjoyed any where else."

CHAPTER XXI.

THE VARIOLOID.

MY health had failed in consequence of too great
exertion and anxiety during the summer session;
I therefore, at its close, resorted to my usual restora-
tive, and journeyed among friends.

I returned to my duties in September, to enter
upon scenes, the remembrance of which still fills
my soul with unspeakable emotion. The Saturday
evening meetings were continued, and the young
ladies of the family selected a season for prayer which
they found well calculated to repress the levity of the
thoughtless, and to assist the Christian in keeping her
heart fixed on God. The time devoted to this exercise was the fifteen minutes that transpired between
the ringing of the bells that summoned the family to
the evening repast. As the warning bell sent forth
its pealing notes, they silently collected in one of
their "prayer rooms," and then bowed down before

their Father in heaven, for a blessing. The second bell was the signal to close their little meeting.

In December, two young ladies, members of the seminary, were attacked with varioloid, which was supposed for a time to be chicken-pox, and which was so slight that it did not, for several days, prevent their attendance at school. In less than two weeks another and another became ill. The cases of Miss C., who boarded with a family very near to us, and of Miss H., a resident in the seminary, became so marked that suspicions were awakened, a council of physicians was called, and to my utter amazement and dismay, they pronounced them decided cases of small-pox, introduced by varioloid.

The school and village were panic-stricken by the intelligence. Every means in our power was resorted to, to prevent its extension. The pupils belonging to town were immediately withdrawn from school, while we, in the seminary, were for three weeks restricted to a range, outside of the door, of only a few yards. Bars were thrown across the street, above and below us. "*Small Pox*," in *whitewash purity*, was blazoned on the walls and fences, warning the unwary traveler to come not nigh the infected spot.

My situation at this time was most distressing. Anxiety lest those in the family should be attacked— for they were not permitted to leave town—the necessity of keeping them cheerful and free from fear, the extreme illness of Miss C. and Miss H., the former of whom was gradually sinking to the grave, forsaken by all save her own mother, and one attendant, the necessity imposed on me of confining my intercourse with her to notes, which I sent by her physician, joined to the apprehensions of the effect that all this might have upon my school, pressed upon my heart, and almost overwhelmed me. The spiritual enjoyment so lately imparted seemed to have forsaken me; "All was dark, and vain, and wild." The judgments of God seemed impending over me, and my feeling was that these were but the beginnings of fiery wrath that would soon be poured out upon me in full measure.

O how strange it was, that, having experienced so much of the mercy of God, in times past, I should now have sought any other refuge. I could not bear solitude; I could not endure my own gloomy forebodings. I flew to books, to anything, rather than to God. He was far from me, and I could not find him in the darkness that enveloped my soul.

One infant child in the village had taken the small-pox from her sister, who had the varioloid. She died and was buried in the stillness of the night. Noiselessly, and almost by stealth, the smitten father sought, at the midnight hour, a resting-place for the dear one among the graves of the household, when no eye was upon him but that of God.

Miss H. slowly recovered, but our young friend Miss C., who had early given promise of devoted at-

tachment to her Saviour's cause, and of mental preparation for a life of usefulness was called home ere
her labors and sacrifices on earth had commenced.
Distressed with agonizing pains, a loathsome object to
herself and to those who beheld her, she yet had
strong confidence in God, and great support in her
sufferings. She died, triumphing in the hope of a
glorious immortality.

A *tarred winding-sheet* prepared her for the
grave, and her ashes repose in a lonely corner of a
solitary field. Coffined in a rude box, we saw her
borne to her last resting-place on earth on the shoul-
ders of four rough, unprincipled men, whose love of
money conquered the fear of death; but we might
not follow her to her rude grave. When with sad
hearts and weeping eyes we looked away from the
melancholy spectacle, we saw the flames ascend that
consumed all the vestiges of her distressing sickness.
We witnessed it all—and O, what a Sabbath morning
was that, when we stood and watched the remains of
our friend passing from our view, and felt that we
might not turn to the sanctuary of God for comfort.
During this gloomy season no friend was permitted
to cheer our solitude, and had any of us been called
into eternity, no minister of Christ would have sent
up a prayer from our deserted bier, or followed us to
our last home.

But not over us alone did the angel of death cast
his shadow. Transmitted from one to another, the

dreaded pestilence extended its baleful influence to distant places, and many who had been exposed to its infection while ignorant of its nature, fell victims to its power.

By the commencement of the succeeding term, in February, the clouds that had so long hung over us seemed passing away. Health was restored to my family; the embargo was removed, the destructive plague was stayed, and once more our school was in successful operation.

CHAPTER XXII.

MARIA'S ILLNESS AND DEATH.

"O weep not for the dead,
No more for them the blighting chill,
The thousand shades of earthly ill,
The thousand thorns we tread;
Weep for the life-charm early flown,
The spirit broken, bleeding, lone,
Weep for the death-pangs of the heart,
Ere being from the bosom part;
But never be a tear-drop given
To those that rest in yon blue heaven."

THE week after the commencement of our term, Maria had a slight attack of varioloid, but so carefully was she kept from intercourse with the family that no alarm was produced. She apparently recovered, and pursued her preparations for an intended visit to Princeton, where she designed spending several months in the family of her uncle, and where she anticipated much intellectual improvement and enjoyment from the privileges and the society that would be afforded to her.

Her literary attainments, her energy and decision of character seemed peculiarly to fit her for great usefulness as a teacher in the seminary, and her active and devoted life as a Christian, gave promise of no common character. Her progress in her studies was such that she always classed with pupils much older than herself. No superficial knowledge of a subject ever satisfied her mind. Study, with her, was a *passion*, one that she never sought to restrain. An interdict upon her books was always a sufficient punishment for a fault, and she asked no greater reward for any good accomplished than the privilege of reading to her mother some book that interested her own feelings. She loved, even in childhood, to steal away from the amusements suited to her age, to some retired spot, to pore over the pages of some work far beyond an infantile capacity. Well do I remember with what interest she twice read over an essay on the subject of *Philology*, when she was but eight years old, pointing out to the attention of a friend some beautiful passages that greatly delighted her.

She possessed great quickness of apprehension, which, while it enabled her to appreciate intellectual beauty, rendered her keenly sensitive to the sufferings of others. Seldom did the tale of sorrow fail to awaken an answering sympathy in her breast, and often, in the days of her childhood, when her mother spoke to her of the distress of some suffering neighbor, has she voluntarily relinquished her own little comforts, that she might carry the offering to the abode of poverty.

She early imbibed a great reverence for the Word of God; "from a child she knew the Holy Scriptures," and a "thus saith the Lord," was always sufficient to awaken in her attention to duty.

Many Christian friends who noticed her strict observance of the Sabbath, and of her private devotions while yet a mere child, thought she was, even then, a babe in Christ.   To uncommon penetration, she united great quickness of thought, and she was always ready with a suitable reply, perhaps serious, perhaps marked by a shrewdness that made her the pet of the passing hour.

When she was about three years old, at the time that I was preparing for my journey to the south to meet my beloved husband, many friends were desirous of retaining Maria with them.

" I must go," she said, "with my mother."

" But," said her aunt, " you will be sick there."

" And mamma will take care of me."

" But the doctor says you may have the fever and die there."

" Well, Aunt E., can't I go to heaven just as well from Georgia as I can from Middlebury ?"

When reunited to her father, whom she scarcely remembered, she seemed to exist in a new world. The varied scenery of a tropical latitude, the successive presentation of new and interesting objects, the affection of friends—whose idolatrous attachment was soon to be corrected—all contributed to increase her natural buoyancy of spirit, and the joyousness of her heart was bursting forth continually in song.

But this brilliant morning of life, so rich in the enjoyment of this purest and best affections, was soon succeeded by a bereavement which made desolate the family circle. From this time, young as she was, Maria searched the Scriptures, to select those promises that were particularly made to the widow and fatherless, and with great propriety and earnestness would she "pray them in her own prayers" to God.

In a journal that she commenced at the age of twelve, she writes, "I have formed some resolutions which with God's help I mean to keep: to read my Bible and to pray, morning and evening. I have begun to read the Bible in course, and I pray God that some of its truths may impress themselves upon my heart, and lead me to Him who is the sinner's friend, and who has said, 'They that seek me early shall find me.' Sometimes, after mingling with the world, and enjoying its pleasures, there is a hollowness in my heart which can not be filled, and yet my hard and stony heart says, 'I will not have the Lord to reign over me.' Sometimes I determine that I will fly to the Saviour, and make the Judge my friend, but then the cares and pleasures of the world take off my thoughts, and lead me to forget my best interests."

At another time she writes, "I have not read much to-day. I am glad I obeyed my mother in this respect; I hope that I shall be an obedient and dutiful child to her. O, what should I do if I were deprived of my mother's counsel and instruction!"

On the Sabbath she writes, "I have been to-day where I have seen books read which were not suitable for this holy day. I am thankful that I have been kept from sinning in this way, but it is not in my own strength, but in the strength of the Lord. I read Christ's Sermon on the Mount. He says that anger towards a brother is murder; how often have I been angry with my brother and sister without a cause. May the Lord forgive me for it."

Again she writes, "I have not been very happy during the past fortnight. The thoughts of my father, so early removed from us, weighed upon me, and I have thought, if my mother should be called away, what I should do without the all-supporting love of God."

On another day. "I wish to record in my journal,". she says, "that this morning I showed a very improper spirit towards my mother, and I should have persisted in having my own way, if she had not prevented me, and made me ashamed of my conduct. At noon I was rude to C. E. I wonder that everybody does not hate me for such things; and why does God bear with me so patiently?"

These extracts, taken promiscuously from a diary, which was kept during only two years of her life, show the tenderness of her conscience at that early age.

Over her defects—and she was not destitute of faults—she often wept bitterly. Again and again would she entreat her mother to point out her failings, faithfully and particularly, that she might try to correct them. Perhaps her failings can all be traced to one great defect—*inattention to trifles.*

Her's was a character strongly marked; her own mind was a fountain whence she drew resources for happiness which rendered her, in a measure, independent of the world, and this very independence, while it preserved her from contamination, by withdrawing her from the society of the frivolous and worldly, led her to neglect many of those little attentions, which, as beings placed together on the great theatre of action, it is our duty to bestow on those around us. Singularly averse to deception, her soul spurned the thought of sacrificing truth and conscience to popularity. Of her consecration to her Saviour's service at the age of fourteen, an account has already been given, in the history of that precious work in 1830, which filled so many hearts with rejoicing. In this surrender of herself to God, there was no sacrifice of worldly pleasure, for she had never sought happiness in such pursuits, but her piety was strikingly evinced by the difference in the *motives* which now seemed to influence her.

She pursued her studies with the same untiring zeal, but she cultivated her mind that she might render herself more extensively useful. She interested herself more in the concerns of those around her, but it was that she might be enabled to strengthen a wavering resolution, or excite anxiety for the salvation of the soul.   Arm in arm with a Christian friend, has she gone forth to the abodes of want, distributing those silent messages of pardon and love which have filled so many hearts with joy and gladness.

The young friend who was the chosen companion of these visits of mercy, once related a circumstance which evinced Maria's moral courage and Christian principle.   In one of their rambles they entered a filthy hovel, where was seated a coarse, brazen-faced, dirty woman, surrounded by a group of children to whom the blessings of clean garments and persons were entire strangers.   Seating themselves on a rickety bedstead, Maria, who was usually the speaker on such occasions, after inquiring after the health, etc., of the wondering occupant, asked if she would accept of one or two tracts.

"Well, you may leave them, if you 've a mind to," was the rude reply.   After a few minutes spent in conversation, Maria said to her,

"Would you like to have a prayer made before we leave?"

"And, pray," said the woman, "who will make it here?"

"I will," said the youthful disciple, "if you will permit me."

"Well, I never," was the rough response, and down she kneeled to listen to the supplication of this babe in Christ, in behalf of herself and her children.   Evidently gratified by the visit, she thanked them for it, and requested that it might be repeated.

Two months after she had indulged the hope of acceptance through a Redeemer, Maria stood up in the great congregation with a band of Christians, on that day hallowed in the affections of every American as the day of his country's freedom and glory, and presented herself, as a " living sacrifice, holy," and, as we trust, "acceptable to God, through Jesus Christ," and avouched the Lord Jehovah as her God and Guide through life.

It was a pleasing sight to see this consecrated band of youthful disciples, *thus* commemorating the day that '' gave a living soul to a young nation's shapeless clay," by this thank offering of themselves, to Him whose dying love bequeathed the blessings of salvation, to a world enslaved by sin. From that time it was evident to those who knew her, that Maria's course was onward.

Many there are who will long remember her labors of love,—her disinterested efforts for their welfare,—her engagedness in every work of benevolence,—her life of prayer. There was so much *expression*, in her prayers, so much of the going forth of the soul, that none who heard her could believe that she was a stranger at the throne of grace. At the weekly concert for prayer on "preparation eve," she was always at her place, and there she loved to unite her heart and voice with the circle of Christian friends, who assembled to supplicate God's mercy on the school.

One little circumstance of the trying winter, that preceded her departure from earth is indelibly impressed on my mind, as almost prophetic of *her* future blessedness. Whenever she saw me weary and sad, she would seat herself at the piano, and turning to me with a smile, " Come, Mother," she would say, " let me sing *my song* to you," and *her song* was always,

> " Jerusalem, my happy home,
> Name ever dear to me.

Many prospects bright and beautiful opened on the future, as she entered upon the spring of 1832. The previous winter had been one of severe trial and to her of intense application; and she was now preparing to spend several months with friends in New Jersey, where as she expressed it, "she should be *feasted* with books."

Returning from a meeting of the Education society, exposure to dampness and cold, concentrated upon her lungs an inflammation which baffled all the efforts of medical skill to remove. The severity of her disorder and the stupor that it produced, precluded all conversation with her during the first week of her illness.

On the fourth day after her attack, her physician, Doctor B., stood by her bedside regarding her for some time with intense interest, then turning much affected from the room he requested me to follow him.

Only those who are mothers—and widowed mothers,—who have felt the death-knell of long cherished hopes strike upon their hearts, can conceive the agony of that moment, when with feelings that entirely overcame him, Doctor B. told me all his fears, and requested that a counsel of medical advisers might be summoned. They were soon in consultation, but gave little hopes of her recovery, and when at evening they again assembled around her bed they unanimously pronounced her case to be hopeless.

I had watched every movement of the dear child—every look and word of kind friends who clustered around her sick bed through that distressing day, at one moment buoyed up by the hope, that youth and kind care with God's blessing would gain the victory over disease,—at another, sinking with apprehension of the trial that might be in store for me. I dared not look into my heart; I was afraid to analyze its feelings, for I was conscious that there was no submission there. And now it came—the terrible truth sunk into my heart,—*she must die*,—and she might be taken from me that very night; so feared her medical attendants. After this lapse of time, when years have calmed the turbulence of feeling, I can not recall the experience of that night without unutterable emotions. They are graven upon my heart as with the point of a diamond. Well, perhaps, was it for me that insensibility for a time, closed up every avenue to sorrow. That was a night to be remembered through eternity.

I was persuaded to retire and seek rest, while my brother and sister with other friends, kindly watched beside the sufferer. In the silence of my chamber, where the feelings of my heart were unveiled to no eye but God's, did I unlock the prison house of my soul, and read its secret anguish. I reviewed the past,—the goodness of God to my school—to my family,—the instructions that I had given to both— how often I had insisted on the efficacy of religion to hush every rising murmur, to give even cheerful acquiescence to trying dispensations. Now I felt that God was saying to me by this afflictive providence, let your own example prove the truth of your assertions.

I had for some time indulged the hope, that this loved one would devote herself to missionary life, and I had often felt that cheerfully I could commit her to the protection of her heavenly Father, should he call her to this work; and I now asked myself if I should repine that He spared her the trials of such a life and called her to a holier employment? The promises of God, rich and comforting, were all spread out before my mind, and while my heart shrunk from the trial of parting, as the image of my dear child in all her loveliness of character and in all that she was to me, rose before me, I turned me to this stronghold and felt that if God would be with me and grant me the supports of His grace, I could resign her submissively. With the simple confidence of a child I laid hold of those precious promises, and pleaded them before that mercy-seat to which I had so often found access through the crucified One. He heard my cries and answered me in mercy, and I went forth from that room in the morning, praising my Father for his wonderful grace to me. From that time no rebellious feelings mingled with a mother's sorrow, and my great desire was, that if my child must be removed from me, her death and my submission might glorify God.

Thus strengthened, I was enabled to attend to my duties in school during the remainder of her life, which continued for three weeks from this time, though often startled in the midst of a recitation lest some approaching footstep was bringing the summons, to go and receive the parting kiss.

In every former illness her impatience to recover, that she might resume her favorite pursuits, manifested itself in all her actions and rendered her restless under her confinement; but from the commencement of this attack there was a resignation of spirit, a passiveness and quietness visible in her whole appearance, altogether unlike her natural character. When informed that no hopes were entertained of her recovery, no agitation of spirit betrayed itself in her looks; she made no reply, but closing her eyes, lay for a time as motionless as if the sleep of death had already fallen upon her.

After many days of deep and distressing anxiety to her friends, who earnestly desired that she might

be able to express her feelings in the near view of
eternity, she fully opened her heart to her mother;
and the only tear that bedewed her cheek while she
lay on her bed of death, she shed while lamenting her
past unfaithfulness in her Saviour's cause. When
asked if she was afraid to die, she replied, "It is a
solemn thing to go into eternity, to appear in the
presence of God."

"But you have hope in his mercy through the
merits of your Saviour?"

" Yes, I *have* hope in His mercy ;—O what should
I now do, without this hope to sustain me;" then after
a pause she added, "but I am afraid of deception,—
I am afraid of my deceitful heart." Many passages
of Scripture were repeated to her, expressive of the
ability and willingness of her Redeemer to save *all*
that would come unto God through Him. She looked
up with an expression that seemed to say, "I receive
into my soul all the consolation and the strength
which these precious promises are calculated to impart."

" Are you willing," said her mother, "to leave
yourself in the hands of your heavenly Father, to live
or die as He sees best for you?"

"I hope *I shall be*," she replied impressively:
"Mother, there are many things for which I should
wish to live;—I have very dear friends."

" You have often, my child, lamented that you were
so early deprived of your father's society and affec-

tion; if you are one of the redeemed in Christ, you will soon join him in his song of praise in heaven."

With an expressive look she replied, "But I leave my mother here."

"If we are the children of God," said her mother, "our scattered family shall e'er long all be gathered into our Father's house in heaven, to go no more out forever."

"Pray with me, my dear mother, that I may be entirely resigned to the will of God."

After this, her uniform answer to the question, "Are you willing to leave yourself with God, to be disposed of as shall be for His glory?" was, "I trust I am willing."

Her distress for breath was such that her friends could converse with her only at intervals, and then but for a moment; but it was interesting to witness the patience and submission with which she bore her sufferings. When I said to her at one time,

"You suffer much, my child."

"O no," she replied, "nothing to what I deserve,— nothing to what my Saviour endured for *me*."

At another time seeing her evidently in great distress, I said, "I wish I could bear some of these pains for you." "I am thankful that you can not;—not one pain would I have you suffer."

She was much affected by the mercies granted to her, and often spoke with great gratitude of the kind attention of friends, who were always ready to minister to her wants and to sympathize with her in her sufferings. "Mother," she said, "we shall never forget this kindness. How merciful is God in granting to me so many blessings."

No murmur or complaint escaped her lips during the distressing illness that was rapidly consuming her vital energies. No enrapturing joys or transporting views of glory, marked her approach to the heavenly world; but the calm confidence of the simple, trusting child,—the peaceful tranquility of the soul, sweetly resting on the bosom of the Saviour, gave a cheering hope to her afflicted friends that she had not been deceived in the great work of preparation for this hour of trial,—that the hope which sustained her was sure and steadfast, based upon the Rock of Ages.

A few evenings before her departure, while weeping friends stood around her bed, expecting each moment would be her last on earth, unable to speak in an audible voice, she drew her mother toward her and whispered, "Mother, as thy day is so shall thy strength be."

"And as *thy* day is, my child, so I trust will be *thy* strength. Is Jesus precious to your soul? Do you feel that you can now commit yourself into His hands without fear?"

"I think I can trust Him. He *is* precious to my soul."

I was much struck about this time with a singular coincidence, in which I recognized a message of mercy from my heavenly Father.   A few days previous to dear Maria's death, a friend had brought to me the explanation of the third verse of the third chapter of Malachi, given by the silversmith of Dublin.   The next day our pastor called, and in his prayer by the bedside of the suffering one, while commending her mother to God's supporting grace, he prayed that as "God had now placed her in the furnace, He would graciously fix his eye upon her and when He sees His image reflected from her soul, say, it is enough and spare the child."

Again the message was repeated.   A day or two after, when my eldest son came as he hoped to accompany the loved one to her uncle's home, he brought me a book of memorials, in which I had requested to have some remembrancers inscribed by absent friends, and there I found recorded by the hand of one of them, this same message of mercy.   I trust it was not thrice sent in vain.

"Mother," said Maria to me, at a time when an interval of ease enabled her to converse a little, "do you remember that beautiful hymn, commencing with,

> "When languor and disease invade,
> This trembling house of clay."

I had begun to learn it just before I was taken sick, and had committed four verses to memory.   I think there are two more and I wish you would repeat them to me, that I may learn *them* too."   I sought the hymn and the verses that she had yet to learn, were strikingly suited to her present situation.

> "Sweet in the confidence of faith,
> To trust His firm decrees;
> Sweet to lie passive in His hand,
> And know no will but His.
>
> If such the sweetness of the streams,
> What must the fountain be,
> Where saints and angels draw their bliss,
> Immediately from thee."

After complying with her request, I asked, "can *you* say, my child,

> "Sweet to lie passive in His hand,
> And *know no will*, but His."

" O yes, mother, it *is* sweet to lie *passive* in His hand."

On the morning of the 17th of April, it was evident that her sufferings would soon cease. Her mind was wandering through the day; and if it is true that derangement exhibits us as we really are, that it displays the ruling passion of the heart—then we might almost envy the purity of mind and freedom from every taint of worldliness, indicated by the remarks of that day. She seemed to have acquired new strength to make her last effort for the good of others. She addressed conversation to different individuals, as though they were present, expostulating with some, and urging others to prepare for a dying hour. She repeated passages of Scripture often during the day, and seemed perfectly to understand and to be able to apply those that were repeated to her.

At one time, supposing that she was addressing one who was a member of the school, but who was not present, she said, with great earnestness, "Ann, let me tell you that a sick bed is no *place* for *repentance.* O the pains and sufferings of a dying hour. Jesus can make a dying bed, 'Feel soft as downy pillows are,' but O the pains and sufferings of a dying hour. I tell you, Ann, that you must not defer repentance to a dying hour." Then pausing, she uttered with fearful solemnity, "Ann, were you ever so ill as to look right into eternity? I tell you, Ann, *don't defer repentance?*"

In a few moments she repeated the scripture, "I am He that blotteth out thy transgressions, for mine own sake." "Do you hope," said her mother, "that all *your* sins are blotted out for Jesus' sake?"

"O Frances," she replied, supposing that she was speaking to an impenitent friend, in school, "if I did not hope so, I should go crazy." She remained quiet for a while, and then repeated in a clear voice, "Him that overcometh will I make a pillar in the temple of my God, and he shall go no more out."

Naming certain friends, for whose conversion to God she had long felt most intense anxiety, she said, "Mother, I can not persuade them to embrace religion; O you can not think how determined they are. What can this world do for them? What will it avail them, if they should gain the *whole* world and lose their souls? I urged the subject upon them, but they turned away with indifference and contempt." The lustre of her eye which seemed to kindle with new intelligence,—the animation of her countenance, almost radiant with celestial beauty—and the impressiveness and energy with which she spoke, gave inexpressible interest to every word that she uttered.

Her last words showed the value that she attached to prayer. "Do they love to pray?" she enquired, after a long silence. Supposing that she referred to the Saturday evening gathering for that purpose, I replied, "Yes, Maria, they love to meet for prayer and there you are remembered." "But do they love to meet in the little family prayer-meetings? I hope they love to pray there." This was a season that had been proposed by herself,—one that had been very precious to her.

Towards evening she ceased to speak or to notice surrounding objects. She lay in all the quietness of infancy, her strength gradually failing till about eight o'clock, when she breathed her life out sweetly on the bosom of her Redeemer.

> "Without a sigh—
> A change of feature, or a shaded smile,
> She gave her hand to the stern messenger,
> And as the glad child seeks its Father's house,
> Went home."

She stands before the throne of God and strikes her

harp in heaven, hymning high songs of everlasting praise to Him, who bled and died for guilty man.

I wish it were possible to describe my feelings, as her soul was departing. Many a Christian mother, I doubt not could give a similar experience, but few could fully sympathize with me in all the circumstances in which this sacrifice was made. I wept, but they were not tears of sorrow alone. The loved and the cherished had departed from me, but in all the dealings of our Father towards us, such mercy was manifested—such support granted—such satisfactory evidence imparted, that she was prepared for the blessed society of heaven—that with Mrs. Graham I could exclaim, "I give thee joy, my darling." Oh, what a holy place was that room, whence the sainted spirit ascended to her rest.

I was as sensible of the presence of my Saviour, as though in the sympathy of His incarnation, He stood before me. I felt that holy angels were on their errand of mercy, to convoy the blessed spirit to her eternal home, and while I experienced in all its bitterness the severity of the trial that was now brought upon me, I found no place in my heart for murmurs or complaints. She was beautiful in death;—for the same serenity and peace that marked her whole appearance during her sickness, rested upon her lifeless features.

LINES TO THE MEMORY OF M. H. C. by H. D. K.

> " They who have looked on death like thine,
> No more should fear to die."

Within a quiet room a couch was spread;—
It was Death's altar, and the victim there
Was young and beautiful.   It was the time
When the glad Spring looked warmly on the earth,
And round the opened window came its winds,
And shook its budded branches, and stole in
With whispers to her ear of bitter thoughts
Of many a bright scene she might see no more.
She turned away, and with her spirit's might,
Flinging the young hopes from her heart, she looked,
With earnest purpose on her only task.
The promise of glad years was on her soul,
The holy loves of kindred, and the smiles
Of a bright world to her; and the kind thoughts
Of a live-hearted girl for her young friends;
And visions of strange brightness, springing up
In the far future; these had all been hers;
And now, she looked upon them one by one,
Yielding the tribute of a death-bed tear
For those sad comforts now, then tearing them
From out her being, that she so might turn
Uncumbered to the strife and better die.
She had been lovely in her life, and when
The beautiful went thronging by, we marked
No look like hers, so speaking of the soul;
But now 'twas more than beauty.   Through the hall
Steps took a desolate hush, and words were breathed
With whispered earnestness that left no hope;
And those that saw the meek and holy calm
That reigned in her lit eye, and heard of peace
And hopes better than earth's, and of a home
Where she should soon find peace, while in her look
All that is this world's beauty took the light
Of heaven's irradiance; O they did feel
That death and loveliness are not sworn foes.

Then came, while yct the parting pang was stayed,
A brighter hour—with fcvcrcd throb no moro
The maddcned pulse leapt on its burning way;
Bright with returning life the kindled eye
Beamed joyously, and hope half lit her torch
To mark the welcome change.   Delusive spell!
So brighter beams, along the brow of hcaven
The midnight meteor, ere it sinks in night.
With fitful ray, so shoots tho farewell flash
From out the scpulcher of wastcd fire.
In the deep, cloudless west, with holy light,
The deep-hued sunset burned, her last on earth;
So calmly turned hcr rcvercntial eye
On the fast-fading glow; she seemed to gaze
On some near seraph band, aud hold communion
With sister spirits of anothcr sphere.
Her hour had come, and she was of the dead;
Yct o'er the ruins of her fallen hopes,
With warring life entombed, and loveliness,
Triumphant was the Christian's hope, and rose
On beauty's wreck, like star of morn on night,
Her hope of heaven and immortality.

CHAPTER XXIII.

WILLIAM'S REMOVAL TO VIRGINIA.—CHANGES.

MANY hopes were entertained that Maria's death, so suggestive, so triumphant, might prove a blessing to the school, and be followed by a revival of religion. There was much seriousness and solemnity for a time, but the dreaded cholera then made its first appearance in the land, and though not in our immediate neighborhood, all other subjects were forgotten, in anxiety, or apprehensive terror, as it gradually pursued its onward march. The impaired health of my eldest and now only daughter, rendered change of air and scene necessary, and she accepted an invitation to spend the summer with the friends in New Jersey who had been disappointed in the visit that they had expected from Maria.

A severe attack of what threatened to be cholera, laid me on a bed of suffering for three weeks, but kind and affectionate pupils watched over me, allowing no "hired nurse" to bestow that care which they declared it was their privilege to share.

My youngest son, having just completed his collegiate course, was now about to go forth to enter upon life's struggles. It was necessary for him to assist me in liquidating debts contracted during this period of his life; he therefore concluded to seek some employment in one of our southern states. I indorsed several notes for him, and hired money literally "*on usury*," in order to meet present demands. This necessity brought upon me new trials—trials which sometimes threatened to cut the brittle thread of life. They are past, and I thank God that *such* trials can never again bring sleepless nights, and days of mortification, disappointment and anguish.

By hastening his journey William was enabled to join his brother in Philadelphia on the morning of his marriage, and to proceed with the newly-wedded pair to Virginia, which had been selected as the place of their future residence.

Dissatisfaction with the arrangements which the trustees of the seminary had made respecting the boarding department, decided me to relinquish my situation in Middlebury, and accordingly, in the autumn of 1833 I closed my connection with the institution. During the previous summer, M. G., a former pupil, visited me, and very precious is the remembrance of the days that she passed with me. A few weeks after, in the midst of her preparations for entering upon a missionary life, she was suddenly called to her rest. She had been for a long time under my instruction, had been to me as a daughter, and her death revived, in all its bitterness, my recent bereavement. Well prepared for the self-denying work to which she had consecrated herself, she was expecting to sail with Mr. A. for Borneo, in the spring. The Lord accepted the sacrifice and spared her the trials to which she would have been subjected.

A. P., another loved and adopted one, who had been recently married entered into her rest only two weeks previous to dear Maria, and as I thought of their youth and their prospects of usefulness, I could scarcely repress the murmuring inquiry, "Lord, why is the peace of a dear family invaded, the young left motherless, and the missionary of the cross prevented from entering upon the work assigned to her, while I, worn out with trials and almost useless, am spared to be a burden to myself and to my friends?" I knew such feelings were wrong, but these deaths deeply affected me.

CHAPTER XXIV.

> "Then come what may, we'll humbly wait;
> His arm was never bared too late;
> The promise will not, can not fail,
> Though dark the night, the morn will break,
> His own the Lord will not forsake;
> The prayer of faith shall yet prevail,
> And we shall deem the trial sweet
> That laid us waiting at his feet."

ELIZA had returned from her visit to New Jersey, but her failing health again demanded a change of climate, and she journeyed to the south, for a brief sojourn with her married brother. We parted in great sadness of spirit, she to pursue her journey with strangers, to her southern home, I to commence my pilgrimage *anew*, to form new acquaintances, a wanderer from the place that had so long been my home. None knew, save Him who searcheth the depths of the heart, what I endured, as I went forth on a dark, rainy, gloomy morning, once more to abide among strangers. I believe that, unsupported by the grace of God, I should have sunk beneath the trial.

I spent one year in Woodstock, a year, like many that preceded it, distinguished by trials and mercies. Here I found myself in new circumstances. My school was composed of those professing all creeds. Many of my pupils were from families who were decidedly opposed to the great doctrines of evangelical truth. With the peculiarities of the parents I was wholly unacquainted, and though I soon found out that I was watched by scrutinizing eyes, all united in endeavoring to make my residence among them comfortable and happy.

Fully aware that my success as a teacher would depend much on gaining the affection and confidence of the children, I entered cautiously upon my work. I had no *sectarian* feelings to gratify, for to such, I trust, I have ever been a stranger. The Episcopalian, the Congregationalist and the Universalist was before me, and I sought not to proselyte, but to instruct the mind, and to win the heart to Jesus.

At the commencement of my term I gave no direct religious instruction, but, while reading the Scriptures, I occasionally threw in explanatory remarks— religious anecdotes—illustrations of certain passages —information respecting ancient customs, etc., till I found that the pupils had become interested in the morning exercises. By degrees the truth was pressed home upon the conscience, and evidently produced some effect.

About this time, Mr. B. came to labor as an evangelist in Woodstock, by invitation from the Congregational church, and great was the blessing that descended upon the people. My school shared largely in this blessing, and several of my pupils consecrated themselves to the service of God. The good work was not confined to any denomination, but the inquiry, "What must I do to be saved?" was heard in every part of the town. I certainly did not approve of *all* the measures adopted at this time by Mr. B., on account of which "there arose no small stir about that way," but I could never unite with those who raised the cry against him. After he had departed from them, many of whom had enjoyed the benefits of his ministry in their own souls or in their families, I considered Mr. B. an injured man, and as such I defended him. An eccentric one he certainly was, and yet God saw fit to bless his labors, and many, I have no doubt, will, through his instrumentality, enter into the kingdom of heaven.

I remained in Woodstock only one year, having been induced, by the urgent entreaties of a suffering sister, to consent to make my home with her during the ensuing winter. Accordingly, in the autumn of 1835, I again changed my residence, feeling that truly "Here I have no continuing city," and took up my temporary abode in New York.

The nine months that I spent in that city were employed in relieving my sister from her family cares and burdens, in teaching her children, and in seeking to find my place among the benevolent operations of the day.

In January, with my brother and sister, I united with the church that had just been organized under

the pastoral charge of the Rev. Dr. Skinner, and rich
was the feast that I enjoyed from his preaching.

While in New York I was urgently and repeatedly
solicited by a friend to undertake the editorship of a
magazine designed expressly for the improvement of
young ladies. Several of my friends were of opinion
that the experience I had acquired in my years of
teaching, aided by the multiplicity of facts that I
had collected during those years, peculiarly qualified
me for such a work. After much deliberation and
prayer I came to the conclusion that God had not
then called me to engage in such an undertaking.

I was also invited to become a missionary teacher
in Illinois, but having been satisfied that the compen-
sation offered could not meet necessary expenses, and
having no capital of my own on which I could fall
back in trying emergencies, I was compelled to give
the negative to this plan. When I left Woodstock
the promise had been made to me that I should be
assisted to establish a school in New York in the
spring; the spring opened, but for reasons that I
never fully understood, and cared not to fathom, the
promise was not fulfilled.

CHAPTER XXV.

> " Spirit of everlasting grace—
> Infinite source of life, come down,
> These tombs unlock, these dead upraise,
> Thy glorious power and love make known.
> Breathe o'er the valley of this dead,
> Send forth thy quick'ning might abroad,
> Till rising from their tombs, they spread
> In full array—the host of God."

WHILE preparing to visit my children in Virginia, I received an invitation to spend a day or two in Bloomfield, N. J., to ascertain the practicability of opening a Seminary in that place. After complying with the request, I concluded to make the experiment, and in July, 1836, once more found myself a stranger in the midst of strangers.

My first term of three months passed rapidly by, and at its close I received an " unanimous call," to make a permanent settlement among that people. I accepted the propositions that were made and passed the month of October, with my children. I proposed to my eldest son to unite with me in what I felt would be an arduous undertaking. He desired time for consideration and here for the time being the matter rested.

During this visit, in company with a number of friends, I made an excursion to Weyer's Cave, which was situated only a few miles from my son's residence. This is one of the grandest productions of nature, where man is emphatically taught his littleness and impotency. The vast apartments, with their lofty arches,—the deep, unfathomable abysses, that bid defiance to mortal vision,—the graceful drapery that ornamented many of these halls, and the solid pillars, which seemed like columns supporting the dome of some gorgeous temple—all emphatically proclaim "the hand that made *us, is Divine.*"

On the first of November,.I reopened my school in Bloomfield, and soon after it was evident that the Holy Spirit was awakening in the minds of Christians a spirit of prayer, for a blessing to descend upon the church and people. I was rejoiced at the prospect, and hoped much for the school. Returning one evening from a prayer-meeting, which had been characterized by unusual solemnity, I resolved before I retired to rest to converse with one of three pupils, who were members of the family in which I resided. One of these was so thoughtless—so very trifling—that though I had repeatedly sought to impress religious truth on her mind, it made no permanent impression. I therefore determined to pass her by for this time, and seek an interview with a more promising subject.

As I rose, at the sound of approaching footsteps, to call one of her companions, I learned that both had retired for the night, and with a feeling of disappointment, I said, "Well, Mary, come in yourself; I wish to converse with you a few moments." Scarcely did I ever before enter into conversation with an impenitent person with greater reluctance, for only two days previous to this term, when I had remarked to her, " Mary, you are *so trifling* in your manner, that every word I speak seems *to rebound*," she laughingly made such a reply, as strikingly illustrated the truth of the remark.

In the interview which had now as it were been forced upon me, I determined, since she was *the one sent to me*, to be faithful to her. After much effort to *impress* truth upon her heart, I prayed with her and we retired to rest. For three days she scarcely spoke or smiled, but evidently sought to be near me. Her distress then could no longer be concealed, and she came to me for counsel and for prayer.

One morning while in school her feelings became so uncontrollable, that she requested permission to leave the room. On her return, which was delayed for some time, I perceived that the expression of her face was wholly changed. Instead of the troubled, anxious look, which had so vividly portrayed the conflict of her soul, a sweet peace and calm serenity assured us that whatever might be the *cause* of the change, the terrible conflict was past, and from that hour increasing evidence gave us the blessed assurance, that her hope was founded on the Rock of Ages

A few days afterwards, having occasion to pass through the place where her parents resided, at her request I called to give them the welcome intelligence, which I knew would fill their hearts with rejoicing.

The mother wept for joy;—the father, with eyes filled with tears and with a quivering lip, exclaimed, "O how manifestly do I see the hand of God in all this." He then related to me the experience of a night—*the very night*, on which I had my first conversation with his daughter. Feeling unwell, he had retired to rest at an early hour, but his slumbers were disturbed by a distressing dream. He supposed that his child was drowning before his face and that he was unable to rescue her. Filled with terror for her and exhausted with his own ineffectual efforts to save her, he awoke, in great distress, and could sleep no more. While pondering on the dream, he was led to the inquiry, "should she be called into eternity, unprepared as she now is, what would be my feelings in view of her future condition, and what my anguish in reviewing my own unfaithfulness?" That night he spent in meditation and prayer, and I have always believed, that to those prayers I was indebted for the *necessity* that *compelled* me, contrary to my previous intention, to commence my efforts with her, and for the blessing that followed those efforts.

The deep feeling of interest increased. At the commencement of the session, *only one* of the members of the school—which then numbered but twenty-five,—was a professed follower of Christ, but for weeks before its close, every individual indulged the hope of acceptance through the Redeemer, and with the exception of two or three who were quite young, all have since given satisfactory evidence that this was no delusive hope.

This revival was characterized by a peculiarity worth noticing. With the exception of the conversion of Miss L., almost all in town and school, seemed for a time to walk in darkness. Though apparently willing to give up all for Christ, they did not at first enjoy the blessed evidence imparted to the soul, of peace with God, resulting from a belief of sins forgiven. They desired and determined to serve the Lord, but the resolution was made in much mental darkness. Gradually as they persistently walked in the path of duty, light broke upon their minds—beams of mercy shed their radiance over their souls—and they became established in the faith.

CHAPTER XXVI.

ESTABLISHMENT OF THE BLOOMFIELD FEMALE SEM-
INARY.—REVIVAL OF THAT YEAR.

"What, though strong temptations rise,
Fiery darts my way oppose—
Threatening storms ascend the skies,
Or affliction's furnace glows?
God is faithful, God is true,
He will still my strength renew."

MY son, having concluded to accept my proposition to unite with me in the establishment of a boarding-school, in Bloomfield, I was joined by my children in the spring of 1837, and we commenced our joint labors in May with twenty boarders.

In the arrangements and instructions of the school a similar course was pursued to that adopted in Middlebury, and as we now had the control of the family, a short season was set apart, morning and evening, for private devotion. This season the pupils were *required* to spend alone in their rooms, in the hope that while it was gratefully improved by those who loved to pray, such a retirement, even for a few moments, might lead the minds of the thoughtless to God.

Early in December, the increased attention of the young ladies to the morning instructions, and the solemnity that pervaded our weekly Saturday morning prayer meeting, filled many hearts with the hope that the Spirit of God was again about to descend, with His blessed influences, upon the school. A few moments were devoted, every afternoon, by Christians in the family, to supplicate God for such a result. I held conversations with many of the pupils; some in the family seemed almost ready to yield their hearts to the Saviour. But the holidays approached, and the interest excited by the expectation of a reunion with friends, and of partaking in the festivities of this annual recess drove from their minds all serious feeling, and they returned to their studies apparently more thoughtless than ever.

I had requested the pupils to prepare a composition to be read on the Wednesday succeeding their return to school, on the theme, "The experience of a week," hoping that, as during this short period of separation, one year would close up its account for eternity, and a new one commence its existence, they would be led to serious thoughts and feelings. Instead of this almost every composition was marked by a levity entirely unsuited to such a season. On this account I declined to read them, and occupied the time in remarks upon the feelings with which we should examine the transactions of the past year, and enter upon the duties and responsibilities of the new one.

Christians in school became more and more solemn, and more earnest in prayer; the interest gradually increased, and at family worship on Sabbath evening, much feeling was manifested. As I met my Bible-class, numbering between twenty and thirty, on the first Sabbath in the year my heart was too full to pursue the usual course of instruction. I told them the feelings of my soul, my solicitude respecting them; I reminded them of God's visit of mercy to that class a year before; that when the revival commenced at that time there were eight impenitent members of the class, and that before its close, as we had reason to hope, all of that little company had chosen the Lord Jesus as their Friend and Portion. Now, as I glanced my eye over the class, to my surprise I again numbered *eight* impenitent members. The coincidence was striking to every mind, and this circumstance gave rise to many remarks which could not but affect the feelings. I believe that each one of that little circle, as the question was asked, "Christian, what will *you* do for the conversion of your impenitent companions?" "Sinner, what will *you* do for the salvation of your own soul?" silently resolved, in that moment of deep solemnity, to awake from her sleep and call upon her God.

During the succeeding week the children of God bowed in penitence before the mercy-seat, and pleaded most earnestly for a blessing upon their own souls and the souls of those who had no interest at the throne of grace.

The quarterly meeting of the Maternal Association came, in its course, this week, and it was deemed advisable to give a general invitation to the young ladies in town who might be disposed to meet with the mothers and children to listen to the instructions of Dr. J. and the Rev. Mr. W., who had been invited to address them. As the meeting was held in the school-room of the Seminary, all our pupils were present. The room was crowded, and the fixed and solemn attention of every hearer gave evidence that the Spirit of God was there.

On the following Sabbath the usual winter arrangement, of having the morning service in the church and the afternoon service at West Bloomfield, commenced. I had always disliked this plan, and at this time was particularly annoyed by it, from the fear that many of the hours of God's holy day would be unprofitably spent; but God overruled even this circumstance for the advancement of his cause. After dinner I invited all those young ladies who had no hope in the Saviour to meet me at four o'clock in my room, and requested those who had hearts to pray, to retire, at the same hour, to entreat the blessing of God on the effort.

At the appointed hour eight young friends came to visit me, and scarcely had I commenced speaking to them of the priceless value of their immortal souls, when the silent tear and suppressed sob gave evident tokens that God himself was speaking to their souls, by the still small voice of his Holy Spirit. I read to them a portion of Dr. Scudder's address to youth,

"Christ knocking at the door of the heart," and urged upon them the duty of opening that door to Him at once, and of an immediate surrender of their whole souls to the Saviour. We could not sing; the feelings of that moment were too deep for any expression save that of prayer, and together we bowed before God, and asked for mercy. Solemn and silent that weeping band retired to their solitary rooms, feeling all the gloom and distress which arises from the reception of the truth into the heart, that the curse of the Almighty rests upon the soul of the sinner; and as the supplicating cry went up from many hearts, thus smitten with a conviction of the evil of sin and the fear of the wrath to come, every Christian felt her soul go forth in earnest petitions to her heavenly Father for mercy and pardon on these wanderers from God. During these moments of deep solemnity A. E., as she thought, submitted her heart to Jesus, and as all assembled around the domestic altar for the evening sacrifice, an infidel could not have doubted that the Spirit of God was there.

Our Sabbaths were always solemn seasons, but the solemnity of *this* day spoke to every heart. A statement of the exercises of one Sabbath will show in what manner truth was brought to bear upon the mind. After breakfast the members of the Bible-class seated themselves around a table with a teacher to aid them, and spent an hour in studying their Bible lesson. The class met for recitation in the afternoon, and after its close I was employed, till summoned to the evening repast, in conversation with individuals, or with several together, as seemed most desirable. At evening worship the pupils were examined by my son respecting the morning's sermon, and such remarks were made as were naturally suggested by the subjects then presented. A hymn and prayer closed the exercises. These frequent changes prevented weariness, and at the same time truth was continually impressed upon the mind.

These Sabbath exercises, in connection with the preaching of the gospel, were greatly blessed to the conviction and conversion of many dear youth to God, and we generally found that their serious impressions commenced during the hours of the holy day.

As day after day passed, on the following week, the Spirit of God gave increasing evidence that He was verily in our midst, making the most trifling solemn, and leading others to cast themselves on the Saviour for pardon and salvation. With trembling anxiety we watched the progress of the work, for while truth was producing its legitimate effect upon the hearts of some, we could not but fear that others would be affected only by sympathy, and really suppose that they had feelings which existed more in the imagination than the heart. The trial of another week showed the reasonableness of our fears. I look back upon *that week* as one of the most remarkable in its experience of any through which, in any revival, I ever passed.

CHAPTER XXVII.

SCOTCH ELLEN.—ALICE E.—COLORED CONVERT.

A CIRCUMSTANCE that occurred at this time, led us to fear for a while that God had forsaken us, and we were consequently filled with dismay; but even this was overruled for the furtherance of the blessed work.

We had in the family a Scotch servant girl,—a chambermaid and waiter—whose very eccentric conduct and singular conversation, awakened our suspicions that she was under the influence of some powerful hallucination that had unsettled her mind. From general remarks made by her,—for the truth of which I can not vouch—I learned that she was living at Rockaway on Long Island, when the Mexico was wrecked on that coast;—that she witnessed the dead bodies as they were washed ashore, strewed along the beach and that she then determined to exert her influence to have a *chapel* erected on the spot, for poor mariners. But in this effort she had hitherto failed, and she now besought me to address a letter to Queen Victoria, asking her to advance a sum sufficient for the accomplishment of the work. Disappointed in her application to me, she persecuted the young mission-ary—who was during that winter performing pastoral duty for Mr. S., while he was absent in a southern city, seeking restoration to health,—and with urgent solicitations sought to enlist him in this "benevolent object." When repulsed by him she became very anxious to unite with the church, repeatedly calling upon him, until wearied with her importunities, he was obliged to close his doors against her. This excited her almost to frenzy, and for several days we felt it necessary to watch her with careful attention.

It was our custom on the Sabbath, while at the tea-table, for each one in turn, to repeat a verse from the Bible, in proof of some subject proposed in the morning. As I was about to commence this exercise on the succeeding Sabbath, noticing a general disposition to levity, which the pupils seemed unable to repress, I looked around to ascertain the cause, and as my eye rested on Ellen, the picture she presented upset my gravity and overcame the seriousness and sadness of my own spirit. She had dressed herself with most elaborate care and appeared in flounces and furbelows. Around her head she had wound a stiff white muslin apron, with a broad full ruffle that encircled her face, and which was fancifully arranged in a large bow on one side,—the ruffle standing out around the ends, while the top was surmounted with a huge bow of blue ribbon.

This *fixture*, placed on a head by no means small, with a face like a full blown *red* rose and ornamented by two or three monstrous puffs of bright orange colored hair,—all overtopping a body of no mean dimensions, as it was poised on one foot, the better to catch the voices of those most distant from her, presented a spectacle too striking for the gravity of any at table, and for a few moments we were unable to proceed. At night she refused to retire to rest;—and though she refused to the last, compliance with our wishes that she would leave the family, the fear that she would become a raving maniac, was such, that on Monday morning my son compelled her to accompany him to New York. She refused to go directly to her friends, but "would call," she said, "on the British consul and request him to write to the Queen, in behalf of her new chapel." After this she returned occasionally, and annoyed us by her visits.

Notwithstanding all our efforts to turn the minds of the young ladies from this subject, the oddities and strange conduct of this girl, wholly absorbed their attention and thoughts, and I could but exclaim as I looked upon their altered appearance after her departure, " And Satan came also among them,"—and diligently had he performed his work. There was a general spirit of levity among those, who a few days before were weeping and trembling on account of sin

With but few exceptions I had little confidence in the reality of the conversions of those, who a week before had professed to love the Saviour. They were almost as trifling in their conduct as they had ever been, and exhibited little of the *unction* that distinguishes the new born soul.

Christians were alarmed—discouraged,—and my own soul was oppressed with a burden that was almost insupportable. "In my distress, I called upon the Lord" for direction and assistance, but He did not appear for our relief. The week passed without any favorable change, though it produced the effect of humbling the children of God. I met them at our usual season for prayer on Saturday morning, and read to them a few verses from the first part of the fifth chapter of Isaiah; "Now will I sing to my well-beloved, a song of my beloved touching his vineyard," &c., and then drew a comparison between that and the preceding weeks; and endeavored to show them the causes of this difference—directing their attention to the artifices of the adversary to turn their thoughts from God, and the *ease* with which he had succeeded in his efforts. It was evident, I said, that we had grieved the Holy Spirit and that he had departed,—and I earnestly besought Christians to examine their hearts anew, to ascertain what delayed the blessing, and to feel more deeply that the situation of their impenitent young friends was perilous. I then proposed that all who could pray, should engage to spend all the time not necessarily devoted to other duties, from Saturday to Monday, in deep, fervent and humble prayer, for the return of His Spirit to our hearts, and requested all who were willing to do this, to rise and sing with me, the following stanza :

> " Here, in thy courts I leave my vow,
>   And Thy rich grace record;
> Witness ye saints, who bear me now
>   If I forsake the Lord."

It was a moment of deep and portentous interest; I felt that eternal destinies were involved in the fulfillment of that vow.   From that morning all trifling ceased.   The Spirit of God drove out the tempter and took possession of their hearts.   Strengthened for the work that I felt I was called upon to perform, I spent all of Saturday afternoon and evening and a part of the Sabbath, in visiting and conversing with every pupil in the family, and in consequence of these conversations which were designed to search deeply into the heart, five of their number relinquished the frail hope to which they had clung, and which they now saw had not produced the peaceable fruits of righteousness.

Among these were A. E., and L. E.   Both had again and again deceived themselves in their hope of salvation, and when they were compelled once more to admit that a deceitful heart had led them astray, they could scarcely endure the thought.   The effect on L. E. was to rouse all the rebellious feelings of a proud heart. The struggle was severe and long continued, but at last she yielded, and sat meek and lowly at the feet of her Saviour.

For several days the feelings of A. E. were those of utter hopelessness and wretchedness. She wept and prayed—but the gloom of midnight darkness was gathered around her soul. She dared not attempt to trust her soul with God; she was sure that He would not receive one who had so often mocked Him. On Monday morning Doctor J. visited the school, and the Holy Spirit seemed to direct and bless every word that he uttered. After he left us, the classes were called as usual to their respective recitation rooms, but each teacher felt constrained by the overwhelming manifestation of feeling in her class, to close her book and bow with them before the mercy-seat, to plead for the salvation of souls.

On Tuesday morning Doctor J. again visited us, accompanied by the Rev. Mr. W. After addressing the school, they conversed individually, with all whose minds were deeply impressed. Again we spent the day in prayer,—and thus passed most of the week,—occupying a few moments in attempts at recitations and the remainder of the time in religious instruction and prayer. A. E.'s distress increased. She felt as though this was God's last call to her soul,—yet she held back from the full surrender of herself to Him. I shall not soon forget in what anguish of spirit she sought my counsel and prayers, at the close of one of these days of mental distress. After urging her to come immediately to the *fixed* determination to cast herself just as she was, on the mercy of her Saviour for pardon, in the fullness of my heart I exclaimed,

"Oh, Alice, I feel as though I could take you in my arms and carry you to the cross of Christ, to the fountain which he hath opened for sin."

"Oh, do, Mrs. C.," said she, bursting aloud into tears; "take me there—oh, take me there."

"Christian friends," I replied, "can lead you to the brink of the fountain, but *you must step in*. We can not perform that work for you; but there is One mighty and ready to help."

With deep anxiety we watched the progress of conviction in her soul. Life or death depended upon the choice that she was about to make. She knew this, and yet she lingered and hesitated.

In a note which my son addressed to her, he urged her no longer to "halt between two opinions," but to come at once to *some* decision—to commit that decision to writing—to sign her name to it, and then carry it to Jesus, as the solemn, the final determination of her soul. In a conversation that he held with her during the same evening, he presented her with two resolutions, diametrically opposite in their character, one of which she should adopt. When he proposed the decision to return to the world, to resist the influences of the Holy Spirit of God, to "cast away fear, and restrain prayer," and to bid farewell for ever to heaven and her Redeemer, her whole soul shrank from such a decision; "then," said he, "why not at once solemnly subscribe your name to the surrender of yourself to the Lord for time and for eternity? Choose which path you will henceforth pursue before you retire to rest."

This startling proposition brought her at length to feel her guilt and danger in delaying, and the necessity of immediate submission; and we trust that she did then give herself to Christ, to be His for ever— willing, as she expressed it, to do any thing, or to be any thing, if she might be permitted to devote her life to His service. We trust she made this decision in the sincerity of her soul, and her subsequent life has confirmed this hope.

After this week of deep and powerful interest, the feelings of the pupils subsided into a calm though serious state. They returned to their regular studies, which had not been wholly neglected, but they found time to attend two prayer-meetings every day. Many indulged the hope, during this interesting season, that they had begun to live the Christian life, and most of them, by their subsequent course, gave cheering evidence that the Holy Spirit had begun a good work in their souls, that would be perfected in heaven. With the exception of a primary class of little children, there was scarcely one in the school who did not profess to love the Saviour.

Many cases might be recorded as interesting as

those already given, but with one other I close the account of this blessed work.

P., a colored woman, had several months previous to this, been a servant in our family, and for two years had been a member of the church of Christ. Her perfect indifference and inattention to family and public worship during her residence with us, led me often to expostulate with her, but without effect. Soon after leaving the family her health failed, and she had all the symptoms of confirmed consumption. Alarmed at her danger, she was led to examine the foundation of her hope, and found herself unsupported by the sustaining grace that she expected; her hope was like the spider's web; the fear of eternity destroyed it. In her distress she came to us, with the hope that "some of the meetings might do her good." I found her in great anxiety respecting the salvation of her soul. She had wandered from God—was, as she apprehended, rapidly approaching the grave, and feared she was unprepared to meet her Judge. She remained in this state of mind through the week, attending all the meetings, and listening with fixed attention to every word of instruction, when, at its close, she gave herself, as she hoped, "into the hands of her Saviour," to have Him do with her just as He pleased. She remained with us some time, eagerly seizing every opportunity of listening to the Word of God, to religious books, and tracts, and it was pleasant to see with how much interest, those who were commencing their Christian course, sat down beside this poor ignorant girl, to read to her the word of *her* God and *their* God, and those little messengers of mercy that speak of their common Saviour. The health of P. was finally restored, and she still lives to honor her profession by a consistent life and conversation.

With heartfelt gratitude to our heavenly Father, for this merciful visitation did we unite in the song, "The Lord hath done great things for us." To Him be all the glory. Here let my journal speak the feelings of my heart recorded at that time.

"Truly my cup of blessings runneth over, and I will praise the name of the Lord for ever. I have earnestly desired that this Institution might be emphatically the Lord's school, and he has owned and blessed it. If He will permit me to be the instrument, in any way, of cultivating mind for His service, of leading the youthful wanderer to the fold of the Great Shepherd, I will bless Him for all the trials by the way, by which he has led me to such a service. None who have not been placed in similar circumstances, can know the feelings of that teacher's heart, who bows with her youthful charge before the throne of grace, and listens to one and another of these loved ones, as they come with their affecting errands, to our common Father. These are among the sweetest moments of my life, and here, in the midst of our interesting family my heart feels at home."

CHAPTER XXVIII.

SUMMER OF 1838.—MISS A. J.

DURING the summer of 1838, and the succeeding winter, some of our pupils gave pleasing evidence of consecration to the Saviour's service. Among them was one, amiable in disposition and irreproachable in conduct, who had not hitherto felt the necessity of the application of Christ's blood to cleanse her soul from sin. Informed by a young friend that her sister was indulging the hope that her sins were forgiven for Jesus' sake, in the midst of a conflict of contending emotions, the great question arose in her mind, "what must *I* do to be saved?" She spent the sleepless hours of the night in tears, in vain endeavoring to solve the problem of acceptance with God. She saw clearly that she was a sinner;—she felt too that she was justly condemned by God's holy law. "How then can a man be just with God?" She turned to her past life, but no beam of light irradiated the darkness that filled her soul. How could she *make herself fit* to approach a holy God, whose laws she had so often violated? Her goodness on which she had so confidently relied, had "passed away like the morning cloud." Rising in the morning unrefreshed and unhappy, she sought in a retired apartment, the peace which none but a reconciled Father can impart. Again and again she read His gracious promises and implored His mercy. Discouraged at length by her unsuccessful efforts to obtain the peace for which her soul agonized and prayed, she burst into tears and springing from her seat threw herself once more upon her knees before God, with all the intensity of an earnest spirit, exclaiming, "Just as I am I come to thee—in all my vileness;—Lord take me and cleanse me in the blood of the Redeemer, I give up all hope of making myself better;—I yield myself soul and body to Thy service forever." This simple language of the heart fulfilled the requirements of the gospel, and here our young friend found the peace so long sought in vain.

To how many souls does the very *simplicity* of the salvation of Jesus prove an obstacle, sometimes almost insurmountable. We look for some great work to be accomplished by us in the way of preparation, hoping by such means to recommend ourselves to the favor of our heavenly Father, but driven from our vain refuges and dependencies, we at last turn to Jesus as the only hope of the sinner, and trusting in the crucified One, find pardon and salvation.

CHAPTER XXIX.

PROFESSOR P.'S DEATH.—MY OWN ILLNESS.

" Saviour, I look to Thee,
Be not thou far from me,
'Mid storms that lower ;
On me Thy care bestow,
Thy loving-kindness show,
Thine arms around me throw
This trying hour.

Saviour, I look to Thee,
Thine shall the glory be,
Hearer of prayer !
Thou art my only aid,
On Thee my soul is stayed,
Nought can my heart invade,
While thou art near."

NECESSARY attention to domestic duties, during the spring vacation of 1839, so exhausted my physical strength that I was quite unfitted for my summer work. I however entered upon it, but scarcely had the examination of our pupils and the arrangement of the classes been completed, e'er I was summoned to the dying bed of my sister's husband. I found him scarcely able to give me a sign of recognition. To my remark, " you are very near your rest, brother," his reply was, " Yes,—sometimes light—sometimes dark—heaven." To the question put by his pastor, " If he felt that his trust was in Jesus ?" he said, " Yes," and these were apparently his only lucid intervals.

Just before his departure, he commenced singing a low plaintive air so sweetly, that it seemed as if his spirit had already parted from the body, to unite in the song of praise in heaven. An hour passed and he was with God.

As I stood by that bed of death, I could not but think how perfectly adapted are the consolations of the Christian religion to every class of men. The man of learning, of towering intellect—the babe in Christ— the illiterate son of poverty—all drink at the same fount, all are supported and comforted by the same simple truths. Jesus Christ and him crucified, is the theme that imparts peace to every soul. Surely, this speaks its Divine origin.

What a breach was made in that domestic circle! Who but God, could speak comfort to that widowed heart? Who but her heavenly Father who had inflicted the blow, enabled her to pass through those trying scenes, herself the victim of disease and suffering of no ordinary character—her children left destitute— bereft of father and home? We laid the remains of the beloved one in the narrow house,—left the eldest son with friends in the city, and accompanied by the afflicted widow and her remaining children, I hastened back to Bloomfield, where my duties and responsibilities in the Seminary, demanded my presence. But nature had been too severely taxed, and disea.e was preying upon my system.

During the July recess, a small party of friends

accompanied me to Boston, Nahant, &c., in hopes that I might be recruited by change of air and scene, but I returned little benefited by the excursion. For three months I suffered intense agony from an abscess, which sufferings but for the powerful anodynes that were administered, would have destroyed this frail tenement. My recovery was pronounced hopeless by three attending physicians, and yet through the influence of disease and medicine, I was too much affected by delirium or stupor to be sensible of my danger. Sometimes, a lucid interval with a few moments' relief from pain would occur, and as the thought of death would present itself to my mind, it was invariably met by the verse, "I shall not die, but live, and declare the works of the Lord." To the watchful care of my beloved children and friends, do I consider that under Providence I owe my recovery from this distressing illness.

With an enfeebled frame I recommenced my duties at the beginning of the next term, feeling more deeply than ever my nearness to eternity, and my obligations to my heavenly Father, and that what I expected to do for the cause of Christ, must be done quickly. I felt *pressed on* to new and continual efforts. Soon after the commencement of the term, my soul was drawn out in frequent supplications to the throne of grace, for the descent of the Holy Spirit on our school and family, but none around me seemed to participate in my feelings. Professors of religion as they looked upon the thoughtless ones with whom they daily associated, appeared to forget that those friends so pleasant in their social intercourse, would soon have passed their probationary season, and that *then* the redemption of their souls would cease forever. Day after day I endeavored to impress religious truths on the minds of our pupils, but the careless and indifferent air of some and the impatience with which others listened, showed but too plainly that God was not in all their thoughts. Often did I retire to my closet with the melancholy exclamation of the Prophet, " If ye will not hear me, my soul shall weep in secret places for your pride."

Weeks passed on and there seemed to be a small increase of feeling in the hearts of a few, but the holidays with all their frivolity and festivity, drove even this little seriousness from their minds, and they returned so thoughtless that unbelief suggested that it would be impossible during that winter, to excite any interest in the subject of religion. This desponding feeling was, however, immediately met by the question, " Can it be that one who has been corrected and disciplined as I have been, and who has access to such precious promises for encouragement to perseverance, can now yield to the temptations of the adversary?" I dared not do it, and again I sought strength and aid from my heavenly Father.

The first Monday in January, 1840, was observed by the church as a day of fasting and prayer, with special reference to the expected Presbyterial visitation during the following week. For three days of that week, we had preaching in the afternoon and evening and a general solemnity pervaded the minds of the community. Christians in the family began to awake from their spiritual sleep; there were deep searchings of heart and renewed dedications to God; and the minds of the impenitent were evidently open to receive the truth.

It was at this moment so full of interest and importance, that again my heart began to fail and I found myself shrinking from duty,—really fearing lest the increased labors and excitement of such a season of intense anxiety, should lay me in my grave. Every feeling rose in opposition; unbelief suggested that my life was too important to my family— to the school;— that such a sacrifice could not be required. Well was it for me, that my heavenly Father provoked at my selfishness, did not set me aside and refuse me the privilege of laboring in His blessed cause. I became alarmed at my own selfish feelings, and in the retirement of my closet, searched into the inmost recesses of my heart, and I trust repented of my great sin;— nor did I leave the mercy-seat until I was willing to sacrifice ease, health, and life itself if need be, that I might be permitted to be the instrument of good to one soul. From that time I felt impelled to "go forward," and I bless God that he enabled me continually to feel, that all my interests were committed entirely to His keeping and that while He should continue me on the earth, my work should be to do the will of my Father in heaven.

CHAPTER XXX.

> "People of the living God,
>   I have sought the world around,
> Paths of sin and sorrow trod,
>   Peace and comfort nowhere found;
> Now to you my spirit turns,
>   Turns a fugitive unblest;
> Brethren! when your altar burns
>   Oh, receive me into rest."

I HAD, previously to this, conversed with several of
the pupils, but I now determined to endeavor to *enter
the heart* of every one in school. God blessed the first
effort, and three among the most interesting of our pupils, became exceedingly distressed on account of their
sins, coming, day after day, to be directed in the way
of life. The promises of the gospel—its urgent invitations, were presented to them; their rebellion
against God, in rejecting the only atoning sacrifice,
and their consequent helplessness, was pressed upon
them; but to every entreaty to cast themselves at
once on the Saviour for pardon, their plea was, the
way to the cross was all dark, they could not find
the Saviour, they did not believe He would have
mercy on *them.*

After a Sabbath of much anxiety, I was requested
by a young friend to converse again with W. J., whom

she had left in great agitation; I found her alone, bowed down before her God, and there she trusted that she had found a Saviour. I had a long and interesting conversation with her, and was much pleased with the docility with which she received the message of grace into her soul; and her conduct in after life strengthened the hope that this was indeed an unreserved surrender of herself to her Redeemer's service.

I then sent for M. J. Poor girl! No hope dawned upon her mind; she could not believe that Jesus would receive her if she made the attempt to serve Him, and she seemed determined not to make the attempt. She was greatly distressed, and when I told her that W. J. had submitted to God, she wept aloud. I prayed with her, and then urged her to raise her own voice in supplication for pardon, through the blood of the crucified One. Instead of an audible expression of her feelings, she prayed in a whisper, and seemed to be earnestly crying for mercy. As she ceased, from time to time, I repeated some promise calculated to encourage her to trust in the Redeemer. I continued with her an hour, and she still continued kneeling, declaring that she could not retire to rest with her present feelings. After again urging her to faith in Jesus, I left her, and found a solemn company assembled in the study.

W. J. was weeping with a heart full of love for her new found Saviour. Near her sat H. T., with her face buried in her hands, shaking with emotion, while two sympathizing teachers were seated beside them, scarcely knowing what to do or say.

The distress of H. was almost agonizing. A sense of her great sinfulness weighed upon her soul, and she was sure that God would never pardon her; I said to her, "H., there is but one sin which shuts the door of mercy upon the sinner's soul, and I trust that you have not yet committed that sin."

"I don't know, Mrs. C., I am afraid I have."

She then related a circumstance of her early life which had led her to indulge this fear. When about nine years of age, she was one day reading her Bible, and came to the verse "all manner of sin shall be forgiven unto men, but the blasphemy against the Holy Ghost shall not be forgiven. And whosover speaketh a word against the Son of man, it shall be forgiven him; but whosoever speaketh against the Holy Ghost, it shall not be forgiven him, neither in this world, neither in the world to come." After reading it over, she said to herself,

"I dare commit this sin."

She was frightened at her own remark as soon as it was uttered, but the circumstance soon passed from her mind, and was not recalled till three or four years afterwards, while listening to a sermon on the sin of resisting the Spirit's influence. She then concluded that her condemnation was scaled, and the effect on her mind was to close her heart to conviction, and to produce misanthropic feelings. To no individual had she revealed the sin of her early days; had she done so, she might have found relief, and repented of her transgressions. But now she felt certain, that so long as she continued to indulge the belief that mercy could not reach her case, there would be no repentance; she therefore resolved to confide her secret to me. This communication gave me direct access to her heart, and I was soon enabled to convince her that had she really committed the unpardonable sin, instead of now mourning over its commission, she she would be too hardened to fear deserved punishment, and too indifferent to seek for mercy. The feelings of which she was then conscious were a sufficient refutation of the fears excited on that account. This conversation in a measure relieved the terrible distress that preyed upon her spirit, and gave her some hope that even so great a sinner as she felt herself to be, might be benefited by the atonement of Christ. It was a late hour when those two girls retired to pass a sleepless night.

Monday came, and Tuesday passed, and still there was no change of feeling. At evening H. came to my room and begged that she might speak to me.

"O, tell me what I shall do, Mrs. C., I can not live so."

I knew that her situation was perilous; she was almost tempted, in despair, to drive away feeling, and, as she vainly hoped, distress, from her mind. I said to her, "H., I have urged every argument that the Bible presents, to induce you to trust in the Saviour; I have repeated promises that might affect the most unbelieving, but they have produced no effect upon your heart; I have one plan more to propose, and with God's blessing, it may lead you to the great decision. Go to your room and read seriously and attentively such and such promises (repeating several to her), read till you do believe that God is *able* and *willing* to perform them; then take the dedication of the returning penitent, in Doddridge's "Rise and Progress," and read it attentively; carefully count the cost of giving up all for Christ, and settle the question seriously, whether you can relinquish every thing for Him. If you feel that you can do this, then take pen and paper, write down a dedication of yourself to God, sign your name to it, as to a solemn covenant, and read it deliberately before your Father in heaven, upon your bended knees, telling Him that with His help, you promise to serve Him for ever, and asking, with confidence, for the influences of the Holy Spirit to renew your heart."

She was struck by the singularity of the proposal, and promised to attempt it; and her prayer, while with me seemed to be an unreserved consecration of herself to the Redeemer. The next day she came to tell me that she had complied with my request, and her smiling, speaking countenance assured me that there was peace within.

In the meantime M. J. had become worn out with intensity of feeling; sleepless nights and anxious days almost laid her upon a bed of sickness. At my recommendation she followed the same course that H. had adopted, with the same happy result; she also found peace in believing.

C. L. had been for more than three weeks weeping on account of her sins. The daughter of Christian parents, her father a missionary to the dark and ig-norant portions of our own land, I felt assured that earnest prayer ascended daily from the domestic circle for this child of the church, so far separated from kindred and from home. When I urged her to trust in the Redeemer, she would reply that she could not find the way. Once she said, "There is a mountain between God and my soul so high and dark that my weak faith can not surmount it." There she remained —just there—day after day. Nothing said to her seemed to give her any assistance. I trembled lest, discouraged, she should turn from God and salvation: with much prayer, and with much anxiety as to the result, I proposed to her also the plan that had been so successful in the cases of M. and H. She seemed interested by the proposal, and taking a copy of Dod-dridge with her—for she was not at that time a member of our family—she spent the whole of the next day at home, in her chamber. When questioned as to the cause of her absence, she replied, "I went to my room, as you directed me, and there, I hope, I gave myself to the Saviour, but I could not go to school that day." Her subsequent history gave pleasing evidence that this was the work of the Holy Spirit.

CHAPTER XXXI.

> " Serve God before the world; let Him not go,
>   Until thou hast a blessing; then resign
>   The whole unto him ; and remember who
>   Prevailed by wrestling, e're the sun did shine;
>   Pour oil upon the stones, weep for thy sins,
>   Then journey on, and have an eye on heaven."

R. E., a young lady of thirteen, came to us at the commencement of the session from a family entirely devoted to the world. She had passed much of her time in the city of New York, though a resident of the country, and for a season previous to her connection with our Institution, had attended a fashionable boarding school, where once a week the pupils were amused with fancy balls, for every one of which a new dress must be prepared. At one of these balls she was attired in the costume of a Turkish Sultana, and the dress that she wore on that occasion cost, as she said, one hundred dollars. On almost every evening that she was not engaged at the ball, she was taken to the theatre or some other place of amusement.

It may easily be imagined what was her preparation of mind and heart to enter into our family, and listen to religious instruction; yet at an early stage of the revival, her mind became impressed with the importance of the subject. It seemed to open a new world to her view. She had lived, she said, long enough for mere pleasure,—it was time that she began to *think*. Of the plan of salvation through a crucified Redeemer, she was wholly ignorant, and it was very interesting to see with what child-like simplicity she listened to the simple truths of the gospel, as they were unfolded to her mind. They came to her with all the freshness of novelty. "The Lord opened her heart to attend to the things spoken" to her, and she did not delay to yield herself wholly to the Saviour. There were no excuses offered,—no cavilings at the plan of salvation,—no fears expressed lest she should not feel the requisite *amount* of conviction,—no doubts as to the power and willingness of Jesus to save her. With the dependence of a child she trusted in His promises and cast herself on His mercy.

Before she had done this, and while her mind was agitated by the thought, "what shall I do when I return home, if I become a Christian?" she wrote to her mother and fully expressed her feelings. Her reply, dictated either by policy or respect for religion, expressed her desire that her child might truly become a Christian, and R. was thereby greatly relieved from much anxiety.

When one of her brothers heard of the change in her feelings,—for as soon as she decided to live for Christ she made it known to all her friends,—he wrote her several letters expressive of his anger at the determination that she had avowed. He warned her "not to listen to the instruction of her fanatical priest-ridden teachers, who had their object in getting up such a state of things," declaring that he would write to her father, who was then absent, to remove her from school. I was much pleased with her reply which she requested me to read. She spoke of her determination to live a Christian life, and assured him that she did not act rashly or unadvisedly as her mother already knew and approved her choice : with affectionate earnestness she urged him to forsake the world, and live for eternity. After this he wrote to her mother, that we were intending "to compel her to join the church." This brought a letter to R. from her mother, in which she referred to the information communicated by her son and hoped she would defer such a step till time should test the sincerity of her conversion, then if she wished to make a profession of religion, she should not be opposed. She urged her to be a Christian in heart, and begged that she would not "put her hand to the plow and look back." I was pleased with the letter and could not but hope that the mother knew something of Christian feeling.

Letter after letter was received from irreligious friends, yet she still held fast to the cross of her Redeemer. A few days afterwards she said to me, "I fear my brother will come and take me home, and he will talk to me all the while about my religion, and I am afraid that I shall answer him in a wrong spirit;" then after a pause, she said with a smile, "But I can take my Bible and read that, and then I shan't heed him."

She remained until the close of the session, but was not allowed to return to the Seminary. After her return home, all correspondence with teachers and pupils was interdicted, and we saw her no more. Several months afterwards I received a letter from her, declaring the continuance of her affection for me and her increasing love to the Saviour. I replied to this clandestine letter, as I believed it to be, exhorting her to hold fast her confidence in God, and directed my reply to the care of her father. She never wrote again, but I trust that she is now, as the head of her own family, fulfilling her high duties and responsibilities.

L. A., an interesting pupil of eighteen, was of a peculiarly amiable disposition, and during a season of religious interest in the school the previous year, evinced great tenderness of conscience and much feeling on the subject. From the commencement of this revival, she had manifested great opposition of heart, was unwilling to attend meetings or to hear conversation calculated to show her her character and situation. Week after week she had been the subject of earnest supplication, and as one after another had yielded herself to her Saviour we almost feared that L. had repulsed the Spirit of God from her heart. In this state of feeling she visited New York. Her return was anxiously expected as we feared that the little impression made upon her mind would be certainly obliterated. Another young lady had also eagerly accepted the invitation of friends and had gone to spend a few days at home.

A church fast was appointed for the 18th of February. Our pastor had proposed that each family, on that day of fasting, should select certain individuals as the subject of special prayer, and these two young friends were among the number chosen by our family.

That was a solemn day,—a day to be remembered through eternity. The morning was spent by the several members of the family, in the retirement of their chambers alone with God;—and God was verily in our midst. I had proposed to spend an hour previous to the public services that were to be held in the afternoon, in prayer with the teacher and pupils. Half an hour before the time for this meeting, the two objects of our solicitude returned from different parts of the country. The circumstance was too striking to pass unnoticed, and when we met to offer our supplications at the throne of grace, with renewed earnestness did prayer ascend for these beloved ones.

M. was entirely overcome by her feelings and wept aloud, while L. sat unmoved evidently struggling with emotions that she was determined to repress.

The day passed, but no one of those for whom we had made intercession had been given to our prayers. My faith began to waver, and as I pondered on what might be the cause of such a failure, I came to the conclusion that my unfaithfulness had come up as a mountain between God and their souls. I tried to repent—to renew the dedication of myself to God. Every effort plunged me deeper in darkness. I dared not restrain prayer for those for whom I had felt so much concern, and yet the fear haunted me that my prayers would prove a curse to their souls. I believed this revival would cease if I continued my efforts and yet I was impelled to continue exertions. No one, unless placed in similar circumstances, can have an idea of the distress of my mind. To no earthly friend did I dare to reveal it. I began to doubt the genuineness of every conversion in the family and school, and though I did not relinquish hope for myself, I really believed that unless I was removed no good could visit any soul under my influence.

I continued in this state of mind for several days, when I opened my whole heart to my pastor, for I felt that I could not endure such distressing emotions another day.

After I had finished my "tale of woe," Mr. S. laughed, and said, " I am rejoiced that you have told me this; now I am convinced that this is Satan's work, for I have had just such temptations during the past week. Depend upon it, you have been yielding to the Tempter's power." The long conversation that ensued, strengthened me much, and I was from that time enabled to resist what I then saw was sent as a trial of faith and patience.

That same day we learned that one of the number, for whose salvation so much interest had been excited, had become a child of God. Thursday, of the following week, was observed as a day of prayer for our colleges and seminaries of learning, and then I noticed a great struggle in L.'s feelings, in consequence of which, after the evening meeting I sent for her. At the first question that I put to her, "Are you yet resisting the spirit of God?" she burst into tears, and sobbed as if her heart would break. She was sure that she had sinned beyond the reach of mercy; she confessed the dreadful opposition of her heart to God. "Oh," said she, "I am not the same being that I was last winter; then I was ready to listen to instruction—now my soul rises in rebellion." After endeavoring to make the plan of salvation plain and simple to her mind, and to show the perfect adaptation of this plan to her guilt and necessities, I said,

"Now, L., can you not trust such a Saviour, who declares that His blood cleanseth from all sin?"

"I think I can," was the prompt reply.

"Will you do it?"

"I will, Mrs. C., I will trust Him to-night."

I prayed with her, and she, in broken petitions, attempted to cry for mercy. As she arose to leave the room, she threw herself upon my neck in great agitation, kissed me, laid her head upon my shoulder, and remained weeping for several minutes, and then, with another kiss, she rushed from the room. She spent the night, as her sister informed me, in prayer, in weeping, and in reading the Bible. In the morning she was ready, for the first time, to attend the early prayer-meeting, and as she was leaving the house of prayer she approached the pastor, and offered him her hand. To his question,

"Have you yet given your heart to the Saviour?" she replied, very decidedly, "Yes, sir, I have." From that time the change in her feelings was so marked that no one could doubt its reality. Like Mary, humbly she took her seat at the feet of Jesus, to be instructed in the way of salvation.

She entered upon her Christian duties like one who had "counted the cost," and knew where to apply for strength to perform them. No doubts clouded her mind, for she trusted in her Saviour in the simplicity of faith, and seemed at all times to feel that now, having cast her soul on Jesus for salvation, He would not leave her to perish. In conversing with her I was often reminded of the first verse of the fifth chapter of Romans, "Therefore, being justified by faith, ye have peace with God."

Many other interesting circumstances connected with this revival might be named beside those already related. Every case of conversion is interesting, and well may there be joy in heaven and joy on earth, when sinners estranged from God are led to submit to his government. About twenty young ladies in the family and school, professed to consecrate themselves to the service of the Saviour, and gave us much hope that they had indeed become the children of God.

For ten weeks during that season of God's special visitation, we had public meetings every evening, and during three of those weeks there was preaching every afternoon. Morning prayer-meetings at half-past six o'clock were well attended in different parts of the town. So great was the desire of the young ladies to attend the public exercises, that they cheerfully devoted hours in which they had not been accustomed to study, to the acquisition of their lessons, so that few of the regular recitations of the school were omitted.

There were many characteristics of this revival that seemed to me to be particularly worthy of note. There were deep searchings of heart, great fervency in prayer, and much spirituality among Christians, and all seemed to have been baptized anew with the Holy Ghost. This was not a time for the children of God to sleep at their posts, for the enemy of souls was not idle. Parents were warned that what they did for their children, must be done quickly, for many of the children of the church, one or two of whom belonged to the Maternal Association of Bloomfield, had, within a few weeks been called into eternity.

O how can parents who themselves know something of the priceless value of the immortal soul, live at ease, while surrounded by impenitent children, who are every moment exposed to eternal death. When will they unite that fervent prayer, and lively faith, and faithful discipline which will ensure obedience to themselves, and submission to God? When shall it be said of the believing parent, as of Abraham of old, "I know him, that he will *command* his children, and his household after him, and they shall keep the way of the Lord."

At the first communion season that followed the close of this memorable session, forty-six converts, fruits of this revival, for the first time sat down to the table of the Lord, to commemorate His dying love. Seven of that number were members of the Seminary.

> "When gathering round the Saviour's board,
>   Fair forms, and brows beloved, I see,
> Who once the paths of peace explored,
>   And traced the studious page with me:
> Father, I bless thy ceaseless care,
>   Which thus its holiest gifts hath shed,
> Guide Thou their steps from every snare,
>   From every danger shield their head."

CHAPTER XXXII.

> "Call her no longer thine:
>   Thou could'st not keep consumption's moth away,
>   From her frail web of life. Thou could'st not guard
>   Thy darling from the lion. All thy love,
>   In the best armor of its sleepless might,
>   The spoiler trampled as a reed. Give thanks
>   That she is safe with Him who hath the power,
>   O'er pain, and sin, and death. Mourner, give thanks!"

SCARCELY had the summer session commenced its operations, e'er the Spirit of God was again manifest in our midst. Several of the pupils listened with earnest attention to the truths inculcated; and during the term ten or twelve gave evidence of faith in the Redeemer.

As the summer advanced, it was evident that the health of my only remaining daughter was rapidly declining. For years she had been a sufferer, and such was her devotion to her mother during *her* long illness the preceding year, that nature overtasked yielded to the demands made upon her strength, and we felt that she would not long continue her ministries to her widowed parent.

Her disease baffled the skill of physicians, and as no relief to severe bodily pain could be obtained, but by the use of Morphine, her mind was kept much of the time in a state of stupor or excitement. In several conversations which I had with her, respecting her religious feelings, her replies generally were, "I can neither think nor feel, I am so stupid."

Her most alarming symptoms abated, and for a season she indulged a hope of recovery. But these delusive promises of returning health soon vanished, and she set herself in earnest to examine anew the foundation of her hopes for eternity. Notwithstanding the effect of medicine and disease upon her mind, she felt sure there were times when Christ was precious to her, and she spoke of her wakeful hours at night as often pleasant seasons of communion with her Saviour,—seasons when she enjoyed much from repeating hymns and chapters from the Bible, when all around her were asleep. "But," she would add, with her usual distrust of herself, "I am afraid that the enjoyment arises more from the excitement of Morphine than from really right feelings in the heart." She often lamented her absence from her mother, when she commenced her Christian course. "Could I have been with you at that time," she once said with much feeling, "I should have been instructed in the nature and duty of cultivating spirituality of mind, and how much more devoted a life I might have led."

She became a Christian as she hoped, at fourteen years of age, while residing with her grand-parents in my native state. They gave her good instruction, but entered very little into her feelings or directed her ex-

perience. She returned to me two years after the
event, in such a state of health as precluded all active effort, and after her sister's death in 1832, she
spent a year in New Jersey, in the hope that change
of air and employment might prove beneficial to her.
There holy affections were not cultivated as they should
have been, and she came home to become the object of
much attention to many who loved her for her gentle,
quiet virtues. The circumstances attending a residence of four years in Virginia were also very injurious to her spiritual interests, and she felt that there
she laid the foundation work for bitter repentance.
To her worldliness and unfaithfulness in the cause of
her Redeemer during that period, she afterwards referred with deep emotions, and as the tears flowed
from her eyes, she expressed the fear that her past
hopes had all been delusive. I urged her if such
were her fears, to renew the dedication of herself to
the Saviour—to apply anew to the blood of atonement for pardon, and to the Spirit of God for His
sanctifying influences. The result of this conversation was salutary, and frequently after this she resumed the subject, seeming desirous to understand her
real situation and her prospects for eternity.

At times, she said, she was much distressed with
doubts and darkness of mind. To her, death had always been the king of terrors, and the idea of the
possibility of being called into eternity, without a well-
grounded hope in the Redeemer, was terrible to her

soul. When asked if upon a review of the exercises of her mind, she could give no evidence of her interest in the atonement of Christ, she uniformly replied, that she did ; but she was so fearful of self-deception, I have reason to believe that much of her time was spent in self-examination ; often when I was obliged to leave her for a season, to discharge duties that imperiously claimed my attention, she would beg that no one might be sent to fill my place—she preferred to be alone.

During the last two months of her life it was interesting to see how subdued was her spirit—how patiently she bore her severe sufferings. Once after I had engaged in prayer with her, she said, " Mother, there is one expression which you use in prayer, that I do not think is right."

" What is it, Eliza ?" I asked.

" You speak of the *bitter cup* that I am called to drink, and it ought not, I am sure, to be called a *bitter* cup."

" But, my dear child, is not such suffering as you endure, bitter ?"

" Yes, Mother, perhaps so ; but then I have so many mercies—it seems *all* mercy."

' I never again used that expression in prayer. She spoke frequently of her enjoyment during her sleepless nights, when all was quiet around her. She derived much profit and satisfaction from Philip's works, especially his " Eternity Realized ;"—Mrs. Dwight's

Memoirs, also deeply interested her. But the book to which she loved most to listen was the Bible, and often would she say to me, "O Mother, you always select exactly the chapters that I love to hear."

On the 1st of November a new session in the Seminary commenced, and for a few days the confusion unavoidable from such a change, disturbed her mind, but she soon regained composure. On the evening of the 16th we perceived a very perceptible change for the worse, and it became very apparent to her friends that her departure was at hand. Although I had repeatedly conversed with her on the state of her feelings in view of death, and told her we had no hopes of her recovery, I dared not trust myself to say that ere that week should close she would probably be in eternity.

Day after day she grew more feeble, till, on the 20th, I requested her pastor to break to her the opinion of her physician that she must soon leave us. Her aunt remained with her, while I retired to pour out my full soul to God. She received the decision of her physician with perfect calmness—told Mr. S. she had no fear of death—that all anxiety on the subject of her soul's salvation was entirely removed from her mind, and that she was ready to depart whenever her Saviour should summon her away. She had sometimes feared, she said, that mother supposed she was reluctant to express her feelings, but it was not so; her hesitancy arose from the fear of distressing *me* by expressing the belief that she was so soon to be removed. After Mr. S. had prayed with us and departed, Eliza requested to see me alone.

"Mother," she said, fixing her eyes with deep interest upon me, and speaking with difficulty, for she was much exhausted, "should I be suddenly taken away, say in a few days, or to-night, could you follow me, in your thoughts, to the throne of God, and feel that I was among those who were engaged in singing His praises?"

"Tell me, my child, whether, if God should remove you this night, you believe, that through the merits of your Redeemer, you should join that happy company?"

"Yes, mother, I believe that I should."

"Then, Eliza, I could think of you, and bless God, as rejoicing in the presence of God and the Lamb."

"One question more, mother; do you feel that you can give me up when the Saviour shall call me away?"

"Yes, my child, I bless God that He enables me to feel willing to resign you to Him; the struggle has been severe, but He has supported me, and I feel assured that He will not forsake me in the trying hour."

"O, I am so glad that you feel so, mother," she said, "you have been a precious mother to me, but I have often been an undutiful child, and I know I have often tried your feelings."

I said to her, "my dear child, if it is any comfort to you to hear me say it, I can tell you that you have been a great comfort to me; in all my cares and trials you have sought to lessen them by sympathy or participation. In sickness you have watched over me, and I feel, that under Providence, I owe it to your untiring efforts and watchful care that I survived my last terrible illness; and I cannot but fear that your present sufferings are the result of your faithful attendance on that sick bed."

"I can say, with Legh Richmond," she replied, "when my heart is too cold to bless God for any other mercy, I can thank him for giving me such a mother."

I was too much overcome by my feelings to converse.

"Mother," she continued, "did you not tell me you could resign me into the hands of God? Why, then, do you feel thus?"

"I trust, Eliza, I am willing to submit to the will of our heavenly Father, but nature will feel—my poor heart deeply feels this trial."

"God will take care of you, mother; it seems wonderful to me that I have so little anxiety respecting you, but I know that it will be but a little while before we shall meet again. I would not be selfish—I know that you are needed here—but O, what a joyful meeting that will be, and it will be so soon. Mother. there is no *time* in heaven."

This, and the preceding conversation with Mr. S., entirely exhausted her, and she lay for some time apparently unconscious. Late in the evening she revived a little, but was soon so distressed that her physician thought she could not survive till morning. She was perfectly sensible—aware of her situation—and entirely calm and composed. Seeing me weeping, she called me to her, "Mother, do you remember your promise?" she said, emphatically. I asked her if she could trust her soul without fear in the hands of her Redeemer. She assured me that she could do it—that her Saviour was very near, and that she had no fear of death.

Many friends watched by her bedside during the hours of that weary, anxious night, every moment expecting her departure; but the morning of Saturday dawned, and found her still an inhabitant of earth; and there she lay, on that bed of suffering and pain, till the following Thursday—spared, I have no doubt, to enable her to exhibit the power of religion to sustain and to fill the soul with joy unspeakable in the midst of great bodily suffering.

I had many interesting conversations with her during those days of anxiety and watching. Never did a cloud darken the bright prospects of eternal blessedness, never a doubt arise as to the reality of her trust in the Redeemer. She loved to talk with me respecting the angelic throng who surround the throne of God. "O, mother." she once said, with much animation, "do you think I shall know my father in heaven? and Maria too—and other friends—what a happy company I shall find in heaven!" We then had a long conversation on the recognition of friends in the heavenly world. "But," she said, at its close, "this will not be necessary to constitute the happiness of the Christian there—the presence of the Saviour will be sufficient."

She dwelt much on the great mercy of God, manifested to *her*—one who had served Him so unfaithfully—to be so blessed in a dying hour; it was wonderful, but she added, "it is all through the merits and blood of Jesus." Through her illness, and especially as she drew near to the close of life, she was tenderly alive to the comfort of those around her, and often expressed her fears that their attendance on her would injure them. She earnestly desired once more to see her brother William, and several times expressed the wish that he might come; "but," said she at one time, "I have so many mercies, that these desires ought not to be named."

Speaking, at one time, of her great desire that her death might be blessed to the good of the school, I asked her if she had any message to leave for the pupils. "O, yes," she replied, "tell the impenitent, from me, that I urge them to prepare for death while they are in health. On a dying bed they will need all the support that religion can impart; let them learn from me that they have no security for life.

Tell Christians to be faithful in the discharge of their duties. O, tell them, mother, not to neglect the duty of conversing freely and frequently on the subject of religion, as I have done. Tell them I consider it a punishment from God for my backwardness in the performance of this duty, that now, when I desire to converse, I am unable to do it."

These remarks were made at different times, often interrupted by severe returns of pain and exhaustion.

Respecting a young relative whom she had wished much to see, and who visited her a few days previous to her departure, she said, " R. cannot know how much he has gratified me by this visit. O if I could only say something that would affect his heart,"— then after a few moments she added, " God can bless even a few words. O mother, it would be worth dying for if my death could produce any good effect on him."

On the Wednesday afternoon preceding her death, as she was reclining in her chair—my sister and myself seated by her side—Mrs. S. came in, and we had some conversation on the blessedness of heaven and the recognition of friends in that happy world. She joined with much animation in the conversation and expressed her full belief that such a recognition would take place, and that they would remember the events which had transpired on earth. I said to her, " Eliza, this is the afternoon for the meeting of the Maternal Association ; you would like to be remembered there ?"

" O yes," she replied, " I have a right you know, to be remembered there ?"

" And have you not," said Mrs. S., " some message to send to mothers ?"

" Yes," was her ready reply, and then she hesitated and turned her eye very expressively towards me.

" I can interpret that look, my dear," I said, " it says that you feel there is an impropriety in sending a message of that kind to those who are mothers, and are so much older."   She smiled assent.

Fatigued with the effort she had made, she lay upon her pillow with her eyes closed.   Struck with the tranquil expression of her countenance, I repeated aloud, " I will keep him in *perfect peace*, whose mind is stayed on Thee because he trusteth in Thee."   Both Mrs. S. and my sister observed that the same passage was passing through their minds, as they looked upon her.

" O," said I, " could we but look into that mind and witness all its views and emotions, as it approaches eternity—" interrupting me, with a most expressive look, she replied, " I wish you could do it !"

Such were the scenes occurring from day to day in that sick room, and such the serenity which led our pastor in one of his visits to exclaim,

> " The chamber where the good man meets his fate,
>   Is privileged beyond the common walks of virtuous life,
>   Quite on the verge of heaven."

After one conversation with her pastor, she said to me,

"Mr. S. asked me one question, mother, that tried me for a moment, but it was a very judicious one. I had not thought of it before, and I was glad afterwards, that he asked me." I wished to know what it was.

"Do you not recollect how I looked at you once, while he was talking with me?—it was at that moment."

I did remember observing a look of distress rest for an instant on her countenance and then, passing away, it was succeeded by a bright and peaceful expression.

I said to her, "Tell me, my child, what was then passing through your mind?"

She replied, "Mr. S. asked if I felt willing to submit myself to God to be disposed of as He should see fit. I told him that I was willing. He then said— does this submission proceed from a willing surrender of your soul to God, or are you willing to die because you see no prospect of recovery? For a moment I was bewildered; is it possible I thought, that my submission can arise from *necessity* alone? My thoughts instantly reverted to my past feelings. I had supposed I was willing to die or to live, as God should see fit to direct—can I have been mistaken? Then I thought of the desires I had had, should health be restored, and I asked myself now should God raise me from this sickness and direct me to a situation which should offer hardship and trial all my days, but one in which I might do much to promote His glory, would I be willing to engage in such a service? and my heart replied, yes—'I can do all things through Christ strengthening me,' and then I *knew* that I felt submission to God's will, not from necessity but because I love Him and His cause. Mother, that was a good question—*it led me to think*—tell Mr. S. so."

The last connected sentences that she uttered were to her brother R. who had just returned from listening to a lecture from Dr. Cox on the subject of history. Supposing it to be of a religious character, she said to him,

" Brother, turn me in bed, and then tell me about the lecture—if it is proper."

On being told that it was not about heaven—" nor God, nor Jesus Christ?" was her query.

" No, none of these things."

"O then," she replied, "I do not wish to hear it."

Through the whole of Thursday, she lay most of the time apparently insensible. Every passing moment we thought would be her last. Towards night she was seized with violent coughing, which we feared would suddenly and painfully terminate her existence, but this passed away and perfect unconsciousness succeeded; and although there were times during the night when she seemed distressed with pain and would cry out, " Mother, dear mother," we could not perceive that she was conscious of distress. One painful struggle almost awakened feelings of rebellion in my heart; for a few moments the conflict was terrible, but our heavenly Father had compassion on the wounded soul and sent the comforts of the Holy Spirit to impart new strength and confidence in Him.

Our pastor surrounded by our family and pupils, bowed before God, in supplication that the solemn scene might be sanctified to all, and that a speedy and peaceful entrance into the heavenly mansions might be granted to the sufferer. At four o'clock in the morning her spirit quietly and peacefully entered into rest, and my heart rose in gratitude to God—to the God of the widow and fatherless—that He had at last housed this suffering one, from the storms and tempests of life. For *her* my soul rejoiced; but when I looked around for the loved one, who was always so ready to minister to my wants—to sympathize in all my trials—to mingle all her feelings with mine, my heart was indeed desolate. True, I was blessed with dear children and kind friends, but they could not be to me what that dear child had been. Still I would not have recalled her to earth. She makes the fourth of my dear family who, I trust, await me in the realms of bliss, and very delightful is the hope that our whole family will yet stand before the throne of God—an unbroken circle—redeemed by the blood of Jesus. To God be all the glory.

On Saturday, the remains of my dear child were consigned to the grave. None but those who have passed through the trial, can know with what feelings the bereaved mourner turns from the grave, where lie enshrouded buried hopes and earthly prospects. That casket which has so long sheltered the spirit now inhabiting the realms of glory, becomes a holy object, and we turn with shuddering at the thought that we leave it to become the prey and food of worms. But the tear is dried and the heart is lightened of its burden, as faith points triumphantly to the glorious resurrection morn, when this corruption shall put on incorruption, and this mortal shall become an immortal body, which redeemed by the atoning sacrifice of Jesus, united to the spirit, shall stand forever in the presence of God.

" And ye are left alone,
Who nurtured those fair buds, and often said
Unto each other, in the hour of care,
'These same shall comfort us for all our toil;'
Yes, ye are left alone. It is not ours
To heal such wounded. Man hath too weak a hand,
All he can give is tears.
But He who took
Your treasures to his keeping, He hath power
To bear you onward to that better land,
Where none are written childless, and torn hearts
Blend in a full eternity of bliss."

CHAPTER XXXIII.

WINTER OF 1840–41.

"'Tis sweet to feel that He who tries
   The silver, takes His seat
Beside the fire that purifies,
   Lest too intense a heat,
Raised to consume the base alloy,
The precious metals should destroy."

WITH what a weight of feeling did our annual Thanksgiving of 1840, which occurred but a few days after the departure of my blessed child, dawn upon me. Not that I felt that I had nothing for which to thank my heavenly Father, but as I kneeled before Him such a rush of overwhelming emotions swept over my soul, as almost took from me the power of thought and feeling. But I did praise Him—praise Him for the very trial that was bowing me to the earth—praise Him for his mercy to my suffering child—for removing her from a world of trial, and for taking her to Himself before she had wept on a mother's grave. And Christmas came cheerily on, with its joyous greetings and sunny faces, but to my soul it spoke only of the remembered past. One year ago and dear Eliza was full of engagedness in her preparation for the Christmas offering. It was her hand that prepared each little memento of affection—that spread the table and uncovered it to the gaze of the curious group,—each eager to receive the gift of the season, and there were glad hearts and happy faces all around us. The sun rose brightly on the Christmas morning of another year; but it shone on sad hearts, on *one* at least that could not drive back its feelings to their prison house. *My* precious offering had been given to God; and though he returned richly of the consolations of the Spirit to my soul, I was forcibly reminded of the lines which dear Eliza had copied for me, a few weeks subsequent to the departure of her beloved sister for her heavenly home.

> "It is not when the parting breath we watch with anxious hearts,
> It is not in the hour of death, when those we love depart,
> Nor yet when laid upon the bier, we follow slow the corse,
> And leave it in its dwelling dark, that most we feel the loss;
> When past the last, the solemn rite, and dust to dust hath gone,
> And in its wonted channeled course, the stream of life rolls on,
> Oh, who can tell how drear the space once filled by those most dear,
> When well known scenes which they have loved, and all but they are here?"

Illness and trials of a peculiar character succeeded, and the winter passed away without any special interest in the subject of the soul's salvation. Our prayer-meetings and bible-classes were well attended and solemn, and a few professed to have passed from death unto life.

Considerable work was accomplished for the missionary cause, and a valuable box of clothing and other things prepared for our friend Mrs. L. of the Armenian mission.

The vacation of April, 1841, I spent in C. with the sister friend of my beloved Eliza. Very delightful was this intercourse, though it forcibly reminded us of the departed one. In that dear family I spent two pleasant weeks; and though the winds blew and " the storm beat upon that house," it diminished not the comforts of its inmates. With many regrets at leaving my friends at the Manse, did my eye watch their dwelling as it receded from my sight, till it became a speck in the distant landscape.

Nothing can exceed the beauty of the prospect that greets the eye on every side of this chosen spot. In front, gracefully winds the noble Hudson, bearing on its bosom steamer and sloop and tiny boat, all subservient to the pleasure or business of man. In the distance, elevated and romantic country seats meet the view, and the city of Hudson on one side, and the pleasant village of Athens on the other, give a pleasing variety to the scene. On the west of the dwelling, the gentle undulations of the land that gradually swell into sturdier proportions, charm by their beauty and variety, while beyond these the lofty summits of the Catskill mountains tower far above the clouds. There too in full view, though so far distant, stands the " Mountain House,"—the resort of the lovers of pleasure as well as of the grand and beautiful in nature,—perched on the topmost crags, like an eagle on his eyrie.

CHAPTER XXXIV.

PERSONAL TRIALS.—DR. ATWATER.

> "Many a shaft, at random sent,
> Finds mark the archer little meant;
> And many a word, at random spoken,
> May soothe or wound a heart that's broken."

DURING the summer of 1841 events occurred that involved me in deep distress, and that kept my mind in continual agitation and perplexity, in which my children deeply sympathized. They were the result of the ungrateful conduct of one for whom I had done much, and in whose welfare my heart took a lively interest. Friends were implicated and alienated, until it sometimes seemed as though God himself had forsaken me. So distressing was the whole affair to me, so distracting to my mind, so injurious to my nervous system, that my health was seriously impaired, and it was with difficulty that the duties of the teacher were performed.

In October, accompanied by Miss N., one of our teachers, who had been to me as a daughter since dear Eliza was taken from me, I visited some friends of my early days, residing in New Haven. There I once more met the venerable man who had been, in my youthful days, my spiritual father—the guide and teacher of my inexperience and ignorance—the friend who, in the days of thoughtlessness and folly, had arrested my attention and directed my feet from the paths of sin to holiness; whom, under God, I shall bless through eternity for his untiring efforts for my salvation. I had not seen Dr. Atwater for thirty years, and it was delightful to renew a friendship so long interrupted.

> "I do remember him.   His saintly voice
> So duly lifted in the house of God,
> Comes with the far-off wing of other years,
> Like solemn music.   I do remember him;
> The comforter and friend.
> Farewell, thou who didst lead me
> To the Redeemer's sacred board a guest,
> Timid and unassured—yet gathering strength
> From the blest promise of Jehovah's aid
> Unto the early seeker."

With much anxiety at the close of the year did I retrace the dealings of God with me.   I reviewed the past, not to write bitter things against unjust calumniators, but to bring my own course to the bar of conscience, and to the view of the heart-searching God, and after the severest scrutiny I could not feel that I should pursue a different course, were I obliged to retrace my steps.   I felt that though justice might never be done to me in this world, unto God I could commit my cause, and that "my judgment was with my God."

No record remains of souls renewed during that troublous year; but much was accomplished for the missionary cause, and I trust that many hearts were made glad by the offerings of affection to the treasury of the Lord, and to the domestic circles of many who are laboring for the dark-minded in far-off homes.

CHAPTER XXXV.

REVIVAL OF 1843.

THE year 1843 opened with more encouraging prospects. "My faith looks up to Thee," would, perhaps, well express the feelings of my own soul. Our first Bible-class, in January, was unusually solemn, and many hopes were entertained that these impressions would be abiding, but, like Ephraim and Judah their goodness seemed "like the morning cloud and the early dew." The studies and employments of the week banisbed serious thoughts. Giddy and trifling, "God was not in all their thoughts." Surely there must be great defects in their home education, when the children of the pious exhibit such a decided aversion to the subject of religion so early in life. How little are parents aware that the first impressions of childhood are generally the most abiding; and thus many characters are formed before the parent has awakened to a sense of his responsibility, or the danger of his child.

" For character groweth day by day, and all things aid it in unfold-
ing;
And the bent unto good or evil may be given in the hours of
infancy.
Scratch the green rind of a sapling, or wantonly twist it in the
soil,
The scarred and crooked oak will tell of thee for centuries *to*
come;
Even so may'st thou guide the mind to good, or lead it to the
marrings of evil;
For disposition is builded up by the fashionings of first impressions."

Bible instruction has always been a delightful exercise to me, and in looking over the records of that year I find that, during the six years I had taught in Bloomfield, we had, in different classes, been through the Gospels, twice through the Acts, once through Romans and the Epistles to the Corinthians. A great amount of instruction has been communicated, how often without the unction from on high, God only knows. That He ever condescended to bless *any* effort, is cause of unceasing gratitude; that He has not done it oftener should excite deep humility. But the promise is sure, " He that goeth forth and weepeth, bearing precious seed, shall doubtless come again, rejoicing, bringing his sheaves with him."

Much of the months of January and February, when not occupied with the duties of the school, were spent in preparing articles for the Persian mission;

and by the first of March they were on their way to their destination, under the care of our friends, Dr. and Mrs. Perkins, who were returning to their work, after a brief visit to their native land. When the articles were completed, we spread them out for the inspection of our pupils and other friends of missions, among whom the Rev. Doctor Armstrong had been invited. To my question, "Dr. Armstrong, is this a useless work?" he replied, "You cannot calculate the amount of good that this offering may do for the missions. Were you to sell every article for its full value, the money would not benefit them as much as these presents."

We had scarcely completed our missionary work, ere the special influences of the Holy Spirit were manifest in our midst, and the song of praise arose from many a new-born soul. The term had commenced in discouragement and trial—it closed amid a shower of mercy.

During much of the session most of the pupils had exhibited a levity of spirit, an inattention to their studies, and an utter disregard of religious instruction that often sent their teachers to weep in secret over their pride and folly. But,

> "Just in the last distressing hour
> The Lord displayed delivering power,"

and the hard heart was melted, and the thoughtless awakened to serious concern for the salvation of their souls.

There were some circumstances preparatory to this work, that, perhaps, it were well to record. While Dr. Armstrong was in town, some hopes were entertained that a spirit of inquiry and an increased attention to the subject of religion were awakened in the congregation; it was therefore proposed that there should be preaching afternoon and evening for several successive days. When this intention was made known in the Seminary, appearances strongly indicated a decided dislike to the measure, and many remarks were made, exhibiting the determination of the pupils to keep aloof, as much as possible, from all serious influences. Indeed, many formed the resolution, that unless compelled to do so, they would attend none of the meetings. I was exceedingly tried to know how to proceed *wisely* at this difficult crisis. Should I insist on attendance at the meetings, their opposition to the truth might be increased; if I allowed them to neglect these means of grace, it might be fatally injurious to those for whose salvation my heart was continually pleading. Friends could not aid me, for they were perplexed and alarmed at the rebellious feelings exhibited. We carried our case to our Father's throne, and entreated to be directed aright. My mind became calm and settled. I decided to keep them, for a time at least, at home.

No remarks were made to the pupils in regard to the appointments of the week, though morning instruction was continued as usual. When the church bell sent forth its first summons to gather for worship in the sanctuary, it was almost amusing to see the looks of surprise cast from one to another, that they were not bidden to accompany their teachers to the house of God. Evening came with its precious privileges, but still they were not there to listen to the Word. They professed to be delighted that they were not " worried" with lectures and admonitions. Another day came and went, and still they were not invited to the feast. Then arose angry feelings— " Well, if Mrs. C. does not care enough about us, to *let us go* to the meetings, we are sure that we do not care ;"—they were evidently chagrined at being passed by.

The succeeding day was to be the last of these privileged seasons, and I was distressed to know how to proceed. Should I persevere in the course thus far adopted, it might seal the eternal destiny of some of these poor deluded ones fatally, irrecoverably. I pleaded for wisdom—for guidance. Like Hezekiah, I spread this overwhelming subject before the Lord, and my mind seemed directed and strengthened.

Without any comment I simply requested every young lady in the family to prepare to accompany me to the religious services of the afternoon. A few asked for permission to remain at home—none were excused—and wondering what had produced such a sudden change in the conduct of their teacher, all fol-

lowed her with various feelings to the House of
Prayer.

Dr. Armstrong preached, and as he had a beloved child in that interesting group, no wonder his
heart and eyes overflowed as he warned them "to flee
from the wrath to come." Desirous to ascertain the
effect produced by this solemn appeal, I said, after our
family worship, that if any were desirous to attend the
public exercises of the evening, they could do so by
applying to me for permission. I had scarcely reached
my room, e'er one and another sought for this permission, until twenty or thirty had assembled there.
With what subdued expression and earnestness did
they now prefer their requests ;—with what evident
sincerity declare their wish to hear the word of God—
and with what solemn awe and heartfelt gratitude did
the teacher conduct them to the place of instruction
and prayer.

After our return home, I disclosed to Dr. Armstrong all my trials and struggles of heart and mind—
told him the situation of the school --the rebellious
spirit evinced—the course I had adopted—and asked
for his counsel, his sympathy, and his prayers.

" My dear friend," was his remark at parting, "it
is a trite but true saying, that the darkest time is
just before day-break, and this I believe, will be your
experience. This term will not close without a blessing to this school. For weeks we have borne its
spiritual interests to the throne of grace, at our family

altar, and the present aspect of the pupils assures me, that a blessing is near. Take courage—go forward; and trust the Lord."

Animated and encouraged we did go forward; the interest and the solemnity hourly increased, and the whole appearance of the school was changed. In the course of two weeks, twenty-four indulged the hope of pardon through a Saviour's blood.

Oh how affecting it was to see those who a few days before, preferred any society to mine, now crowding to my room for instruction and prayer, and how delightful to bow with those dear ones before the mercy-seat, and listen to their supplications for God's mercy on their own souls and on those of their impenitent companions. They were now as eager to confess the wrong feelings that they had indulged, as they had been to justify themselves in their disobedience and rebellion. With one accord they met at all times, when opportunity offered to unite in singing the praises of the Redeemer and to pour out their hearts before Him.

The last day of the term was one of peculiar interest. A new tie bound heart to heart, and the joyous anticipations of "Home, sweet home," were mingled with grateful remembrances of the past and sorrow at the expected separation. The day was closed with appropriate and profitable addresses by our pastor and my son, which were calculated to leave a salutary impression upon the minds of the pupils.

In view of the merciful visitation of the Holy Spirit, we could only cry, "Not unto us, not unto us, but to Thy name be all the glory." Blessing and honor, and glory to Him, who turned our mourning into praise, and who so richly verified His own promise, "He that goeth forth and weepeth, bearing precious seed, shall doubtless come again with rejoicing, bringing his sheaves with him."

CHAPTER XXXVI.

LEILA'S DEATH.—WILLIAM'S CHILD.

"Ye who mourn,
Whene'er yon vacant cradle, or the robea
That decked the lost one's form, call back a tide
Of alienated joy, can ye not trust
Your treasure to His arms, whose changeless care
Passeth a mother's love? Can ye not hope,
When a few hastening years their course have run,
To go to them, though they no more on earth
Return to you?
    And when glad faith doth catch,
Some echo of celestial harmonies,
Archangel's praises, with the high response
Of cherubim and seraphim, O think—
Think that your babes are there."

THIS season of spiritual enjoyment was followed by
a bereavement most distressing. A beloved grand-
child given to me, as I trusted, in some measure to
supply the loss of my departed one, and bearing her
name—of whom I often said "this same shall comfort
me," was stricken by disease. With trembling anxiety did her parents and friends watch beside the
couch of the sufferer, as she gradually declined—feeling more and more assured that her heavenly Father
would soon recall the treasure He had so kindly lent
us. It was to me a melancholy pleasure, that this illness occurred during our vacation, by which I was
enabled to assist in ministering to her wants, and in

soothing the excitability occasioned by a constantly raging fever. Her only indication of distress, was a low moan accompanied by difficulty of breathing; no cries proceeded from her, and not once did she refuse the most disagreeable medicine. Once only she seemed amused with her playthings, and when I showed her the little book of pictures, which she had often been delighted to have me explain to her, I said to her, "Lelia, tell Grandma' how the little girl does when she prays to God," she looked up with a smile, and directly clasped her little hands together as she was wont to do when in health.

But a few hours before her death, as I stooped to raise her from the sofa on which she lay, she clasped her arms around my neck and raising her head laid it on my bosom and slept for an hour. These are sad but pleasant recollections. In mercy was she given to cheer the lonely hours of a weary life, and for nearly two years sweetly did she perform her mission of mercy. The Lord *gave*,—and I blessed him for the precious boon;—He *took* her to Himself—"a lamb, untasked, untried,"—and I blessed Him still for His mercy to her. So early removed from the sins and sufferings of life, what blessed scenes opened upon her vision; what pure and holy joys filled her soul with wonder, gratitude and love. Gently did the dear child breathe her life out on the bosom of her Redeemer, and went to join the blessed, who strike their harps to the praise of God and the Lamb.

> "Those feeble feet, unsteady,
>   That tottered as they trod,
> With angels walk the heavenly paths
>   Or stand before their God.
> Those eyes, so curbed in vision,
>   Now range the realms of space—
> Look down upon the rolling stars,
>   Look up to God's own face."

> " 'Tis sweet, as year by year we lose
>   Friends out of sight, in faith to muse,
>   How grows, in paradise, our store."

" Woes cluster—rare are solitary woes ;" and such seemed now to be the discipline of our Father. Scarcely had our dear Leila been transplanted from earth, a delicate and fragile flower, to bloom and expand for ever in the paradise of God, than the sad intelligence was received that the youngest of William's family circle—a lovely child of twelve months, had also been removed to the same bright home in the better land.　Other trials succeeded, but often did I comfort myself, when exhausted in body and mind, with the thought, rest will soon come to the weary one—full, perfect rest—holy rest and forever.

How many seasons there are in the life of woman when she must feel and suffer *alone;* "when," as Charlotte Elizabeth justly remarks, "the dearest friends must be comparative strangers.　There are depths of thought and mazes of feelings not to be explored by human eye—throbs of secret anguish beyond the alleviation of human sympathy.　Alone, man enters the world, and alone he must launch forth upon eternity; and between the two periods there is many a moment when, despite himself, man is compelled to feel what it is to be *utterly alone*."

When the stricken heart is thus left desolate, how does the remembrance of the sainted ones come over the soul, like the beautiful rays of the setting sun—soft, melting, and melancholy. But does this dark picture present no light amid its shadows? Yea, many. Precious seasons of spiritual comfort—domestic affections lightening life's burdens—friendship's cheering voice, sympathizing in the hour of trouble—merciful answers to prayer—children renewed and prepared for heaven. Surely, then, we should rejoice in the government of God, and cling to the cross of the Redeemer, until He becomes to our souls, "as the shadow of a great Rock in a weary land."

> "Who is *alone*, if God be nigh?
>   Who shall repine at loss of friends,
>   While he has One, of boundless power,
>   Whose constant kindness never ends,
>   Whose presence felt enhances joy,
>   Whose love can stop each flowing tear,
>   And cause upon the darkest cloud
>   The bow of mercy to appear."

11*

CHAPTER XXXVII.

> " It is a heavenly theme;
> I bear a voice Divine, no idle dream,
> Calling to duty and to self denial,
> In face of many a stern and bitter trial;
> Reverberating, when the day is bright,
> Soft whispering in the gentle hush of night;
> Chiding when earthly pleasures round me rise,
> Soothing when sorrows fill my weeping eyes;—
> " Go preach the Gospel! fly to every land,
> Obey the risen Saviour's last command!"

THE following year passed by with its clouds and sunshine. Here and there I can recall one and another who, by the grace of God, were led to think upon their ways, and to turn their feet unto God's testimonies. One dear friend, a teacher in the Seminary, bade adieu to home and friends and native land, to devote her life to the service of her Redeemer, in the far-off isles of ocean. She passed away from us like a bright dream, which left its sweet influence on the heart; but we yielded her cheerfully to the call of duty and of God.

Another loved one also, who had proved herself a devoted child to me ever since my own Eliza had slumbered with the dead, and who for six years had labored by my side as a teacher in the Seminary, departed to assume the responsibilities of married life.

> " Methought 'twere well to bear the frowns
> And meet the trials of a heartless world;
> If sometimes there may cross our earthly paths
> A kind and loving spirit that may walk
> Awhile with us, adown life's 'vale of tears,'
> And help us in our way to heaven."

During the following winter of 1845-6, we were favored by a gracious visitation of God's Holy Spirit, and several of our pupils then, as we had reason to hope, consecrated themselves to the Saviour's service. O, how do such refreshing seasons strengthen the faith and nerve the exhausted energies of mind and body for new duties and responsibilities.

The multiplicity of my cares at this times, prevented me from recording many interesting scenes which would be, in the retrospect, "like the music of Carryl, pleasant and mournful to the soul." Faithful teachers greatly aided, by their efficient efforts, in the good work, and many, I doubt not, were permitted to be instrumental in placing new gems in the Redeemer's crown.

The summer and autumn of 1846 was signally chronicled in the Seminary as a season of great missionary enjoyment. Two missionary families—Mr. and Mrs. Crane, from India, and Mr. and Mrs. Hutchings, from Ceylon, who were at that time residing in our village—greatly contributed to our enjoyment; and their society, in connection with fre-

quent intercourse with dear friends who were soon to
give the parting hand to the loved circles at home,
greatly tended to increase our zeal in the missionary
work. With great assiduity did the members of the
school engage in assisting in the preparation of a New
Year's present for the devoted ones who were soon to
make their home, for many months, upon the bounding billows.

We rejoiced that another band of devoted Christians
were ready to join those who are laboring in India,
and it was pleasant to see the unabated zeal which led
those veterans in their Master's service, Scudder and
Spaulding, with their self-sacrificing companions, to
return to those labors and privations in which they
had already passed twenty-four years of their lives.

But for only two short years was one of this precious company permitted to labor in her new and foreign home. Faithfully did she perform her work,
and early and sweetly did she sleep in Jesus. " Dark
and inscrutable are the ways of God to man, but there
is comfort in the thought that what now seems mysterious in the Providence of God, will hereafter be made
clear." She was a precious gift, lent for a few short
years, but early needed to increase the gems in the
Redeemer's crown.

" Give joy to the departed one,
Whose conflicts all are past;
Whose song of triumph has begun,
And shall for ever last;
Where raptured saints and angels join,
In strains seraphic and Divine."

CHAPTER XXXVIII.

VISIT OF MR. AND MRS. HUTCHINGS.—REVIVAL.

THE winter of 1846–47, was one of severe bodily suffering ; the effect of dyspepsia and derangement of the nervous system. But these trials were trifles in comparison with the mental suffering which often came over my soul like a dark cloud, bringing with it storm and tempest, and it was not till convinced that the mind was affected by the derangement and prostration of the physical energies, that relief was obtained.

But notwithstanding that sore trial, the Lord did not leave me wholly comfortless. Though I was called upon to suffer, others in the family experienced signal mercy. Our Father poured out his Spirit upon the school, and the anxious inquiry for the way of salvation came from many a bursting heart. Unable most of the time to converse with the pupils, I could only while lying on my sofa send up broken petitions to my Father God, for the aid of His Holy Spirit, to perfect the work that he had begun in our midst.

For several weeks, in the early part of the session, our dear missionary friends, Mr. and Mrs. Hutchings, whose return to the field of their labors had been prevented by the continued ill health of the former, had tried to make us a visit, but her indisposition or my illness had hitherto postponed it; but now just when their prayers and their instructions were most needed, the Lord sent them into the family, and for ten days they both labored with untiring effort to bring souls to Christ. During this time fifteen indulged the hope that they had passed from death unto life, among whom was the eldest daughter of Mr. Hutchings.

One of our teachers who entered with much zeal into the work of the Spirit, gave me the following account of one of the pupils, who, naturally reserved and timid, shrunk from observation.

"It was during the period of deepest solemnity that I found H. A., one evening at twilight, standing alone by the stove, which was near the door of her room. In reply to a few questions, cautiously and sympathizingly addressed to her, she expressed her willingness to yield her heart, at that moment, to the Saviour, and entering her room we bowed together at His feet. After I had earnestly commended her to Him and besought his blessing upon her, she unhesitatingly offered a full and simple-hearted consecration of herself to her Redeemer and to his service. From that hour she cherished the Christian's hope, and quietly but sweetly witnessed for Christ. We hope much *for* her and *from* her."

Removed afterwards to the companionship of t'.e gay and worldly, and having no Christian friend to direct her steps or warn her of her danger, she made no public profession of her faith and was classed by many with those who had no hope. " But the memory of that twilight hour and its visible results, to those who recalled the deep interest of those bygone scenes, forbade the belief that she was at heart a worldling. At length when years had kept that cherished memory,—kept it yet undimmed—the Spirit of God came with special power upon the Church, and upon the hearts of the community where she resided. Then her pastor sought her out and found her still indulging the hope of her earlier years.

"Never had she relinquished that hope—never had she ceased to perform as she could, the duties it implied. And now having received anew the baptism of the Holy Spirit, she sought and found a place among the sympathizing friends of the Redeemer."

H. E., came into the family in the year 18—, a wild, reckless, neglected child—apparently destitute of those affections and sensibilities that give interest to the female character. Often was I tempted to withdraw myself from the incessant demands that she made upon my patience and forbearance, and return her to the guardianship of the only friends who seemed to care for her; and as often was I deterred by the improvement that she made in her studies, and by the earnest entreaties of those friends to bear with her a little longer.

Sadly had her early education been neglected. The mother who would have watched over the years of childhood, had been removed by death, and for a time none seemed to care for her soul or to aid in training the young immortal for usefulness and happiness. Thanks be to God that at last He deeply enlisted Christian sympathy for this unloved, forsaken child. Here was mercy—mercy in store for the wayward. In this season of God's power His grace at last touched her heart. Her tendency to despondency, arising partly from temperament and partly from the circumstances of her early training, gave its own dark hue to her religious experience. She looked upon herself as *justly* condemned by God's holy law, but for a long time no rays of sunshine from the Redeemer's cross beamed upon her soul.

Slowly did she open her mind to the conviction, that "the blood of Jesus Christ, cleanseth from all sin,—that it could avail to cleanse even her polluted heart. Fearing and trembling, she did at length trust in the merits of her Saviour. Eventually she united with the church of Christ, and is now a refined, cultivated, affectionate girl, fitted for almost any situation and desirous of living only for the glory of God.

During this revival all our teachers were indefatigable in the performance of their duties, and many souls I doubt not, were given them, who will be crowns of rejoicing to them in the great day of the Lord.

CHAPTER XXXIX.

> " Home, kindred, friends, and country—these
>   Are things with which we never part;
>   From clime to clime, o'er land and seas
>   We bear them with us, on our heart,
>   And yet 'tis hard to feel resigned
>   When they must all be left behind;
>   But when the pilgrim's staff we take,
>   And follow Christ from shore to shore,
>   Gladly for Him we all forsake.
>   *Press on,* and only look before;
>   Though humble nature mourns her loss,
>   The spirit glories in the cross."

THE summer of 1847 passed away rapidly. Preparations were in progress for the departure of one of the members of the Seminary to make her home in the heart of China. Our new pastor, the Rev. Mr. D., was invited to address our missionary society at its anniversary, and it was arranged that our missionary friends should be married at the close of these exercises. It was a deeply impressive scene. Several clergymen were present, among whom were Mr. Richards and Mr. Rankin, both of whom expected to spend their lives in the same far-off land.

The report of the secretary of the Society, which closed with a farewell address to Miss F., awakened mingled emotions of joy and sorrow. For seven years had she been connected with the Seminary, during three years of which she had been a teacher, and a portion of the time a member of the family. She had peculiarly endeared herself to us all by her amiable disposition, her quiet, dignified deportment, and her cheerful sacrifice of self to the welfare and comfort of others. Truly, she was unto me as a daughter. Many were the gifts of affection that assured the missionary couple of the sympathy and friendship of those from whom they were soon to separate.

Educated in the same community, members of the same church, the newly-married pair were doubly one. The farewell meeting—the last parting scene—are registered in the deep recesses of the heart. They went forth amid the tears and prayers of many, who rejoiced to yield them to the work of the Lord, while their hearts were sinking at the sad farewell.

Many friends accompanied them to the ship. Ere they cast loose from their native land—after prayer had been offered and the benediction pronounced—several friends commenced singing "Shall we whose souls are lighted." Scarcely had the assembled throng joined in the hymn, ere a beautiful bird alighted upon the rigging of the ship, over the heads of the missionaries, and clear and shrill his notes were distinctly heard, above the song of praise, on the deck; and thus he chanted his lay until they had finished, when he also ceased his notes and winged his way to some other resting-place. To the superstitious mariner, accustomed to bode good or evil much from auguries and signs, this was a cheering presage of a fortunate voyage, and one of the owners was so much interested in the incident that he declared his perfect confidence that success would attend them.

God did bless them, on the sea and on the land, and though domestic bereavements, failure of health, and prostration of strength, have often threatened to lay them aside from their work, they labor on, and are happy "to do and to suffer" for Jesus' sake. Of the other two missionary friends who witnessed the nuptial ceremony, one was early called home to God. His work was cut short by infinite wisdom, and he rests from his labors. The other, with the companion who accompanied him to that benighted land, has returned to his native country with the hope of regaining the health and vigor which had become impaired by unwearied efforts in the cause to which they have consecrated their lives.

God bless them in their restoration to health, and speed them back to their foreign home, and to their labor of love.

CHAPTER XL.

REVIVAL OF 1847–48.—CASE OF H. M.—CONVERSION AND DEATH OF H. C.

THE scenes of the winter of 1847–48 will live in the memories of those who were engaged in them, through the countless ages of eternity. Well might we exclaim, " Praise to our God for the unspeakable gift of a Saviour, and praise to our blessed Redeemer for the manifestation of His mercy to me and mine. My own mind had previously been much disturbed with " fightings without and fears within ;" yet again He had planted my feet upon the Rock of Ages, and poured in upon my soul the light of life, the peace that passeth all understanding. Yea, more, His Spirit had subdued the proud heart—had given penitence and faith to those who had long trifled with their soul's salvation—had gathered many precious lambs into the fold of the good Shepherd.

It is impossible to recount all the cases that occurred

that were well worthy of record. The conversion of one of our teachers, a gay, trifling young lady, many of whose family friends and associates were of the same character, and around whose heart, binding her to earth, were stronger ties even than those which existed beneath the parental roof, was an event, I have no doubt, to cause joy in heaven, as it did among the people of God on earth.

Her caviling spirit exhibited itself on all occasions. The doctrine of election was peculiarly obnoxious. "If I am *elected* to salvation, my soul is safe: if not, no effort of mine can avail to effect it." Wearied with her pertinacity and her refusal to yield her assent to any argument employed, I finally proposed to her to *adopt* that opinion, and to *act* upon it, only changing the premises, "I will believe that I am elected to salvation, and therefore I will *comply with the conditions.*" This presented the subject in a new aspect; she caviled no longer.

Her convictions were deep and pungent, and the struggle in her soul was agonizing; but breaking away from the enchantments of the world, she fled to Jesus and he received and sustained her sinking spirit. She freely yielded all to Him, and He strengthened her, giving her a good hope through grace, as an anchor to her soul, sure and steadfast. From this time her efforts were untiring to induce her companions to listen to the invitations of the Gospel, and a word in season, with a prayer offered in her behalf, often led the inquiring sinner to the cross of Christ.

Two prayer-meetings were commenced in the family, which were held every morning, at each season of private devotion, and the same course was pursued in the evening. The calls on me were incessant, and urgent were the requests that I would converse with awakened sinners, to teach them what they must do to be saved; and with those who were indulging a trembling hope of an interest in the Saviour, to guide them aright, and tell them more of Jesus and His salvation. Often did I return to my room after such interviews, the poor, wearied body almost ready to yield and pass away, while my soul has been filled with the peace which only Christ can impart.

It was delightful to see the union of feeling—the affection subsisting between the pupils, and between the teachers and pupils.

One, who in early life had been consecrated by her parents to the service of the Redeemer, but who had caused them much anxiety by her self-will and deception, was placed in the Seminary by her father, with the hope that the religious influence which was now excited, might affect her heart and character, and in this hope he was not disappointed. She was one of the first to come with the earnest inquiry, What must I do to be saved? I shall not soon forget the intense anxiety with which she hung upon the words of instruction, or the desire that she evinced to be led in

the way of salvation; and when she received the Saviour into her heart, it was with such entire consecration of soul and body to His service, as led her at
once to do everything in her power to recommend religion to all around her.

She entreated forgiveness of her parents for past
disobedience, and by every means in her power she
sought to atone for injury done to others. She spent
the summer session with us, and her labors in pro-
moting the welfare and improvement of her fellow
pupils, in the cultivation of her own mind, and in the
cause of missions, were incessant. On her return to
the family circle, so great was the comfort that her
parents derived from her society, and so salutary her
influence upon her young brothers and sisters, that it
was decided she should spend the winter at home.

Scarcely had she begun to realize the blessedness
of the home gatherings, under these new circumstances, ere disease commenced its blighting influence.
A cold, increased by exposure, settled on her lungs,
and bore her rapidly to her grave. From the commencement of her illness she evinced entire submission to the will of God, rejoicing that she was in
His hands; and when in the midst of great bodily
sufferings, her friends could not suppress their tears,
her only reply to their expressions of sympathy was,
" I suffer no more than I deserve."

None could witness the peaceful serenity of her
countenance and feel sad. Every word, every look,

convinced her friends that the grave, with its appalling accompaniments had no terrors for her. She talked of dying with as much composure as she would have spoken of a journey, and none hesitated to speak freely, in her presence, of her expected departure.

Never for a moment did a cloud darken her mind, nor a doubt distress her respecting her salvation. "I *know* in whom I have believed," was the feeling of her heart; "I have perfect confidence in my Saviour," was the language of her lips.

My duties at home prevented my seeing her more than once during her sickness, and that was only a few days before her death.

"You have come," she said, "in answer to prayer."

She expressed great delight at seeing me, and I spent several hours with her,—hours that will not soon be forgotten;—hours of painful yet delightful interest. When I asked her, if she could *fully* trust in Jesus,—if he was a *present* Saviour to her,—if she could cast all her burdens on Him?

"Oh yes," she replied, "He is *my* Redeemer,— He is a precious Saviour, and I am willing to live, to suffer, or to die, as my heavenly Father sees best."

To her mother, she expressed unbounded gratitude and affection, for her unwearied attentions and watchful care. Once while I sat by her bedside, she was speaking to me of her heavenward journey, when a little prattler who stood near the bed, cried out, "I

want to go with sister ? May I not go with sister ?"
Raising her head to look at the little pleader, with a
sweet smile, she said, " No, my dear, you must stay
and be a comfort to mamma, and by and by you shall
come to sister."

When expressing the wish that her mother would
not leave her, clasping her arms around her neck, she
said, " I love you, mother, I love you. Little did I
think that I should be the first called home, but it
will not be long before you will come, and I'll be there
to welcome you. Who can tell but my spirit will
often hover around you here, to comfort you in sorrow
and in trouble ?"

Her father inquired whether she wished " to be
gone, to be freed from suffering, or to be with Christ ?"

" To be with Christ—to be with Christ."

" Are you willing to leave father and mother, and
the rest of the family ?"

" Oh yes, yes,—if God sees best; and how glad
I'll be to welcome you and ma in heaven, and the
children—will they come too ?"

She often spoke of the comfort and instruction she
derived from the visits of her pastor, and expressed
much affection and gratitude towards him. She was
conscious till the last moment, took an affectionate
farewell of her beloved parents, her brothers and
sisters ; and her last words were, "happy—happy."

Thus died one, who a few months previous was living without hope and without God ;—now justified by

His grace, and clothed with the robe of Christ's righteousness, made meet to be a partaker of the blessedness of the Redeemer in glory. For any instrumentality which I was permitted to exercise in this work of preparation, I do bless my heavenly Father, and give Him all the glory.

> "O weep not for the dead,
> No more for them the blighting chill,
> The thousand shades of earthly ill,
> The thousand thorns we tread;
> Weep for the life-charm, early flown
> The spirit broken, bleeding, lone,
> Weep for the death pangs of the heart,
> Ere being from the bosom part,
> But never be a tear-drop given
> To those who rest in yon blue heaven."

CHAPTER XLI.

M. M.—MISSIONARY BOX.

"Thine, Lord, is the whole,
The body, the soul,
All, all, that we have or desire,
Our time, and our health,
Our influence, our wealth,
Our affections, that upward aspire."

M. M., entered the Seminary at the commencement of the summer session of 1847. She had been for three or four years a professor of religion, but as I conversed with her from time to time, and watched her entire indifference to spiritual instruction and religious duties, I was satisfied that the life-giving principle had not been imparted to her soul. During the following winter, she was prevented for some days by indisposition from pursuing her studies, and much of the time she spent in my room. This gave me frequent opportunities to become acquainted with the true state of her feelings, and to get an insight into a heart that had hitherto deceived her. She was solemn and attentive to instruction, and seemed perfectly aware that her hope was "like the spider's web," which a breath might destroy. Soon she gave me pleasing evidence, that she had at length put her trust wholly in the Saviour. From that time she evinced deep interest in religious exercises and duties.   It was a merciful providence that gave me the opportunity to learn her true condition, and to lead her to apply the only remedy—to fly to the only refuge.

Early in the summer, after her return to her home, she was seized with inflammation of the brain,—attended by deliriums that precluded all conversation— which in the course of a few days terminated her earthly existence.

Weeks after she had laid her loved one in the grave, I found the bereaved mother, still mourning over this child of her hopes, and " refusing to be comforted," not only " because she was not," but because no ray of spiritual light had illumined the dying bed of the departed.   She knew nothing of M.'s experience during the preceding winter, and very thankful was I to be permitted to pour the oil of comfort upon that wounded heart, and to be able to say to her,

> " Weep not for her ! there is no cause for woe ;
> But, rather, nerve thy spirit, that it walk
> Unshrinking o'er the thorny paths below,
> And from earth's low defilements keep thee back ;
> So when a few fleet severing years have flown,
> She'll meet thee at heaven's gate, and lead thee on—
> Weep not for her."

The last Saturday of the term, so marked by the manifestation of God's mercy, at the request of the pupils, was observed as a day of fasting and prayer for those who continued impenitent, and to entreat that those who had given themselves to the service of

God, might have grace to resist the temptations by which they would soon be assailed.

It was a deeply interesting day. In the evening, Mr. C., one of the secretaries of the Tract Society, with our pastor, attended a meeting which had been previously appointed, in the schoolroom ; it was truly an affecting scene. Mr. D., particularly addressed those who were so soon to pass away from these soul-stirring scenes, and several prayers were offered in their behalf. Many wept aloud, and our pastor, who had entered with his whole soul into this work of grace in the Seminary, was so unnerved that its influence was felt for several days.

The exercises were closed with the hymn, "Blest be the tie that binds," &c. Many tears were shed as we pronounced the sad farewells and separated, some hoping to return,—others to meet no more, perhaps, till the great resurrection morn shall assemble us before the judgment-seat of Christ.

A circumstance occurred at the close of the session, which exceedingly gratified my feelings. About a month previous to the expiration of the term, I had read to the young ladies a letter from the Rev. Mr. W., asking aid in commencing a library for a Theological Institution at Beybec, and also speaking of the ill health of his wife. I said to the school, that if the session had not been so near its close I would propose to make up a box for Mrs. W., but that I had no time—and I was sure they had not—to make garments, I would therefore let the matter rest until the next summer.

As Hohannes was about to return to his native country, I commenced writing to several missionary friends, and had nearly completed a letter to Mr. W., when the young ladies fearing that the package would be sent away, appointed a delegation to inform me that they had an offering which they wished should accompany the letter. It seems that after my remarks in school, several of the pupils collected at recess and consulted together on the practicability of preparing a small present to Mrs. W. Zeal and energy supplied means, and when they reported their success to me, they had purchased and made about twenty garments of different sizes and kinds. I was delighted with this independent effort. I felt that the benefit to themselves would be of greater value even than to the missionaries, though to them it would prove no mean assistance. By the time that we were ready to close the box, the articles contributed were valued at forty dollars. It was truly a thank-offering to our heavenly Father,—an appropriate expression of love to Him, who had visited us with the refreshing influences of His Holy Spirit.

CHAPTER XLII.

> "There is in *souls* a sympathy with *sound.*"
>
> "It may be glorious to write
>   Thoughts that shall glad the two or three
> High souls, like those far stars that come in sight
>   Once in a century;
> But better far it is to *speak*
>   One simple word which now and then
> Shall waken their free nature in the weak
>   And friendless sons of men."

IN the spring of 1848, for the first time, I visited the home of my youngest son, in the sunny south, and there witnessed the ceremony of laying the corner-stone of the Institution of the Deaf and Dumb, in the city of Raleigh, North Carolina. This city is pleasantly situated, and the many groves scattered over its whole surface, and the long lines of trees that shade the sidewalks, give to it a beautiful and romantic appearance, fully entitling it to be called the "City of Oaks."

Two prominent streets cross each other at right angles, thus forming, at their junction, a conspicuous location for the capitol of the state, an imposing building embowered in trees.

The 14th of April was the great day for the ceremony, to which many had looked forward with eager anticipation. The Board of Trustees, the orator of the day, and the pupils, escorted by a long procession of Free Masons, in full dress, and a band of music, marched from the Institution to the building, passing under an arch adorned with flowers and evergreens. Masonic mummeries were employed; the corner-stone was placed in its proper position—a box, containing appropriate mementoes of the day, and of the occasion, was deposited in the centre of the stone, and corn, wine, and oil were poured upon it, to denote, as the Grand Master told us, the prosperity that they trusted would attend the infant Institution. Pity that one of the fraternity should have diminished the quantity of wine by putting it to his unhallowed lips, as he bore it to his august Master.

Rev. Mr. B., of the Methodist church, gave an interesting address, very handsomely defending the cause of Masonry. He gave us its origin and history, and the *reason* why females are excluded from its lodges. They perform the works of benevolence *in their own sphere*, and in a more feminine way, while the stronger sex engage in theirs in a way more fitted for those who can *go forth* to labor.

In the evening the various companies of Odd Fellows, collected from different parts of the state, with a fine band of music, formed a procession from their lodge room, and halting in front of the Institution, received the governor of the state, the board of trustees, the orator and clergy who were assembled there. Then followed the family and pupils, and very comical were my feelings as I paraded, by courtesy, by the side of the lady of the mansion, through the long avenue of blazing stars and gorgeous regalia which adorned the Odd Fellows, who were arranged on each side as we passed up the broad stairway to the Assembly chamber of the capitol, already nearly filled with fair spectators.

Never before had I witnessed, in the attire of any body of men, such a display of splendid ornaments; and as this was their first appearance in public in full dress, the applause that greeted them on their appearance was deafening. The address of Dr. Peet, the Principal of the New York Institution for the Deaf and Dumb—marked by extensive knowledge and sound sense—was exceedingly interesting. He gave in detail the history of the commencement, the progress and the success that had attended the efforts in behalf of this long-neglected portion of the community. An examination of the pupils in Scripture, history, and an illustration in signs, of various mechanical employments, the passions, etc. etc., followed the address, the whole closing with the humorous exhibition, in the language of signs, of the drunken husband sewed in a sheet and whipped into repentance by his wife. The exercises were exceedingly entertaining, and gave general satisfaction.

It was particularly gratifying to me to witness the
12*

exercises of a Sabbath day among the deaf-mutes. Morning worship on that day is made a season of more elaborate instruction than on other days. They attend church in the morning, and the sermon is repeated to them by their teacher, who, screened from observation by a curtain, translates the words of the preacher into the language of signs. In the afternoon they are taught at home.

On the evening of the second Sabbath that I spent with them, I was invited by my son to give to the pupils some account of the religious feeling that had been manifested in the Seminary during the previous winter. "Be simple and concise," was the direction given to me. As I entered the room, filled by teachers and pupils, sitting in breathless expectation and silence, awaiting the novel communication which I had promised them, it was affecting to see how their countenances brightened, as their teacher informed them of the purpose of my visit. I told them of the revival—described some of the scenes through which we had passed—spoke of the prayer-meetings, of the Bible-classes, of the last fast-day, and of the closing of the school. Warmed with my subject, and somewhat excited by the novelty of the scene before me, I urged upon the mutes the importance of securing an interest in the Saviour. I spoke of their privileges, so superior to those of many of their unfortunate class—these privileges increased their obligations to God, and that therefore greater would be their guilt and danger, if they rejected the Saviour He had provided.

Many wept much. I said that I should soon leave them to return to my home, and that we should never all meet again on earth; but there would be one more time of meeting, before the bar of God, and I wished that they all might be prepared to rejoice with me in heaven.

Their teacher followed with a few remarks and prayer. All seemed very solemn, and some wept *aloud*. After we returned to the house, one of the female pupils sent to request that her teacher would come to her in the study room. She seemed to be in great distress. "O, why, Mr. C.," she said, "have I not known these things before? Suppose I had died while ignorant of these truths, what would have become of me?" He told her that she had often heard them, but had not attended to them, or had not been able to comprehend them—that he had given her similar religious instruction, but she had not felt it. She wept aloud.

"I am going home," she said, "and who will teach me there?"

"Jesus will be there," he replied; "he will be your teacher, and you must pray to Him."

She continued very serious until she left the Institution, which was in a few weeks. How I longed to gain access to the heart, and to unfold the truths of God's word to this dark-minded mute, but her inability sufficiently to comprehend language, to write correctly, or to understand many of the words that I might use in attempting to communicate with her, deterred me.

Never before had my feelings been so deeply interested in these unfortunate beings. Never had I, previous to this daily intercourse with them, any correct ideas of the difficulty attending the attempt to impart knowledge to these vacant minds, and yet their teachers are delighted with their work. " O," said one, " the instruction of the deaf-mutes, with their speaking eyes and bright intelligent faces turned toward you with so much attention and expectation, is a thousand times more delightful than imparting information to those ' who have ears and hear not,'—who have mastered everything but their own brainless skulls."

In the company of my children and their family, I returned to my Jersey home, and to the responsibilities of a new term. Scarcely had I commenced my duties ere I was summoned to follow to the grave my youngest sister, whose physical sufferings for many years had made her life a tried and painful pilgrimage. Her departure could not call forth a tear for her, for we trust that she passed away to a heavenly home, where the inhabitants shall no more say, " I am sick,"—" where there shall be no more sorrow, neither shall there be any more pain."

" There is a blessedness that changeth not,
    A rest with God, a life that cannot die;
A better portion and a brighter lot,
    A home with Christ, a heritage on high.
Hope for the hopeless, for the weary, rest,
    More gentle than the still repose of even!
Joy for the joyless, bliss for the unblest;
    Homes for the desolate in yonder heaven!"

CHAPTER XLIII.

SUNSHINE AND SHADOWS.

THE winter session of 1848-49, opened with strong indications that the Spirit of God was moving with increasing power, upon the minds of some of our pupils. During the preceding year more than thirty, as we hoped, had consecrated the dew of their youth to God, and much of the influence of that precious work, continued to affect the school. Some seed, we trust, was sown, that was not wholly destroyed by the adversary or choked by the pleasures of this life, but was implanted in hearts, open to receive the word, and brought forth fruit in its season.

Often has my heart been cheered by intelligence from those who had departed from school influences without giving the evidence that I desired of their conversion to God, that the impressions here made upon their minds were never obliterated, but continued to disturb and trouble them, till they found peace at the Saviour's cross.

Here, then, may desponding teachers place their

confidence, and in His word may they trust. Blessed be God that He does not require of us *success* in our work. Duty is ours—*results* belong to Him.

The summer brought its trials of fears, sickness, and increasing cares. Several members of the family, whose aid was greatly needed, were laid on beds of sickness, and the cholera, which was spreading death and desolation over many portions of our land, filled our hearts with fearful apprehensions though it came not into our immediate vicinity. Sometimes, my physical strength was taxed to such a degree, that it seemed as though the brittle thread of life would snap asunder. Sad and solitary I would shut myself in my room, and weep bitter tears at memory's shrine.

But they were precious tears, they reminded me of days gone by; days of trial and suffering, when my blessed Master gave me the assurance of his sympathy and of His power to support and strengthen the tried and tempted spirit. To this refuge of the weary I turned for help; I cast myself anew upon his mercy, resolving, henceforth, to *do* or to *suffer* to the extent of my power, all that should be laid upon me, cheerfully and faithfully, if God would give me grace.

Death, also, was busy at his work among friends, and many whom I loved were snatched away from bereaved parents and the dear delights of home affections. One, a dear friend of my departed Eliza, while on a visit to her friends in Vermont, was numbered with the dead, and rests beside the beloved mother whose loss she early deplored. Very similar were these sister-friends in temperament and feelings; and I trust they now rejoice together in their heavenly home. " My rest is in heaven, my home is not here," was the appropriate song of the family circle at our evening worship, after the news reached me of the removal of our friend A. B., to a better world. O the fulness of that love which opens such a prospect to the world-wearied spirit, through the blood of Jesus—which assures the lonely heart of a reunion with the loved ones, who once cheered by their affection the sad spirit of a widowed mother,—whose tender watchful ministries anticipated her wishes and filled her heart with gratitude for such rich blessings. I thank thee, Father, that such treasures have been mine, and that they were not called to weep at the couch of a dying mother. Thou didst in mercy take them home to Thyself, and I rejoice, severe as was the trial, that they were so early removed from the sins and sorrows of earth. Then,

> "Be hushed, my sad spirit, the worst that can come,
> But shortens my journey, and hastens me home."

Another passed away who, a few months previous had been a member of our Seminary, suddenly summoned from earth, and so far as we know, with no preparation for another state of existence. She came among us like a fair flower, which even in the morning was cut down and withered. But where is the soul that never dies?   No bright ray beaming from the Sun of Rightcousness shines upon the darkness of *her* grave, for she loved not the ways of holiness.

While visiting friends in N., in the autumn vacation, I enjoyed the privilege of listening to an address to the Sabbath school of one of the churches of that city, from the Rev. Mr. Van Lennep, a missionary who was visiting this country for a few months.   He spoke of the importance of a division of labor in all departments of human life, and the facilities it gives for the accomplishment of a desired end.   He described the practice of olden times, when frequently the processes of shearing the sheep, of carding, spinning, weaving and dyeing the wool, and of making the garments for the family, were performed by the same individual.   He referred to the tedious process of manufacturing a single pin when one person was obliged to go through with the various operations requisite to bring it to perfection and how few could be completed in a day.   Now it requires eight persons to attend to the machinery necessary for the formation of this insignificant though indispensable article, but thousands can be made by this means in the time formerly employed in the creation of a dozen, because each one has his specific work to do and confines himself exclusively to its accomplishment.   Just so in the moral world ; God does not design that one individual shall accomplish the conversion of the world, but each one has an appropriate sphere in which he is expected to labor, and he is answerable for the success of his *machinery*.

Children, too, have their *machine* which they must watch ; and it is the children of the heathen world. "Let the parents care for the men and women that are going down to perdition ; but your duty, children, is to see that the poor heathen children are furnished with the word of God ; that teachers are sent to them, that they too may be instructed in the way of salvation." For the encouragement of the children that he was then addressing, Mr. Van Lennep said he would tell them what kind of youth the missionaries of the East were often called to teach. Far up the Bosphorus lies the city of Constantinople—a magnificent city, the diameter of which is fifteen miles—three times the size of the city of New York. A boy of thirteen years of age was placed in the school of which Mr. Van Lennep was the teacher. He became much interested in his studies, and the fears of the priests were consequently awakened lest the missionary should induce him to become a Christian. They therefore required the parents of the boy to remove him from missionary influence and place him in a native school, seven miles distant on the other side of the city. The boy was unhappy,—he was cruelly treated—he felt the difference in the schools—he could not study, and he determined to return to his former instructors. On the following morning instead of entering the school with his companions, he secretly and swiftly passed into a lane, and afraid to appear in the streets, or to go in one of the boats, he passed over a bridge that led him a considerable distance off from the direct route, thus lengthening his walk to twelve miles.   He accomplished his fatiguing journey in four hours, and presented himself at the missionary's door, pale, trembling and exhausted.   They received him joyfully, and through the great mercy of God the priests were prevented from withdrawing him a second time from the school.

In this mission school he learned to pray and to love his Saviour, and very recently, Mr. Van Lennep said, he had received a letter informing him that this interesting child had been called home to dwell with the Saviour that he loved.   The missionary then requested the children who heard him, to ask themselves every Saturday night, " What have I done during the past week for the salvation of heathen children?" and he proposed that each one should write down a resolution to this effect, that whenever the time should come when he should begin to think of the future, and determine what should be his employment or profession for life,—he would first ask himself, why ought I not to become a missionary.

CHAPTER XLIV.

> "Spirit of everlasting grace
>   Breathe on this valley of the dead,
> Send forth thy quickening might abroad,
>   Till, rising from their tombs, they spread
> In full array—the host of God."

THE winter session of 1849–50 commenced with goodly prospects. From the first opening of school, I noticed unusual attention to morning instruction, but daily, as the pupils turned to their studies, or to social intercourse, these encouraging appearances were dispelled. The Holy Spirit was evidently impressing truth on heart and conscience, and sinners were as evidently resisting convictions of sin and duty. Thus week after week passed by, until a circumstance occurred that called for censure and discipline. The discipline consisted in prohibiting the offending party from enjoying her usual *social* intercourse with her companions, moving among them as one who had no common interests with them, further than related to her studies. This often proved a severe and salutary punishment, and in this case was followed by happy results.

I conversed with D. C. She felt and acknowledged that she had done wrong, and the conviction, now fo the first time, seemed to enter her mind, that she was a sinner against God.   The conflict within was great; for days no smile enlivened her usually pleasant countenance.   In the midst of these encouraging prospects, the holidays came, with their distracting influences, and our pupils went forth to plunge into their gaieties and festivities, and to return, as we feared, more thoughtless than ever.

Pleasant as these seasons of recreation may be to teachers and pupils, I regard them as a grand device of Satan to turn the thoughts from God, at a period when the closing of one year and the introduction of another, are so well calculated to lead the mind to look, with earnest scrutiny, upon the past, and with deep anxiety into the future.   With feelings of deep solemnity did I commend them all to God as they parted from us, for this transient visit to their homes and friends.   They did return—not merely thoughtless, but seemingly with " hearts fully set in them to do evil "   Many of them appeared to be alarmed lest instruction and the influences of the Holy Spirit should *compel* them to give attention to their soul's salvation.   They were not only trifling in their conduct, but evinced a fixed determination to resist every attempt to lead them to " consider their ways and be wise."

Sick at heart, and almost sinking beneath the dark waters, the cry of " Lord, save, or we perish," went up from a bursting heart.

From my pastor I received much sympathy and assistance. The peculiar state of the school was a marvel to him. Those who had been educated by pious parents seemed to have lost all that tenderness of conscience which is so often met with in those of their sex and age; while others, who had not been thus instructed, knew nothing and cared nothing about religion. The foundation work, therefore, to be done, was immense, and such as to try the faith and tax the energies of the teacher as she had never been tried in all her previous experience.

It was a long and weary time before the first stone above the water showed that the foundation had been successfully laid. But how different were the indicacations of the coming of God's Spirit, from what might naturally have been expected in such circumstances. The "eye" of "the tender and delicate woman who would not adventure to set the sole of her foot to the ground for delicateness," was just as evil towards God and His law and His holiness, and her heart was as unwilling to yield to the Divine claims as that of any other sinner.

If we had ever supposed that any heart in which supreme love to God was wanting was less than totally depraved, or that there was any thing morally good in amiable instincts, we were soon taught differently. Like the flush that sometimes lingers on the cheek of the corpse after death, there is nothing beneath such goodness but corruption. As soon as the power of

the world to come began to take hold of their consciences, it became too apparent that these fair seeming qualities were nothing but frostwork, and the old
truth came up as unmistakeably, that "the carnal
mind is enmity against God, and is not subject to the
law of God, neither indeed can be." The cheerful
and good-natured indifference and thoughtlessness by
which our young friends had hitherto been characterized, speedily assumed the form of fierce and down-
right opposition.

Some, as it afterwards appeared from their own
confessions, opposed through ignorance; some through
pride and vanity; some through fear of ridicule;
some because they were unwilling to have their companions converted; some because they were not willing *now* to be converted themselves: and some—and
these were most bitter of all—because they had stifled
convictions before. Of course such a state of things
was the occasion of most intense anxiety and distress
to all who were either directly or indirectly concerned
in the spiritual welfare of the Seminary.

Believing that not a few must be guilty of such
conduct "ignorantly through unbelief," the pastor at
length preached on Acts ix. 4, 5, "Saul, Saul, why
persecutest thou me, etc.," with an application that
could not well be misunderstood by those for whom it
was principally intended: To some of the leading
minds of the school this truth was brought home by
the Holy Spirit, and during the following week nearly

a dozen were made willing to yield to the heavenly influence.

"For a momen. the shock upon the rest at being thus separated from their companions, was almost overwhelming, and, we began to fear, the effect of sympathy; but for once we were mistaken in anticipating much danger from that source. No sooner was the number of converts *all told*, and it was found that the *majority* were still on the side of the world, than the remaining opposers rallied, and endeavored to build up the walls higher and thicker than ever. So far as it was in their power to effect it, they were fully determined that the work should cease, and had not the Lord again been on our side their triumph would have been complete. We were made to feel, oh how deeply and sincerely, that the work of conversion was not of man but of God; and while we were thus prostrate before Him, He again appeared for our deliverance, and saved us for His mercy's sake." Thus wrote our excellent pastor, in his review of this spirit-stirring work.

The sermon to which reference is made above, so exactly exhibited to the hearts of many their own bitter opposition, that they became alarmed. The suppressed feelings now burst forth. D. C. sought me in great distress. I could only, as I had done before, urge upon her the Saviour's claims, and beseech her to trust in his righteousness alone. After commending her to God in prayer, I sent her, with her Bible and Doddridge's consecration of the sinner to Jesus, to seek, in retirement, reconciliation to Him who only readeth the heart of man.

She came not to tea; the evening passed, and still she was alone with God. At eight o'clock I entered her room, and there she sat, leaning on her hand, her countenance beaming with light from within. I asked her if her peace was made with God.

"I trust," she replied, "that I have cast myself on His mercy—that He has pardoned my sins for Jesus' sake."

I was much gratified with the conversation that I had with her—at the distinctness of her views, and the simplicity with which she embraced the gospel of salvation. I prayed with her, she followed me, and seldom have I listened to such a pouring out of the soul to God. When she had finished, I arose, but she still knelt.

"D., do you still wish to pray?" I said.

"O, Mrs. C., I feel as if I could pray for ever."

"Then let us again go to the mercy-seat."

A second time I commended her to God's mercy and protection, and again went up the earnest petition from this dear child for grace to serve the Lord, in newness of life. This prayer seemed to take hold of the blood of Christ, as cleansing her from all sin. Sweet to my spirit was this season of communion with a new-born soul, just emancipated from the thraldom of sin. How earnestly did she plead for her impenitent father and brothers; how strong and urgent her appeals to the throne of grace; so full of humility, so subdued, so entirely divested of self, and so full of reliance upon the merits of the Saviour. It was good to listen to such a prayer. She requested permission to remain in her room, and I left her, to seek another and a different scene. D. took her stand in the family decidedly for Christ. All felt that she was in earnest, and that this was no *childish* consecration.

D.'s conversion produced a great sensation through the school. Many came seeking counsel; some, with full hearts, to tell me that they had found the Saviour. One of these acknowledged, that before this session she had never had one deeply serious thought. She hoped that *now* she felt her vileness, and her lost condition as a sinner, and was willing to yield herself to the Saviour. I trust that then, prostrate before God, she made a full surrender of herself to Him and His service. Thus taught and influenced by the Spirit of God, they came, day after day, with the great question, "What must I do to be saved?"

CHAPTER XLV.

FARTHER DEVELOPMENTS OF CHARACTER.

On the third day after the Sabbath, deeply were all impressed with the conviction, "surely God is in this place." I read at the opening of school, from Luke, xv. 1–11. I spoke of the joy of heavenly beings over penitent souls.

Why should *Angels rejoice?*

Because they know how to estimate the blessedness of heaven—the terrors of hell and the vanity of earthly pursuits. They know too the value of the immortal soul; they know something of the depth and evil of man's sin—not from having been partakers of it, but from the abundant manifestations of it in man's history;—and they know what a terrible punishment is implied in being forever banished from the presence of God. And as God is glorified in the salvation of every sinner, they rejoice at every new star that glitters in the Redeemer's crown.

The distress of mind evidently increased. Some begged permission to retire to their rooms, some requested to see me alone, and through that and several successive days, we all felt that the Spirit of God was in our midst, with convincing and converting power.

After family worship that evening, I invited those that felt anxiety respecting their soul's salvation, to assemble in my room. I read to them the tract entitled "The Act of Faith," and tried still further to illustrate the *simplicity* of faith by presenting the case of a miserable, destitute outcast, to whom a home with all its privileges should be offered, on the simple condition of yielding obedience and affection to the kind benefactor who makes the generous offer. She trusts in the *promise* of her disinterested friend, and is received and adopted as a child of the family.

As this interesting group separated with varied and conflicting emotions, C. L., begged to see me alone. The hitherto pent up emotions of her soul could no longer be suppressed. Bursting into an agony of grief she exclaimed,

"O, Mrs. C., I have been so miserable all day, that it has seemed as though I could not live."

She then at my request, gave me an affecting account of her feelings during the last few months.

" At the commencement of the session you gave me Abbott's school-girl. I read a few pages until I came to one where the author calls upon the reader to make her choice for or against Christ, at once—saying, that perhaps before that page was read the final, irrevocable decision would be made. I closed the book,—I was

not ready to decide yet,—I loved the world too well
to be willing at present to give it up; I was so young
that it would do to wait until I became a little older.
Yet I feared to finish the book, thinking, foolish child
that I was that *there* the matter would rest for the
present, and that if I did not pass over that particular
page it would make no difference.

": I went through the usual routine of school duties,
still wherever I turned those words followed me. Two
months passed on in this way. The spirit of evil was
warring mightily with the Spirit of God in our hearts
and the appearance of the school after the holidays,
was such that our teachers seemed almost in despair.
A violent altercation that arose between several of the
young ladies, which was referred to you for settlement, gave you the opportunity to press home upon
each and all the necessity of settling a more important
question.

" On the Sabbath when our pastor preached that
searching sermon from the text, ' Saul, Saul, why persecutest thou me,' &c., D. and I sat side by side. It
seemed to each of us, ' these words are spoken to me,'
and throughout the sermon each felt, that the whole
congregation must know it too. That evening D.
made the great decision for eternity, while I passed a
sleepless night still undetermined. The morning
brought no light to me—all within was darkness.

"Having been early instructed in the truth, I had
no doctrinal difficulties: I wished there were some

such difficulties—something new to learn, something for me *to do* to ensure salvation,—then there might be more hope in my case. Thus the few last days have passed in hopeless gloom."

To no one had she applied for sympathy or counsel, and only when overwhelmed by her feelings did she apply to me for the instruction and assistance that she felt she needed. I placed her duty before her; urged her immediate acceptance of Jesus as her Saviour; gave her Doddridge's dedication to study and to use, as her own consecration to God, and left her with her Bible and her God, after commending her to His mercy.

There in the solitude of her own room, she trusted that she yielded her heart to the claims of the Gospel and laid the weapons of rebellion forever in the dust.

The visits of our pastor and Mr. C., who at that time was assisting him in his pastoral labors, greatly aided and strengthened us, and we have reason to believe that many souls,—of those connected with the Institution—rescued from the destroyer through their instrumentality, will appear in the great day as seals of their ministry and crowns of rejoicing.

On one occasion after a very solemn address from Mr. D., a pupil who, on account of her waywardness and folly, had been to me an object of great solicitude, came to seek an interview. She said to me that she felt as if this was her last call—that she had been distressed for some time, but could not yield her heart to Jesus. She complained of the temptation of Satan to defer repentance to a more convenient season, and yet she was sure if she did wait till to-morrow, she would *never* do it.

I repeated, as I had done many times before, the gracious assurance of our Redeemer,

"Him that cometh to me I will in no wise cast out." After a long conversation, I asked,

"Are you *ready now*, to submit to Jesus, and will you do it now?"

With much apparent sincerity and decision, she replied, "I will."

"Come then, let us kneel down and make the surrender?"

I prayed, and spread out the dark picture of her life and heart as they had been revealed to me by her own confessions, as well as by her conduct, hoping *thus* to impress more deeply upon her own soul, its fearful turpitude and its rebellion.

"Now," said I, when I had concluded, "make the consecration of yourself to God just as you are, lay hold of the blessed promise, 'the blood of Jesus Christ cleanseth from all sin,' and resolve if you perish it shall be at the foot of the cross."

She started back, exclaiming, "Oh, I can't, I can't."

Then commenced a hysterical scene, which greatly tried my patience. I bade her with decision to be calm, and by my firmness and composure interrupted and prevented the dramatical effect she evidently intended to produce. I again repeated some solemn truths to her, placed in her hands, Doddridge's Rise and Progress, to read and sent her to her room. There she remained alone through the night, but the morning found her still impenitent.

At the opening of school next day, I read to the pupils, the parable of Dives and Lazarus. I spoke of the fondness of the human mind for supernatural sights and scenes; the origin of superstition; our desire to penetrate mysteries; to obtain information from the spirit-land. In this parable one from the unseen world is permitted to speak to us, and a terrible revelation has he made.

When I returned to my chamber this poor, tempest-tossed wanderer followed me.

" Have you any good news, my child, to communicate respecting yourself?"

" O no, Mrs. C., I came to ask you to present *some motive to induce me* to trust Jesus."

I was heart sick; after presenting so many motives in the school-room not five minutes before, many of which were designed expressly for her, and after having pressed her duty upon her mind so often, with so much earnestness, to hear *this request* from her was really too much.

" No, R.," I said, " I have no more motives to present. If you can resist all that has been urged upon you, ' Neither will you be persuaded though one rose from the dead.'"

Determined to make herself conspicuous, she tormented her teachers and companions with the continual request, that they would present motives which would induce her " to fly to Jesus." To entreat for the Spirit's influence to give her a *disposition to yield,* suited not the natural feelings of her unsubdued heart.

And thus the struggle went on, until we have reason to fear, the Spirit of God ceased to warn and she was numbered among those who having practically said, " Go thy way for this time,"—receives the dreadful sentence, " They are joined to their idols, let them alone."

What a warning does such an example present to the fearful and unbelieving. How does its sepulchral sounds ring through the soul, as we follow such a spirit up to the dread tribunal, and bear back the terrible sentence, " I never knew you."

Many such cases might be recorded, full of fearful interest, in view of which the Christian teacher and friend has often retired with the lamentation of the prophet, " If ye will not hear me, my soul shall weep in secret places for your pride ;" and many instances might be presented, equal in interest and blessed results with those already given, exhibiting the triumphs of grace over the proud, resisting heart.

" Not by might, nor by power, but by my Spirit, saith the Lord of Hosts."

CHAPTER XLVI.

> " Fight the good fight of faith,
>   With weapons proved and true—
> Be faithful and unshrinking to the death,
>   Thy God will bear thee through;
> The strife is terrible,
>   Yet 'tis not long,
> The foe is not invincible,
>   Though fierce and strong."

THE influence of that precious work of grace which had marked the preceding year, rested on the school after they had reassembled for the summer session. Two of those who had professed to trust in the Saviour early in the season, were numbered with the dead. Both had been pupils of great promise, and left bereaved friends to sorrow, but " not as those who have no hope." Weeping friends might anxiously inquire, " shall we see them again ? know them again ?"

Yes, bereaved ones.

" Voices unheard by the dull ear of worldlings, yet comforting as sweet songs of promise, shall answer your questionings. They whisper soothingly to you; you *shall* find them—know them—love them —your fadeless treasures—the sainted dead."

Many circumstances occurred during the term, of

unusual interest. Some there were among the professed followers of Jesus, who were awakened to new, deep heart-searchings, lest they had built their hopes for eternity on a foundation which would fail them in the day of trial. Several members of the school and family publicly united with the church in Bloomfield, and many presented themselves on their return to their homes, as living sacrifices in the temples where their parents worshipped.

A daughter of one of our frontier missionaries, who had been teaching in our family for three years, consecrated herself, at the close of this session, peculiarly to the *home department*, and became a fitting companion for one who had learned to estimate her worth. She came to us alone;—she went forth from us to bless a husband's home with the cheerful radiance of affection and sympathy. The festivities of the marriage, which took place at the Seminary, formed an appropriate sequel to a term full of exciting incidents.

On reviewing the passing events of the succeeding winter session, sad recollections crowd upon my mind, of the unhappy effect produced upon the minds of the young ladies by the recurrence of the winter recess. While some seemed disposed to give us trouble, many there were whose minds were awakened to serious thought, when the holidays came with their blighting influence. How sadly do the indulgences of these festive occasions break in upon brightening prospects, and cut off the fair buds of promise that seemed almost ready to blossom beneath the goodly influence of Christian culture.

The pupils returned to their duties—were kind, affectionate, and attentive to religious instruction; but no deep anxiety to be numbered among the people of God seemed to possess their hearts.

The first of March brought, in its regular course, our communion season, and two of the family came forward, and in the presence of God's people, took upon themselves the vows of consecration. This awakened a new interest in the minds of many. A youth of the same age as one of my grandsons, while witnessing the solemn scenes of that Sabbath, gave himself to God before leaving the sanctuary.

The seriousness increased; and now, every moment when not employed in the instruction of pupils, I was engaged in conversation with the impenitent who sought my counsel. Truly could I say that my soul rested on Jesus; that all my efforts were nothing, only as directed and blessed by His Spirit; and the more deeply I felt this, the sweeter it was to labor in His cause.

Our pastor greatly aided me—God bless him for his labors of love—and as the result several indulged a Christian hope. Our teachers were no idlers in the vineyard, but by their faithful, efficient efforts, were greatly instrumental in leading souls to Christ. From the tablets of one who was an effective helper in this good work, I obtained the following record of a young friend, over whose sad experience our hearts watched with painful anxiety.

There was much in her character to admire—much in the development of mind and heart to mark her as one whose influence would be felt in society; but though kind and pleasant in her intercourse with those around her, we could not, for a long time, gain access to the inner chambers of her heart. She was a professor of religion, and no improper levity, or unbecoming worldliness of manner, afforded any reason to distrust her professions.

" The occasional lighting up of unusual animation—the speedy relapse into the almost constant expression of soberness, through which I soon fancied I could detect deep and hidden grief—the settled air of abstraction to things around her—the talent manifested—the consistency of her conduct, and her efforts for the good of others—all made her more and more a mystery to us.

"Gradually I gained access to her heart, and found that it was disquieted by anxious thoughts in regard to its own state. I endeavored to point her to Jesus, and while she failed to behold him, and grew more distressed, these efforts were gratefully received, and so inspired her with confiding affection, that she made me acquainted with her previous history.

Six years before she had lost a mother of no common excellence, and most sacredly did she cherish the memory of her prayers, and her holy example. For three years she had hoped that she loved her Saviour, but only recently had she publicly professed her faith in the Redeemer. Since that time she had passed through a season of bitter trial, the effect of which I could now distinctly mark. Excessively *proud*, and exquisitely *sensitive*, she had buried her unappreciated sorrows within her own heart, and then, in a little world of her own, she had dwelt alone, and lived a life of suffering. Now she was writing bitter things against herself, and the dark clouds which covered her were growing darker still. She put away all hope that she was a child of God, and spent her days and nights in agony.

"She scarcely took necessary nourishment, and so absorbed was she with the struggle within, that she seemed perfectly indifferent to aught about her.

"At first, she did not refuse to take part in our little meetings for prayer, but now she did so invariably. When for the first time she declined, I sat beside her, and after the meeting was over whispered to her,

"Did you *do right?*"

"Almost a *groan* of agony was her only answer, and she sat speechless and apparently riveted to the spot, long after the room was vacated. Our beloved mother C., labored faithfully with her. Our pastor too, endeavored to pour light upon her pathway; but while she was grateful to all who sympathized with her and labored for her good, she continued still in darkness.

"Her physical system soon began to feel the effects

of such undue activity of mind, and she daily suffered severe bodily pain, in addition to her mental anguish. The physician's efforts to relieve were added to the rest, but he soon declared his skill inadequate to remedy the ill effects of a mind diseased.

"Thus passed the summer—and vacation separated our family for a season.

"C.'s imperfect health did not prevent her return to school at the commencement of the next session. She seemed to be not quite so much agitated and controlled by grief, but the lines of deep sorrow were still strongly marked, and she unhesitatingly, but very far from unconcernedly, ranked herself with those who had no hope in God.

"Our efforts and our prayers for her were unremitted, and as time passed on, though no change occurred in her feelings, we were persuaded that she gave good evidence not only of real piety, but of a rapid growth in grace. Towards the close of the winter, our hearts were solemnized and gladdened by some few tokens of the special presence of God's Spirit, and C. not only manifested a deep interest in the welfare of others, but seemed herself to share largely in the good influence.

"Why then did she close her heart to all hope, and refuse to be comforted? It was a continual mystery to us all. At last an incidental allusion made by her, to one of "Spencer's Sketches," flashed the truth upon my mind. And now so clearly could I see the whole;

so manifest was the agency of the great adversary of souls, that I had not known it all before. There was a *cross* that she could not bear; *She could not pray in the presence of others.*

"For *this* she had endured unspeakable suffering; for *this*, she had relinquished her hope in Christ; around this point Satan had gathered his forces, and hurled his "hellish darts" until it had attained an awful prominence in her mind, and then to make his triumph more complete and her misery more intolerable, he devised the plan of *secrecy* and made her dread nothing so much as the revelation of this cause of all her misery.

"Frightened and excited when she found me in possession of her secret, she earnestly besought me still to preserve it inviolate, and it was only after long and repeated pleadings with her, and a struggle on her part which well nigh exhausted all her remaining strength, that I obtained permission to divulge the cause of her troubles to Mrs. C. and obtain her counsel and advice.

"The power of the great tempter was *broken* now, but it was not *destroyed*. He could no longer deprive her of an humble hope in Jesus—but no counsel, no aid, no effort could remove the difficulty from her way and enable her to join her prayers with ours. Unspeakably painful were the conflicts that she still endured, but her victories were only partial—her sufferings were scarcely diminished.

"Several years have passed since C. left school, and her heavenly Father has laid upon her a weight of sorrow such as few young hearts are called to bear; yet His grace has helped her in hours of trial, when earthly sympathy seems but a mockery of grief, and she could gratefully say, "Though He slay me I will trust in Him." Amid all, the conflicts with her great temptation has been going on, but God has been with her, and when a few months since, a skeptical friend, was through her instrumentality brought trembling to his knees, she knelt beside him and achieved a triumph over the arch-tempter—so joyous—so complete, that to use her own words, she 'would gladly every hour of her future life engage to endure a suffering as intense, if it was to be followed by a joy so far outweighing it.'"

Thus speaks the testimony of friendship; and such or similar experience may have distressed many a youthful Christian's heart. Well does the enemy of souls know how to use his weapons, and often most successfully does he wield them. Sinking amid the dark waters, how often does the cry ascend, "Lord save, or I perish!"

The above is no idle tale of suffering;—no matter in what form the temptation assails us, let faith yield to fear and the soul is wrecked on the rocks of unbelief, soon to be engulphed in the overwhelming billows of despair. Perhaps the success of the arch-deceiver is never more complete than when he instigates the soul to turn from the mercy-seat, to seek relief in the pleasures of the world, for

> "Satan trembles when he sees,
> The weakest saint upon his knees

A prophet has told us respecting his influence and power, "With lies ye have made the heart of the righteous sad, whom I have not made sad."

Though our enemy has great power and great knowledge, blessed be God his power is not omnipotent—his knowledge is not infinite. Precious promises beam upon the soul from the radiant pages of God's holy word.

"There hath no temptation taken you, but such as is common to man; but God is faithful, who will not suffer you to be tempted above that ye are able, but will with the temptation also, make a way to escape, that ye may be able to bear it."

Then trust fully and fearlessly in this blessed assurance, and looking to Jesus for help in every time of need, repel every attempt to gain entrance into the citadel of your heart. Then with the devout Newton may you say,

> "Begone, unbelief! My Saviour is near,
> And for my relief, will surely appear;
> By prayer let me wrestle, and He will perform;
> With Christ in the vessel, I smile at the storm."

CHAPTER XLVII.

> "What matter whether pain or pleasure fill
>   The swelling heart one little moment here?
> From both alike how vain is every thrill,
>   While an untried eternity is near!
> Think not of rest, fond man, in life's career;
>   The joys and griefs that meet thee dash aside
> Like bubbles, and thy bark right onward steer,
>   Through calm and tempest, till it cross the tide,
> Shoot into port in triumph, or serenely glide."

THE summer of 1851 brought but little of the special influences of God's Spirit upon the school, though a few indulged the hope that they "had passed from death unto life," and several minds were awakened to serious reflection.

During the July recess I decided to visit some friends in western New York. Through the intervention of unavoidable circumstances I missed an opportunity of accompanying a party of friends who were about to proceed on the same route; I was therefore obliged to take the evening train on the Erie railroad alone, in the darkness and discomfort of a rainy night.

To add to the disagreeableness of my condition, in the confusion of departure, my basket, which contained sundry comforts for traveling, had been left behind, and not a single *rag* could I command to wipe away the tears that would force themselves to my eyes, as I contemplated my forlorn and solitary state. All night the dismal train went on. No one cared for the " lone woman" whom no one knew; no " friendly Quaker" stepped forward to greet or aid me.

At that time the arrangements of the road were such that it was necessary to change cars at Sufferns, and here new trials awaited me, for so intent were the *gentlemen* in securing entire seats for themselves, that it was some time before I could find a resting place for my weary limbs. I finally was permitted to sit beside a foreigner, whose bundles I was politely requested to watch whenever he left the cars for refreshments.

Much has been written on the subject of railroad courtesy, and much censure has been deservedly cast upon our sex for the ungracious manner in which many receive polite attentions from fellow-travelers. There are those who, by their overbearing arrogance seem to *demand*, as their prescriptive right, the first seat—the best seat—indeed *all* the seats in the car or stage, that they may desire to appropriate to their own special indulgence. But the scene has changed. The much-abused lords of creation have not only abundantly avenged themselves upon the offending fair ones, but they have made the innocent to suffer with them, in the general outburst of indignation. Not only do they retain unyielding possession of their own appropriate seats—to the undisturbed occupancy of which every reasonable woman would concede that they have a perfect right—but they contrive to spread out their ample dimensions so as to convert the whole into a *lounge,* and thus effectually bar out every intruder.

On that dark and rainy night, I myself passed through three cars, in each of which not less than six or eight individuals were cosily reposing, before I could gain permission, with the assistance of the conductor, to watch the stranger's bundles.

But even here the trouble does not end; if a lady succeeds in securing a seat beside some reluctant churl, she must hold high her hooped skirts, or she will find them floating off upon a *sea* whose waters cast up filth and dirt. The *debt* is abundantly paid. Greek has met Greek, and *both* have conquered. As a traveler, I am ashamed of my countrymen. O that the time might come—the " good time" be hastened— when the rights of both sexes shall be fully conceded, and kindness and courtesy take the place of arrogance and rudeness.

A visit to Niagara—the wish of a life-time—was at length accomplished. With the friends of other years, I stood upon the brink of its rushing waters, and as my eye rested upon the tumbling rapids, descending in successive cascades, until they make their final plunge into the fearful gulf, my mind was overwhelmed; I could scarcely speak; the power of the Being, who had produced so magnificent a work, overawed me, and I felt like Elijah, when he hid his face in his mantle while the glory of the Lord passed by. As night threw her dark mantle around us, and objects were seen, indeed, *in the mist*, and we stood upon the beautiful islet, trembling with the ground beneath our feet, the sublimity of the scene increased.

So many miserable attempts have been made to describe Niagara, and so many truly graphic representations given by the pen and pencil of ready sketchers, that the common mind may well be satisfied to wonder and adore, only exclaiming with the inspired writer, "Great and marvelous are Thy works, Lord God Almighty." "The voice of the Lord is upon the waters; the God of glory thundereth; the Lord is upon many waters."

The remainder of the summer, after my return to my home, was marked by no incident of special interest, but early in the succeeding November the news reached me of the death of the mother of one of our teachers, who had endeared herself to me. In this record of life's experience, I can not refrain from giving utterance to the feelings that oppressed me, on a Sabbath full of sad and tender memories, revived by this intelligence, as embodied in a letter to a friend, who has, from our earliest association, rendered to me the affection of a daughter.

"In the stillness of this quiet Sabbath evening (November 16), with thoughts of the past crowding thickly upon my heart, I may pour out a few of these thoughts upon you, not to excite a melancholy spirit, for such is not their effect upon me, but to give a chastened view of the realities of life, and to point to that better land where sorrow and weeping can not enter.

"Poor L! just one week since she became motherless; that beloved parent was suddenly summoned away from the family circle, to her rest in heaven. Friends sorrow not as those without hope; but O, how trying are these bereavements. With what a pang are those cords snapped asunder which have so long bound heart to heart. Well for us if in such visitations we can see a Father's hand.

"I went to the house of God this morning with all my sympathies awakened for our dear desolate one, so early stricken. The service commenced, and the second hymn that was selected was

Come we that love the Lord.'

O what a host of memories did it bring up. It was the last hymn that I sang with my husband. It was Sabbath eve—our children were around us in our quiet happy home,—and as we looked out upon the landscape as it lay reposing in the bright beams of the full orbed moon, we felt that our cup of happiness was full. We sang together, ' Come we who love the Lord,' and we felt that we were

> " ' Marching through Immanuel's ground,
>   To fairer worlds on high.'

" In one week from that time he was treading the courts of heaven, and I, widowed and desolate, was left a weary pilgrim of earth to pursue my journey of years sad and solitary.   And yet God has not left me *alone*.   My husband was removed at a time, when it seemed that I most needed his protection and support, but God was Himself the husband of the widow and the Father of her fatherless ones. He took my beloved daughters to Himself, but He surrounded me with loved ones who have been as daughters unto me; with whom I hope to rejoice before the throne of God.

" And can I murmur when such blessings are mine ? I trust that it is not in my heart to do this; but I do not wish to bury the past in forgetfulness. Let it live to awaken gratitude—to excite to greater energy and devotion in my Master's cause—and to present new motives to strengthen those who are weak and desponding.

" Forty-five years ago, this month, three young friends presented themselves for admission to the church of Christ. As it was then the custom in the Congregational Churches of New England, to examine the candidates before the assembled members, many who felt no peculiar interest in the subject of religion, came in to see how those who but recently had been as gay and thoughtless as themselves, would act and speak on such an occasion.

"We felt the embarrassment of our situation, and the importance of not shrinking from the avowal of our feelings. We knew that many eyes were upon us, and at the close of the examination, we requested that the hymn might be sung which commences with

> "'I'm not ashamed to own my Lord,
>   Or to defend His cause;
> Maintain the honor of His word,
>   The glory of His cross.'

"That hymn was sung at the close of the service this morning. Was it not emphatically a *morning of memories* to me?"

Towards the close of the year a new trial awaited us. Our pastor, who by his deep interest in the improvement of the youth in his congregation, and his earnest efforts to promote their eternal welfare, had endeared himself to many hearts, was invited to become the spiritual guide of a congregation in a neighboring city, and the wants of that church and people determined him to listen to their appeal. Great was the excitement produced by this encroachment as we deemed it, upon our rights, and many were the arguments used to convince him of the superior importance of the field in which he was then laboring.

He left us satisfied that his "steps were ordered of

the Lord,"—and followed by the prayers of many a sorrowing heart that the presence of the Holy One would still attend him and bless his efforts in his new field of labor.

In the midst of these agitating events and feelings, there were some whose minds seemed accessible to the truth and several hoped in the mercy of the Redeemer. Judging from appearances from time to time, could we have had the advantages of a regular ministry,—had our minds been less affected by passing events,—and had my own health been less influenced by these occurrences, so that more thorough attention had been given to the religious instruction of the pupils, there might have been a powerful revival in the school.

Early in March we were much gratified and profited by a visit from the Rev. Mr. Goodell of Constantinople, who gave a very interesting account of the female Armenian school. It commenced with seven girls, all of whom became pious. He told us of their joy when they heard that their fathers and brothers were persecuted for their attachment to Jesus Christ, because they were " counted worthy to suffer shame for His name," and were enabled to stand firm in defence of the gospel. Of fifty-three who had left that Seminary, fifty-one had become hopefully pious.

On the 28th of the same month, our new pastor, Mr. S., entered upon his duties and preached two excellent sermons to us from Heb. xi. 4. " He being dead yet speaketh."

The subject was "Influence," and he illustrated it by reference to Scripture characters,—to the Waldenses, Reformers, Covenanters of Scotland and Puritans of England and America,—to Howard, Harlan Page, &c.

At the close of the session which occurred a few days after his installation, he visited and addressed the school.

CHAPTER XLVIII.

> "O trust in God, the God of our salvation,
> Trust in the Lord to heal the desolation;
> The cause, now precious in His sight!
> He has an arm of boundless might;
> O trust in God, nor yield to fear;
> Our Helper is for ever near,
> In darkness as in light."

MANY indications, during the summer session of
1852, gave, at times, sweet evidence of the presence
of the Holy Spirit. The little gatherings for prayer,
which were usually kept up in the Seminary every
day, but which were now attended with renewed
interest, and by increasing numbers, testified that
the " still, small voice" was whispering powerfully to
their hearts; and many were the interviews enjoyed
with subdued and anxious ones.

On the last Sabbath of the session our pastor addressed the youth of the different schools, who were
soon to separate—many, to see each other's faces no
more. The discourse was well calculated to leave a
salutary impression on their minds, and I trust that
seed was sown that will hereafter bear fruit to the
glory of God.

Our last religious exercises in the Seminary were peculiarly solemn.

I first invited to my room all the professed followers of the Saviour. I read to them Paul's injunction to Timothy.

"Let no man despise thy youth, but be thou an example of the believers, in word, in conversation, in charity, in spirit, in faith, in purity."

I urged upon them the duty of cultivating consistency of character—never allowing themselves to do things, anywhere, which they would not dare to do under the eye of a parent or teacher.

Afterwards I called in those who hoped that they had found mercy at the cross during the term, and sixteen youthful converts seated themselves around me. To these I read the sixth chapter of John, commencing at the twenty-fourth verse, dwelling particularly on the words,

"Will ye also go away?"

I reminded them of the temptations that were so soon to assail them, and of the great difference between their present comparatively secure situation, and the circumstances in which they were about to be placed. The vacation would prove a *test* season to many of them, and well would it be for them if they did not yield to its allurements, and return to the "beggarly elements of the world." I urged upon them ceaseless watchfulness. Their first declension would begin in *the closet*. They must therefore watch, and resist the least disposition to neglect that consecrated place; they must look to Jesus for help—must pour out their hearts before Him, and trust Him for His grace, and it would be at all times sufficient for them.

A large number attended, when I assembled another class to my room. My heart sank within me as I looked around upon this interesting group, going forth, many of them to return no more, without any Christian principle to restrain or guide them. I read to them from Revelations iii. 20, "Behold, I stand at the door, and knock; if any man hear my voice, and open the door, I will come in to him, and will sup with him, and he with me;" and thus He had stood, rejected or disregarded by them, until, to use His own beautiful figure, "His head is filled with dew, and His locks with the drops of the night."

I then contrasted this view of the Saviour's compassion and forbearance with that set forth in the language employed in Proverbs i. 24–31.

"Because I have called and ye refused; I have stretched out my hand, and no man regarded;

"But ye have set at nought all my counsel, and would none of my reproof:

"I also will laugh at your calamity; I will mock when your fear cometh."

Faithfully did I try to address them in that parting hour. Many wept, and all looked sad and solemn. God grant that those feeble attempts to save the soul, though made in great weakness and imperfection, may be followed by a blessing from on high.

Much was accomplished during the year for the missionary cause. Mr. S. addressed the missionary society connected with the Seminary, at its anniversary, in an appropriate and interesting discourse, and the secretary reported that one hundred and twenty dollars had been collected, and three boxes prepared for different missionary stations.

This anniversary was the closing exercise of the school; then followed the sundering of tender ties—the sad farewells—the tearful partings, mingled with smiles of gladness, at the prospect of "Home, sweet home."

Soon after this, yet dearer ties were sundered. A precious lamb, the fourth that had been removed, was taken from the flock, and the domestic circle of my children in Raleigh was again made desolate. A bereaved twin sister, as she looked in vain for the companion of her childish sports, was left to wonder why little Nettie was gone so long away. Many hearts mourn thy departure, sweet babe, whilst thou dwellest with thy Saviour in the better land, for,

> " Art thou not of that band, of whom
> He said with wondrous grace,
> Behold ! their angels always stand
> Before my Father's face."

The vacation was spent with friends in Philadelphia. As it was my first sojourn for any length of time in that city, much of my time was occupied in visiting various places of interest. I first directed my steps towards Independence Hall, and with feelings amounting almost to awe, seated myself in the chairs once occupied by Hancock and Thompson. I looked upon the old "cracked bell" which once pealed forth the notes of freedom to an oppressed nation, and almost felt the blood course through my veins with the energy of youth, as I thought of the noble sacrifices endured, and the noble acts achieved by the fathers of our country.

Nothing in the Academy of the Fine Arts more completely enchained my attention than Wittkamp's "Deliverance of Leyden." The scene was laid at the time when that city was besieged by Philip Second of Spain, in 1574. The Spanish fleet, commanded by Valdes, is moored in sight. Vanderwerf, the Burgomaster, saw nothing before him but impending destruction; the people were dying of famine; emaciated forms and faces, the look of defiance, and the prostration and suffering portrayed upon the canvas, all told the tale of their extremity. The burgomaster stands in the centre of the picture—pale, haggard, yet resolute—surrounded by the clamorous multitude, urging him to surrender, and threatening to sacrifice him if he refuses. With his eyes raised to heaven, he exclaims:

"My friends, since I must die, it is of little importance to me whether I fall by your hand or that of the enemy. I shall die satisfied if I can be in any way way useful to you."

The people were subdued, and Vanderwerf resolved to break down the dykes that kept out the incursions of the sea, preferring to perish by the incoming waves of the ocean, than to trust to the tender mercies of the enemy. The sudden rush of the waters compelled Valdes to draw off his forces, and give to the Dutch admiral an opportunity to advance with his vessels to the relief of the beleaguered city, news of which was conveyed by carrier pigeons to the despairing inhabitants, ere it arrived.

While the scene of distress is depicted in the foreground, on the walls and in the distance on the shore, the uplifted arms, the waving caps, and the exulting shouts—-you can almost imagine that you hear them— are proclaiming the glad tidings of deliverance.

After relief and freedom were obtained, the Prince of Orange offered to them two privileges, one of which they were permitted to choose—immunity from taxation for a certain period of time, or liberty to found a University in their city. They wisely chose the latter, and thus originated the University of Leyden.

At the Laurel Hill Cemetery, two double monuments beautiful in their simplicity, particularly arrested my attention. On the first, these tributes of affection were inscribed,

OUR MOTHER;

SHE TAUGHT US HOW TO LIVE, AND HOW TO DIE.

OUR SISTER,

TO US, A MOTHER—TO THE WORLD, A SPIRIT OF LOVE.

On the other pair :

LIZZIE;

ANGELS ARE CROWNING THY FAIR YOUNG BROW;
WHY THEN DO WE WEEP?

WILLIAM;   .

THINK OF ME AS OF A WANDERER WHOSE HOME IS FOUND.

The Penitentiary, with all its arrangements for the safety, comfort, employment and spiritual instruction of its inmates, has been too often described by admiring visitors to require more than a passing remark. One little incident related to me by a bystander, will suffice to show the estimation in which this retreat is held by those for whose special accommodation it was designed.

A man had been condemned, for larceny, to several months' imprisonment in the Moyamensing prison. On being asked by the presiding judge if he had anything to say in reference to his sentence, he replied,

"May it please your Honor, I would rather go to the Penitentiary." The reason for his request having been demanded,

"It is much more comfortable there," said he, "they are better fed—the work is not so hard,—and *my morals would be safer.*"

The court thinking that such *disinterested* solicitude for the purity of public morals should not go unrewarded, granted his request, and he was sent to the

Penitentiary amid shouts of laughter from the assembled crowd.

Girard College, too, needs no attempts at description; its world-wide reputation and the circumstances attending its foundation, mark it as a spot of curious and special interest. Through the influence of a friend, I was permitted to inspect the interior of the room which contains the relics of the eccentric founder of this Institution. In its centre stands an immense zodiac; and arranged on shelves are models of various kinds, among which is a model of the college prepared by Girard himself, his library, china, sword and gun, hats and boots, clothes—even to his knee-patched pantaloons—chairs, tables, &c., filled the room.

An amusing though somewhat startling circumstance was related to me, connected with the removal of Girard's bones to this room, preparatory I believe, to a new interment. Some persons desirous of viewing the remains of the departed, opened the coffin in the evening, but holding a lamp too near, to their utter consternation, a violent explosion was the consequence. One of their number, more intelligent or self-possessed than the rest, allayed their apprehensions by suggesting that the explosion was the result of confined gases and thus the mystery was accounted for.

An old lady who knew him well, gave me many interesting circumstances of his life. For years, in

his early history, he trundled a barrow in the streets
of Philadelphia. By degrees he increased in wealth
and began to send ventures to sea. Fortunate in all
his speculations, he soon became the owner of several
vessels trading principally to the West Indies. Previous to the insurrection of the blacks and the massa-
cre of the whites at Hayti, many wealthy Spaniards
and Americans consigned their money and other valu-
ables to his care, intending as soon as they could ad-
just their affairs to follow to America. Most of them
with their families were cut off in the ensuing mas-
sacre, and as no person survived to claim the property
thus placed in his hands, it eventually became his own,
and laid the foundation for his enormous fortune.

Soon after the commencement of the winter sessions
of 1852–53, our sympathies were deeply enlisted for
one of our pupils, who was laid on a bed of extreme
suffering.

She was a young lady of great promise, but that
scourge of multitudes of our sex, an affection of the
spine, suddenly prostrated her and for weeks we
watched over her as one who was hovering on the
verge of the eternal world. At times, the spasms
brought on by intense agony, were absolutely fright-
ful; and thus she suffered from week to week, till
months had passed away.

Night after night did we retire to rest, expecting
that the morning would dawn upon a bereaved household, but severe as were her sufferings never did a

murmur escape her lips—never a word express impatience. Early she had learned to love her Saviour, and He did not forsake her in this trying hour.

"It is all right." "My heavenly Father is very kind to me." "Jesus is near to help and comfort me." "Mrs. C., I want you to thank God for His great mercy to me."

Such was the language of a heart imbued with the love of the Redeemer, and such the language of her lips, when able to express her feelings.

But her life was spared;—at the end of three months she was removed on a bed to her own home, and there she lingered till Hydropathic applications restored her to comparative health.

But what effect did this produce upon the young ladies of the family? God had spoken loudly by His providences. He had whispered by His spirit to many a heart,—" Watch, for ye know not what a day may bring forth,"—yet the triflers did not listen. The excitement produced by passing events, occupied their minds and turned their attention from more important subjects.

My own heart was burdened, and often did I feel that I could joyfully turn away to my quiet resting-place beneath the evergreens of the cemetery, and return no more. My soul was sad and dark; in the bitterness of my spirit, I said, " all these things are against me." I had hoped for better things in a spiritual sense—for brighter hours in my pilgrimage, but my mind was distracted with cares, and almost destitute of that peaceful reliance on the Saviour, which in times past I had so much enjoyed.

A severe family trial quickened our supplications at the throne of grace, and seemed to awaken thoughtfulness in some minds.

On the evening of the first Sabbath in February, as the family had been prevented by the inclemency of the weather, from attendance upon the worship of God in the sanctuary, I collected the pupils in the study hall and read to them the sermons that had been preached during the day—having borrowed them for that purpose.

One there was in our midst, who wept the whole evening, and the earnest silent prayer was raised by many, that some permanent impression might be made upon the mind of this hitherto thoughtless one. There was a considerable manifestation of feeling among the impenitent, but Christians stood aloof and "came not up to the help of the Lord."

The attention to religion became general in town, and extending its influence to the school, deepened the anxiety that had been awakened. "I wait for Thy salvation," was my earnest cry, "and in Thy word do I trust."

Three or four pupils were withdrawn from the school, the pretext, headache—the real reason, unquestionably, the fear of their parents, that their children would become Christians.

On the day that has been for many years observed
by the churches, as a season of special fasting and
prayer in behalf of our Colleges and other seminaries
of learning, three members of our family professed to
give their hearts to Jesus, and from that time the
good work rapidly progressed. So occupied was I
with the demands made upon my own strength and
time, that I had little opportunity to look abroad and
enquire into the state of things in town. I felt the
need of faithful, judicious coadjutors in this soul bur-
dening work. Some whose hearts were right, were inexperienced and deficient in judgment, but God's
promise encouraged me, "They that sow in tears,
shall reap in joy." There is no restraint to the Lord,
"to save by many or by few."

On one occasion some excellent remarks were made
to the school, by the Rev. Mr. H., in which he compared the privileges of females in Christian lands, with
those in heathen countries, and their consequent obligations to God. He spoke of the importance of *securing* favorable opportunities for the soul's salvation
and showed that the present was just such a golden
season. He also showed that the influence which
they exerted over others for good or for evil was great,
and that they could not prevent it. He illustrated
this position, by reference to recognized principles in
Natural Philosophy. A footprint gives its impulse to
every grain of sand upon the globe; the rain-drop
affects the waters of the ocean; a word spoken gives

impulse to the whole atmosphere;—just so with influence.

Many thrilling remembrances present themselves to my mind, as I think of the past and recall scenes, recorded only on memory's tablets, but the all engrossing nature of my work effectually precluded the possibility of *written* records, and thus I lost the minutiæ of many passing events, that might have added interest to these details.

One circumstance, however, I recall to mind that interested me much. A young lady who had for some weeks been impressed with a sense of her danger and guilt, as a sinner against God, came at last to tell me that she had been to Jesus for pardon, and it seemed to her that she could see *the cross*, but that the Saviour was veiled from her view. A day or two after, I asked if her faith was strengthened and her hope brighter;—with a face expressive of a subdued and trusting spirit, she replied,

" O Mrs. C., I think that this morning, I caught some glimpses of glory from the *Saviour on the cross*—I do hope that I trust in His mercy."

As I was one day addressing a company of impenitent pupils, my attention was particularly attracted to five young ladies who were seated side by side. They had all come from the same neighborhood and occupied adjoining rooms, forming an interesting group, whose antecedents were such as rendered them hopeful subjects for special efforts. I addressed them collectively and conversed with them individually. They were of an age to appreciate the truth : it had already, in some measure, made its impress upon their minds, and now they seemed ready to open their hearts to the conviction of the necessity of that new birth, which would make all things new to them.

One after another yielded to the heavenly call, and soon the grateful song resounded from thankful hearts, " Hear what the Lord hath done for me."

As the fruit of that season of refreshing from the Lord, I find about thirty names recorded. May it be found in the great day of account that these names are all written in the Lamb's Book of Life.

" Glory to that wondrous Grace,
    Which hath drawn their hearts to God,
Gained for them a dwelling-place,
    In the heavenly, high abode.
Fit them for that holy rest,
    Claim them for Thy service here;
Till among the spirits blest,
    They in glory shall appear."

CHAPTER XLIX.

ENLARGEMENT OF THE CHURCH.—MR. D.'S MISSION-
ARY ADDRESS.—REVIVAL IN THE WINTER
TERM OF 1854.—DEATH OF FRIENDS.

> " If thou would'st reap in love,
> First sow in holy fear ;
> So life, a winter's morn may prove
> To a bright endless year."

THE summer of 1853 was so much disturbed by
various obstacles to permanent serious feeling,—by
the changes rendered necessary in our place of worship on the Sabbath, by the enlargement and repair-
ing of the sanctuary, and by various other causes,—
that no *record* appears of conversions during that session. The seed was sown in hope,—by God's blessing some fruit may hereafter appear, to the glory of
His grace.

Our Missionary Society at its annual meeting, was
again addressed by our late pastor, who had enlisted
the respect and affection of many youthful hearts, and
who cheerfully responded to our invitation to speak to
us once more, on the great work of aiding in the
spread of the gospel through the nations of the earth.

The winter of 1853–54 yielded much fruit to the
glory of God. Many precious souls we have reason

to hope, turned away from the world and sought pardon and peace through the atoning blood of the Redeemer. Teachers engaged earnestly in the work : young converts conversed and prayed with impenitent companions, and many appeared with the anxious enquiry " what shall I do to be saved ?"

Often have I regretted since I commenced this work, that intense anxiety and constant care and labor prevented my recording many passing scenes, that would have added greatly to its interest. The recollections of a teacher, furnish me with the following incident :

" One evening, a group of young ladies were assembled in the hall. A teacher called their attention to the peculiar beauties of the setting sun,—its golden tints richly illuminating the horizon, and fringing the edges of the light clouds with its parting beams. H., being a great admirer of nature, lingered after the others had departed. Miss G. spoke to her of the surpassing beauty of the Sun of Righteousness, who comes to the soul not only to infuse light to the mind, but with healing in His beams to overcome the disease which sin has brought into the troubled spirit. H.'s mind filled with the glory of the present scene, was at once impressed with the all-sufficiency of Christ and her need of His salvation ; and thus commenced her first serious impressions, which resulted through the mercy of God in the consecration of herself to His service."

Deeply interesting was the gathering of the youthful band of converts, numbering between twenty and thirty, who assembled in my room on the last Sabbath of the term, to receive the parting instructions of their Mother-friend.

As on a similar occasion in former times, I read to them a few verses from John vi., "Will ye also go away?" "Then Simon Peter said, Lord, to whom shall we go? Thou hast the words of eternal life." I spoke of the *power* of the adversary to draw the heart from Jesus; of the proneness of that heart to wander; of the only safety of the young disciple, beset on every side by snares and temptations; Jesus the *alone* refuge of His people, their helper in every time of need would not forsake them, and in Him they might surely trust. I then repeated the charge so often given to my beloved pupils, "Never engage in any pursuit, or amusement, upon which you can not ask the presence and blessing of God."

While these interesting scenes were passing in our midst, the family of a beloved sister was shrouded in mourning. The "light of the dwelling" had departed and the hearts of the bereaved ones were desolate. In the midst of his people and of his usefulness—for age had not so impaired his vigor and his power to labor in the cause of his Master as to diminish his efforts,—was this man of God stricken by disease, and the angel of death commissioned to speak to him—"Come up hither," "the Lord hath need of thee" in His holy habitation.

It is unnecessary here to give in detail the character of one who presided so long over an Institution, which has sent forth its hundreds to bless our land and the world, by their successful efforts to build up the kingdom of the Redeemer, and to spread the light of truth among the nations of the earth. The memory of Doctor B., is enshrined in many youthful hearts, and when in his declining years he retired from that sphere of usefulness to the quiet of a country manse, faithfully did he perform the duties of his pastoral office, and stepped as it were from the threshold of the sanctuary to the presence of his blessed Saviour.

Many hearts mourned his departure and testimonials of respect and affection still linger on the lips of surviving friends. Said a clerical friend, who was called to bear his testimony to the worth of the departed, on that day which forever shrouded him from the view of his weeping family on earth, " The highest tribute that we *can* pay to him is to seek to perpetuate his usefulness, by giving to his teachings and example a permanent home in our memories and hearts, and endeavoring to secure to them an enduring influence over our fellow-men."

<blockquote>
"Servant of God! well done!
Rest from thy loved employ;
The battle fought,—the victory won,—
Enter thy Master's joy.
Rest from thy labor, rest;—
Soul of the just set free!
Blest be thy memory, and blest
Thy bright example be."
</blockquote>

On his dying bed, this man of God commended his afflicted companion to the filial care and affection of his beloved children. Faithfully had she performed her maternal duties to them and richly was she rewarded by their devotion to her comfort, and their active and cheerful efforts to promote her happiness, and to cheer and sustain the dark days of widowhood that succeeded. But the crushed spirit, though calm and peaceful, and the enfeebled frame, never rallied. In less than eighteen months she too went home to God, to join the blessed assembly of holy ones, whose names are written in heaven, and who had already preceded her to the realms of glory. She was mourned by a large circle of friends, to whom she was justly endeared by mental and moral worth of no ordinary character. One who knew her long and intimately, writes, " To a mind enriched by education were added the charms of a cultivated taste and of social refinement. Mrs. B. would have shone in any department of life, but by her distinguished and well balanced piety, she was eminently qualified to become what she truly was, a help-meet to her beloved husband in the various and responsible duties of his public and domestic life." " In her death the church on earth lost one of its most prayerful and devoted friends, but the church above has added to her treasures another bright and imperishable jewel."

And I was left alone, the last of that happy group who had, in other days, gathered around the hearth-

stone of the dear old home, where once the bright
and sunny smiles of father and mother shed their
radiance upon hearts full of life and joyousness and
happiness.

Where are they now—that broken family circle.
Through the mercy of God, I trust, reunited in a holier, happier home ; while the eldest of that band of
children still wanders on in her pilgrimage, striving
to fulfil her mission—a miracle of grace, a monument
of God's mercy and forbearance.

> "A stranger—lonely here I roam,
>   From place to place am driven ;
>   I have no home but heaven."

But the thought is indelibly impressed on my heart
that,

> " A charge to keep I have,
>   A God to glorify ;
> A never-dying soul to save,
>   And fit it for the sky ;
> To serve the present age,
>   My calling to fulfil,
> O, may it all my powers engage,
>   To do my Master's will."

With such an object before me, I may well rejoice
that my threescore years and ten are extended, while
I praise the Father that through infinite grace, thus
" to live is Christ, and to die is gain."

CHAPTER L.

> " What matter whether pain or pleasure fill
>   The swelling heart one little moment here ?
> From both alike how vain is every thrill,
>   While an untried eternity is near !
> Think not of rest, fond man, in life's career ;
>   The joys and griefs that meet thee dash aside
> Like bubbles, and thy bark right onward steer,
>   Through calm and tempest, till it cross the tide,
> Shoot into port in triumph, or serenely glide."

WORN out with care, anxiety and labor, it was decided by friends and physician that relaxation for a season was imperatively demanded, and I concluded to spend a part of the summer of 1854 in the quiet homes of friends of other days. During the vacation I spent several days in Mendham, where it was my privilege to attend a communion season, at which I witnessed the accession of one hundred and twenty members to the church of Christ under the ministry of the Rev. T. H. Between forty and fifty of these converts were baptized. The man of gray hairs, and the child who had numbered but twelve years ; fathers and mothers who a short time since knew not the language of prayer, and the youth, lately so gay and worldly, there kneeled at the altar to receive the sacred symbol of consecration to the Redeemer. Among them came one who looked back to the time of her connection with our Institution as the season when she made the surrender of herself to Jesus. Another, for whom my prayers had often ascended to the throne of grace, during this revival yielded her heart to the influences of God's Holy Spirit. What a scene for angels to behold! What an accession to the heavenly company who are

> " Marching through Immanuel's ground
> To fairer worlds on high."

How many are rejoicing in the realms of glory over beloved ones on earth, preparing to follow them to the mansions of everlasting love!

Previous to my departure from Bloomfield, in June, I met the pupils on a sabbath evening in the study hall and solemnly addressed them on the great subject of their eternal welfare, not knowing but it might prove our last meeting on earth. Letters afterwards received gave me cheering hope that four of their number dated their serious impressions from the instructions of that evening, and though one returned to worldliness and folly, the remainder, I trust, obtained that good hope through grace which shall hereafter prove as an anchor to the soul, sure and steadfast. To those precious notes, written in the flush of the first love of the young convert, I immediately replied, and soon I followed these with a letter addressed to all the pupils in the school.

"Dear Ones All,—I think of you. O how often, morning and evening, the prayer ascends to your Father and my Father, in your behalf, and the question arises, which I put to you with maternal anxiety, 'Is it well with thee?' *Well*, as it respects bodily health, mental improvement, and spiritual preparation for a better world? Do you ever think of the deep solicitude with which parental affection watches to catch every intimation of a loved daughter's improvement—of the glow of satisfaction that lights up the countenance when the precious assurance is given 'it *is* well with thy daughter,'—of the disappointment depicted in that mother's face as the word falls heavily on her ear, 'your daughter refuses obedience—she is an idler in the vineyard?'

"From the general appearance of the pupils in the Seminary, I anticipated a session of great improvement and pleasant intercourse; and I love to turn my thoughts homeward, and in my mind's eye, picture you assembled on our beautiful green for recreation, at evening twilight, or as gathered for study or instruction in the hall of old Harmony. Often the question arises in my heart, when shall I take my accustomed place in their midst, and sympathize in their joys and sorrows? As this gratification can not yet be enjoyed, remember my parting words, 'I have no greater joy than to hear that my children walk in the truth.'

"The fascinating scenes of earth are rapidly passing away; like the 'fairy frost work' of a beautiful vision, they leave only the wreck of broken vows of promise, the blighting of many fond anticipations, the gloom and sadness of joys and comforts scattered and destroyed. Secure while you may a hold on the anchor of hope, on which you may safely rest when the storms of life threaten to overwhelm you.

> " 'Lean not on earth—'twill pierce thee to the heart,
>   A broken reed at best, and oft a spear;
>   On its sharp point peace bleeds, and hope expires.'

" Give the dew of your youth to the Saviour's service; trust me, nothing will elevate your characters like this. Nothing short of this will prepare you to be blessings to a degenerate world.

" Enter, then, at once on woman's true mission. Exert the influence which it is your privilege to extend around you, and then, when you have blessed your generation by holy effort and example, you will pass away from earth, loved and lamented, to meet the many who have been prepared, through your instrumentality, to join in the great anthem of praise with the countless throng of the redeemed, saying, ' Blessing and honor and glory and power be unto Him who sitteth upon the throne, and to the Lamb, for ever and ever.' "

At the commencement of the winter season I resumed my duties, and my heart sent up its earnest petitions for the salvation of souls around me. Verging rapidly towards that period of life which the

Psalmist pronounces "the days of our years," I felt that what I would do must be done quickly.

I was disappointed in the aid I expected. A few gave their efforts and their prayers, but the greater portion of God's children seemed more intent on the question, "who will show *us* any good?" than on the inquiry, "Lord, what wilt thou have *me* to do?" It seemed too, as though Satan had been let loose upon us, and at times I was ready to forsake my charge, and seek a quiet resting-place, where I might die in peace. I felt that too heavy a burden was laid upon me in my declining years, and I shrank from the trial. With a sorrowful spirit I sought strength and direction at the mercy-seat, and there I was assured that the sustaining grace of an ever present Saviour was granted, and that an Almighty arm was around me. Thus supported, I resolved to await His direction, and to be governed by His providence. I spent a Sabbath with friends in the city, a quiet, retired, and holy day, for the rain prevented my attending the worship of God in the sanctuary. I spread out my case before the Lord; I made a new consecration of soul and body to His service, and I resolved to remain and die at my post, if such was the will of God concerning me, though trials should cluster around me, and duties and responsibilities crush me to the grave. And they did come, with a force that almost destroyed me. The cases of ——, with all their attendant circumstances, came over my soul like the surging billows; but the Lord mercifully brought them to submission. The results to one, for a season, were especially happy. Possessing a strong mind, an indomitable will, and a proud spirit, H. had never been conquered, and when compelled to admit that she had so sinned against others that a public acknowledgment was inevitable, she was driven to look into her own heart, and see its alienation from God. A little incident that occurred in the school-room, helped to increase serious thought and feeling. Overcome by severe exertion of body and mind, at the close of evening worship, I fainted and was taken to my room. H. expressed much sympathy for me, and her fears that I should not recover. A friend who stood near said to her:

"Mrs. C. is prepared for a sudden summons, but H. would you be ready should such a call be made to you, to appear before your Maker?"

" Oh no, Miss W.," she replied, with much feeling, " I should not. I am intellectually convinced of the truth, but my heart is unaffected."

Then, while the voice of prayer was heard in several surrounding rooms, she threw her arms around the neck of her friend, and kissing her, retired in tears to her own chamber. Conviction of her great sinfulness followed, and she was thence led, as we hoped, to trust in Jesus for salvation.

Previous to this a few had indulged the hope that they had passed from death unto spiritual life; and from this time there was a steady increase of feeling, which gave us the comforting assurance that the Spirit of God was with us of a truth. The whole work was characterized by deep impressions of God's truth,—solemn and still—with little excitement or outbursts of mere sympathy. Christians awoke to their duty, and many labored much to bring their companions to the cross of the crucified One. The session with its labors and blessings passed by, and the account was closed for eternity, and we praised and extolled the King of heaven for His wondrous mercy to the rebellious children of men.

"The winter was over and gone,—the flowers appeared on the earth,—and the singing of birds was heard in the land,"—and our study hall again became the home of the student. But increasing years were pressing upon me the necessity of lessening my labors in the school-room.

A record of the feelings with which I completed my seventy years of pilgrimage, can not be irrelevant in this place. "May 23, 1855. This day completes my threescore years and ten. What a world of memories have been revealed to my soul. How have I retraced the steps of my eventful life and traveled over the past, stopping by the way to shudder at the precipices; to tremble at the tempest and the billows that at times threatened to overwhelm me; to recall the trials, the privations. the hardships, such as few missionaries can recount in their list of tribulations; the

flicted, tempest-tossed and not comforted,' my way all hedged up, 'fightings without and fears within,' His Spirit has whispered 'peace—be still, and know that I am God.' 'Thy Maker is thy husband and thy Redeemer the Holy One of Israel.' 'The Lord hath called thee as a woman forsaken and grieved in spirit. For a small moment have I forsaken thee, but with great mercies will I gather thee. In a little wrath I hid my face from thee, but with everlasting kindness will I have mercy on thee, saith the Lord thy Redeemer.'

"Trust—trust in Him and He shall bring it to pass, has been written upon my guide-board through life, and now through grace I can say, 'My heart trusted in Him and I was helped.'"

The anniversary of the society which had for so many years been almost identified with my very existence, had now arrived, and for the last time I was to preside at its annual celebration.

Many beloved friends, teachers and pupils of other days were gathered within our walls, to offer the parting hand to the mother-friend who was " passing away," and to give expression to the feelings still warm in their hearts.

Mr. V. D., who had recently returned from a tour on the eastern continent, addressed the society in an interesting and impressive discourse, and our secretary in her report, gave us a summary of the operations of the society, since its first formation in Bloomfield, in 1837.

Much had previously been done in the Seminary in Vermont, to aid the cause of foreign and domestic missions, and two heathen children in Ceylon had been adopted as beneficiaries of the Missionary Society, who were placed in the female school at Oodooville. When the Missionary Society was organized in Bloomfield, those children were transferred to that association, and others were added from time to time, till the names of nine were recorded on our books.

Of these, three have married and have exhibited the blessed example of Christian families amid the darkness of Paganism. Two died in the faith while yet members of the Seminary, and four are still in the course of their education.

For the Foreign Missionary and other kindred societies, $2,415 have been collected; which with fifty or sixty boxes of clothing, sent at various times to different parts of the world, valued at $2,736, makes the sum total of $5,151, as the appreciable results of our missionary efforts.

But how inadequate are figures and ordinary statistics to measure the results of Christian effort.

And now my exhausted energies and " often infirmities," reminded me that I must retire from the weight of responsibility that would soon place me by the side of my *sleeping ones*. Added to this consideration, was a desire to leave my testimony to the unmerited grace of God and His wonderful mercy manifested in all His dealings with the wanderer.

I had long contemplated the possibility of accomplishing such a work, and retirement from the duties of the school would alone enable me to enter upon the task.

I therefore, at the close of the summer term resigned my situation, and closing my connection with the Seminary, sought a quiet, retired home, far from the din of business, where I could occasionally,

> "Hear the stir of the great Babel
> And not feel its power."

It was not without many conflicts and trials of feeling that I bade adieu to scenes and spots hallowed in my recollections as the places whence ascended the first accepted prayer; the first lispings of praise from hearts and lips unused to the songs of Zion. And that consecrated room—rendered sacred as the birth-place of souls,—as the chamber from which arose to the abodes of the blessed the spirits of my departed Eliza, and of the precious lamb that I had hoped had been given me to take her place, and soothe my sorrow,—"did I not feel," as I turned away from all these, and

> "Through the shadowy past,
> Like a tomb searcher, memory ran,
> Lifting each shroud, that time had cast
> O'er buried hopes."

In accordance with the wish expressed by several friends, I subjoin a summary, as correct as my papers will allow me to make it, of the number of pupils who were under my instruction from the commencement of my labors in Vermont until 1855, when I withdrew from my connection with the Seminary in Bloomfield.

The number taught in these different places amounts to about one thousand eight hundred and fifty.

The number of teachers and pupils who have consecrated themselves to the work of foreign missions, from these several Seminaries, is sixteen; but of those who have gone out as missionaries to the West, or as teachers of youth, no accurate estimate can be made.

In like manner we can not speak with certainty of the number who, in the judgment of charity have passed from death unto life.

CHAPTER LI.

TRIALS OF TEACHERS.—WANT OF DISCIPLINE AT HOME.—ILLUSTRATION.—OBSTACLES IN THE WAY OF EDUCATING YOUNG LADIES.

> "Where shall a teacher look, in days like these
> For ears and hearts that they can hope to please?
> For beck'ning pleasure leads them wide astray,
> They burst the bonds, and cast the yoke away."

MUCH has been said and many treatises written, to impress on the mind of woman the extent of her influence on society, and especially on the little circle gathered around her in her own beloved home. That such enforcements are called for, in this age of fashion and worldliness, no one can deny, or too deeply deplore. We need but to take a view of a modern school-room to fathom the trials to which many a conscientious teacher is subjected, to understand fully that we have reached the times portrayed with so much feeling by the Prophet, "The child shall behave himself proudly against the ancient." "As for my people, children are their oppressors, and women rule over them. O, my people, they which lead thee cause thee to err."

No discriminating observer of the present generation can fail to observe that the reins of government are not, in most cases, in parental hands. Disguise it as many strive to do, the "I can't" and the "I won't" of the child controls the parents.

"Father," said a very precocious young lady, just entering her teens, "you need not say one word about my taking music lessons; I don't like it, and I won't study it."

Stepping to her side, and laying my hand on her shoulder, I said, "Young lady, we require our pupils to learn, and to obey, the fifth commandment."

The foundation of the evil complained of, lies in the neglect of the parent to enforce the *first* lessons of obedience. These *first lessons*, it is true, must be taught by the mother; she always *is*, or she always *should be*, near to check the impetuosities of child-hood, to repress the first outbreaks of passion, to impress on the infantile mind the importance and the beauty of truth, and to teach her child that from the decision of parental authority there can be no appeal.

But while such holy responsibilities rest upon the mother, if she is to be successful she must have the entire sympathy and will of her husband. Forgetting, in the whirl of business, the Divine injunction, to give "honor unto the wife as unto the weaker vessel, as being heirs together of the grace of life, that your prayers be not hindered," forgetful that he derives his *name* from the significant appellation *House-band*, which unites all domestic interests in one, too often he suffers the weary, perhaps nervous partner of his life to plod on from day to day in her slow progress of educating her offspring for God's service, with scarcely a word of encouragement—oftentimes in direct opposition to her will: because, forsooth, he is absorbed in business through the day, and so seldom can enjoy the society of the little ones at home, that he must be allowed to indulge them in their demands upon his yielding spirit. No wonder that children disregard the commands of a mother who, in these trying circumstances, possesses not firmness of principle and gentleness of spirit to enforce obedience.

Pass from household to household, and how often is the heart of the Christian pained by the general failure to compel prompt and entire submission to the authority of the parent. The examples presented of the influences of such training are too abundant to need further illustration. They are scattered broadcast over the land.

Mothers of the present day! I fearlessly appeal to your hearts and consciences—is not this the general training of thousands of our children who are rapidly growing up to take your places in the community?

Forgetting, or perhaps ignorant of the fact that the impress of the first few years stamps the future character of the candidate for eternity, the training process is deferred till the child, as the parent hopes, shall have attained an age when it will yield to reason and to moral suasion. Thus the parent becomes the subject of the "*Young Dominion*," and the juvenile lord reigns triumphant in the domestic castle.

Thus prepared to assert his or her rights in all circumstances, our "young patriarchs" are transferred to the supervision of teachers, who are expected to transform their youthful charges into models of propriety, gentility, and scholarship.   Would the parents encourage the disheartened instructors, by their co-operation in the great work committed to their trust, there might arise some hope of success, but alas! such co-operations are "few and far between." Memory reveals a case of years departed.   A mother—a lovely Christian mother—placed in my care two interesting children.   "They have many faults, Mrs. C.," she said, "but you need never fear to make me acquainted with them.   Correct them when they go astray, and you will always find that you have my confidence and co-operation," and she always sustained me in my efforts to train these children for God's service.   Our covenant God brought them both, as we trusted, into the family of His disciples.

A few years passed, and this beloved mother became a saint in glory.   The father, unfit to manage spirits that required a wise and guiding hand, filled with care, and borne down with sorrow, suffered these daughters to assume the reins of government, and by his blind confidence in their ability to control themselves, entirely paralyzed the efforts of their teachers for the good of his children.

Many similar cases loom up before my mind, clearly illustrating the effect of so unwise a course. Many have been placed under my care, upon whose word, according to the testimony of the parent or guardian, no reliance could be placed. Something in the course of regulations or discipline displeased the young lady—false statements were made to the parents, and notwithstanding the previous testimony, that the child would deceive, these statements were believed, the teacher treated with disrespect, perhaps with abuse, and the pupil withdrawn from the school.

And what, in most cases, is the plea of the mother? 'My child has a very *peculiar disposition*, she is exceedingly *sensitive*, and can not bear reproof, and the teacher does not understand her temperament, and consequently does not manage her aright." Such remarks are often repeated in the presence of the offended child, and as a necessary consequence the confidence of the pupil in the ability of the teacher to instruct wisely and judiciously is destroyed, and her influence for good lessened, or wholly neutralized.

The following extracts are taken from a paper on Female Education, read before the American Association for the Advancement of Education, at its annual meeting in 1852, by R. L. Cooke:

"Thus many a teacher labors under the imputation of incompetency or unfaithfulness, when every energy of soul and body has been brought into exercise, and that too with reasonable success, because unreasonable expectations have been excited in the parent's mind, which have not been and never can be realized. Said a mother to me some years since, whose daughter had been five months a member of our Seminary:

" 'I do not see that my daughter has corrected all her bad habits since she has been with you. She is almost as careless as she was before she came to you. It was to overcome these habits that I sent her from home.'

" 'Do you expect, madam,' I replied, 'that we are able, in one term, to undo what, under your maternal care, it has taken sixteen years to establish? We are not omnipotent; in the short space of time that you have allotted us, we can not break up habits or overcome propensities which you have not been able, in a lifetime, either to prevent or to subdue.'

"Another serious obstacle to the discipline of the female mind, arises from the rapidity with which our pupils are required to advance in their studies.

" 'Progression is the watchword of the day; we must *think* fast, or fall behind the spirit of the age.' 'Knowledge must be attained with a degree of rapidity approximating, in some measure at least, to that which characterizes everything else, otherwise time could not be afforded for its attainment at all.'

" An ambitious mother, or perhaps a daughter vain of her position or her looks, are alike in haste to introduce to the world this scion of luxuriant growth, that she may early 'enjoy life,' or catch some of the butterflies of the day, that are ever ready to flit around the new comer, and to lend their influence to the increase of folly and vanity.

" Probably in no enlightened country on the globe are children more anxious to be esteemed, or earlier permitted to become men and women than in our own ; it has been with much truth remarked, that in the United States there is no such period as *youth ;* we jump at once from childhood to fancied maturity. In female education is this evil most apparent and most serious in its consequences. As soon as a young lady has attained that age when she begins to appreciate the advantages of a well-stored mind, and the influence that it will secure for her in society—when she is prepared to profit most, by instruction—the usages of society, perhaps the mistaken eagerness of parents themselves, call her away from her studies to assume her position in society, soon, it may be, herself to become the head of a family, destined to train other immortal minds, while as yet her own is only just dawning into maturity. The idea that young ladies who have reached this point will perfect their education by the aid of private tutors or by personal application, after they have given up the duties and the tasks of the school-room, is a delusion that deceives at first, but is soon abandoned. The consequence of this is that the general standard of female education with us is low compared with that of England, and perhaps most of the countries of Europe. But while these various obstacles are well calculated to discourage conscientious teachers, and to excite the heart-sickening inquiry, 'who hath believed our report?' many bright oases are sprinkled over the desert, and upon their ' tent in the wilderness' many bright sunbeams shed their cheering warmth to gladden the heart that would otherwise sink in despondency. Not unfrequently the affection of grateful hearts is permanently secured, and the seed sown in years gone by, springs up to be replanted in other soil, perhaps to furnish fruit in the juvenile vineyard of the youthful mother."

As the wearied, worn out veteran, at the close of a long life of labor, casts her eye over the great map of earth, and views, in imagination, many of her loved ones whom she has followed with her prayers, occupying stations of usefulness as missionaries in our own or foreign lands—as mothers or heads of families—or as teachers, seeking to obey the Divine injunction, "freely ye have received, freely give," and feeling that to their influence and example the welfare of the rising generation is committed—will not the aged pilgrim, with such a prospect before her, close her eyes upon the " memories" that reveal the thorns and briars of her pathway, and thank God that she was suffered to be a co-worker with the Redeemer in training hearts and minds for such a glorious work.

And how sweet is the thought that, as one after

another is passing away from earth, and increasing
the " attractions of heaven," that,

> " Our best affections here
>   Are not like the toys of infancy ;
>   The soul outgrows them not,
>   We do not cast them off."

> " When, soon or late, we reach that coast,
>   O'er life's rough journey driven,
>   May we rejoice, no wanderer lost,
>   A family in heaven."

THE END.

www.ingramcontent.com/pod-product-compliance
Lightning Source LLC
Chambersburg PA
CBHW021728110726
47902CB00005B/1389